MW01275109

Pryor & Cummings

The GAIA Incident

By
Rod Pennington

*e*PulpPress.com
Jackson, Wyoming

Pryor & Cummings

The GAIA Incident

ISBN13: 978-1-57242-097-7

*e*PulpPress.com
P.O. Box 8906
Jackson, Wyoming 83002

CHAPTER 1

A T 3 A.M., every desk in the subterranean combination office/ laboratory was empty except for one.

Nick Blake, a scruffy grad student with a riot of hair, was hunched over the keyboard on his cluttered desk. His round, acne-pocked face appeared to sit on his plump torso without the benefit of a neck. Spending more time at his desk than at his apartment, the top of his work space was littered with candy wrappers, Post-it notes, a variety of take-out boxes and an overflowing ashtray he normally kept hidden in his drawer.

Pausing, without taking his eyes off his monitor, he reached for a can of Red Bull but misjudged the distance and came up short. He turned his head, located the can and tried again. Picking it up, he discovered it was nearly empty. After a deep, long-suffering sigh, he took a final pull then tipped his head back to get the last drop. Next, he tried to crush the can but with his lack of hand strength, the best he could do was twist it out of shape but not flatten it. With another sigh, he tossed the empty can in the general direction of the recycle bin about twenty feet away. The can hit the rim of the bin and clattered to the floor next to the three other cans he had already finished. As he reached for his pack of unfiltered Camel cigarettes he grinned at the sign some wise-ass had hung on the wall next to his desk.

This is a Smoke-Free Facility
Thank You for NOT Smoking!

Blake shook out one of the three remaining cigarettes in the pack and shoved it into his mouth. He chuckled as he reached for the BIC lighter next to his keyboard. All things considered, if anyone figured out what he was doing, violating the office no smoking policy would be the least of his problems.

Other than the glow of a few exit signs, the only light in the room was coming from the 32-inch monitor on Blake's desk. With the cigarette dangling from his lips, his fingers danced across his keyboard. He suddenly gasped as he read the information on his screen.

Blake rubbed his chin as he slowly reread the screen to be sure he was seeing it correctly. He had come close too many times without actually finding the motherlode. Satisfied, he leaned back in his chair and intertwined his fingers behind his head. "Eureka," he muttered.

Blake bristled when he heard a sound at the far end of the room. Wheeling around, he thought he saw movement but there were too many dark shadows so he couldn't be sure.

"Hello? Is somebody there?"

Blake searched his desk for a potential weapon but the best he could come up with was either a stapler or the wireless keyboard from his workstation computer. Before Blake had to choose, he relaxed, let out a nervous sigh and smiled.

"Oh, it's only you."

Blake's eyes widened and the smile vanished when he saw the weapon aimed at him. Before he could utter another word, a perfectly placed shot rang out and Nick Blake was dead before he hit the floor.

CHAPTER 2

THE SUN HAD only been up for about an hour and the sprawling campus was just starting to shake off the morning cobwebs and was coming to life. Like so many other universities, it was in the center of a neighborhood that had seen better days. Sitting on over three thousand acres, the campus itself was clean and modern. The area went downhill fast the farther you got from the campus.

A knot of people, some curious students and some employees denied entry to their workspace, were milling around on the outside of the crime scene tape. All eyes and all conversations were focused on the front of a small, futuristic building with 'GAIA Institute' etched in marble over the entrance.

A meticulously restored cherry red 1958 F-150 pickup rolled up to the sawhorse 'police line' barricade blocking the parking lot access and a young uniformed officer held up his hand indicating the driver should stop. The bored, fresh-faced rookie rolled his eyes as he sized up the man behind the wheel of the restored truck. He sighed and shook his head as he waited for the driver to manually crank down his window.

The man behind the wheel was barely closer to forty than fifty and looked like he had been rolled out of bed with only a couple of hours' sleep after a lost weekend bender. Which wasn't that far off. His blue eyes were bloodshot and he had three days of mixed black and gray stubble on his face that looked thick enough and coarse enough to dull a cheap disposable razor.

"I'm sorry, sir." The rookie made 'sir' sound like a pejorative. "This area is closed."

The man behind the wheel eyed the nameplate on the officer's uniform and noted his badge number then made no attempt to cover his yawn.

"Thank you, Officer Polling. Badge 83471." The scruffy man glanced at the analog clock embedded in the dashboard of the Ford and yawned again. "When he asks, and he will, please inform Lt. Garrison you turned me away from the crime scene at 7:26 a.m."

"Excuse me?" the young cop said, suddenly interested and with a hint of panic in his voice. "Are you Detective Pryor?"

Pryor checked his rearview mirror and put his truck into reverse. "Pryor, yes. Whether I'm still a detective is a subject of some debate."

Despite the crisp morning air, small beads of sweat started to form on the young officer's forehead as he realized he had almost stepped on a potential career-derailing landmine. "I'm sorry, sir," he said, and this time he meant it. He picked up the sawhorse and waved Pryor through.

Not willing to risk any dings in the vintage pickup's custom paint job, and not much caring what the other people at the crime scene thought, Pryor parked his truck at an angle, taking up three of the remaining spots.

Pryor sat behind the wheel for a moment. He drew in a deep breath through his nose then let it out through his mouth before finally opening the truck door and stepping out. A bit over six feet tall and a rock-solid one hundred and eighty-five pounds, wearing faded blue jeans and a rumpled slept-in flannel shirt, he looked more like a day laborer arriving at a construction site than a detective showing up to investigate a homicide.

Pryor headed toward the building but pulled up short when he heard a familiar voice behind him.

"I thought you were suspended," said Detective Danny Holden.

Pryor turned and smiled at his ex-partner. "That's what I thought, too."

Pryor and Holden had ridden together for nearly eight years and had had the highest clearance rate in the homicide division. Of course, since they were a great and productive team, in the infinite wisdom of the police department, they were split up. Each was promoted to senior homicide detective where half their job was keeping newbie detectives from making fools of themselves. It was a full-time job.

Holden was only a few years older than Pryor but they had been tough years. A high-functioning alcoholic with three ex-wives, Holden had long ago given up the battle of the bulge. He had been adding about five pounds a year for the past five years. His suit jacket was tight on him and his belt had already passed its last notch, so Holden had punched an extra hole instead of trashing it. Holden didn't care. In a college town, where the most frequently heard mantra was 'Defund the Police', he had had enough. He had already turned in his retirement papers and his current wardrobe would make it for eleven more days.

"You look like shit," Holden said.

"You look two donuts short of a coronary," Pryor replied.

Holden handed Pryor the extra-large take out cup of coffee he had just bought from an enterprising food truck vendor who had pulled up when he saw a potentially hungry and thirsty crowd had gathered in front of the GAIA Institute. "You look like you need this more than me."

Pryor accepted the cup but, from experience, sniffed it then made a face. "Good lord, Danny," Pryor said as he handed the cup back to his ex-partner. "What the hell did you put into this?"

"The envelope said it was organic raw cane sugar."

"How much did you put in?"

"What does it matter?" Holden answered with a laugh. "It's organic and raw. It has to be good for you."

"Keep telling yourself that," Pryor answered as he turned and headed toward the food truck. A half-dozen giggly people reeking of cannabis smoke residue were ahead of them in line. Trying to channel their inner-hippie, the mix of three females and three males were all dressed pretty much alike in bright, ill-fitting clothes and all had long, shoulder-length hair which had not seen a shampoo bottle recently.

They all eyed Pryor and Holden, exchanged glances then all tried to suppress their giggles.

"Good lord," Pryor muttered as he glanced at Holden. "Did I miss the Woodstock Revival notification?"

Holden winked at Pryor. "What's that odd smell, detective?" Holden asked as he opened his coat so the sextet could see the gun and badge clipped to his belt.

5

"I'm not sure, detective," Pryor answered as he sniffed the air. "You think while we have all of this extra time waiting in line here for a coffee we should call K-9?"

"Recreational marijuana is legal in this state, man," one of the glassy-eyed stoners offered.

"For anyone over the age of twenty-one," Holden answered with a smile. "What's your date of birth?"

"Why are you hassling us? We're not bothering anybody," the stoner protested as he looked at his posse for support. All of them were busy studying their Birkenstocks. He was on his own.

"I'm just making conversation while we're killing time waiting in this long, long line when all we want is a single cup of coffee," Holden answered.

The six stoners exchanged glances then all stepped aside and the leader said, "Why don't you officers go ahead of us?"

"Why thank you," Holden said with a smile.

Pryor grinned as he stepped up to the window. A large Hispanic man in a white t-shirt with the food truck's logo on the front and wearing a matching doo-rag struggling to contain his abundance of hair, grinned down at him. Apparently, he had been enjoying watching the Albert and Danny comedy hour.

"Large, black. No lid," Pryor said to the man in the window who nodded. An instant later, Pryor had his drink in his hand and blew across the top of the cup before taking his first sip. As they walked away, Pryor chuckled. "I haven't used that gag since we were partners."

"The classics never get old," Holden answered.

Pryor nodded in the direction of three men and one woman in front of the GAIA Institute in deep conversation thirty yards away. "This can't be good." Pryor's and Holden's immediate supervisor, Lt. Wilson Garrison, was getting an earful from the mayor, Caldwell Jackson. Mayor Jackson was a garden variety local politician with higher aspirations. He certainly looked the part. He had a full head of hair, with never a strand out of place, and he also had the most important qualification for a career politician. He lacked any core guiding principles he wouldn't forsake for enough votes.

So far he had managed to advance his career by being good at judging which way the wind was blowing and identifying which ass to firmly press his lips to. He could also count. With the police department representing less than one percent of the registered voters, he seldom found their backsides appealing enough for a little romance. The same could not be said for their backs. A knife between the shoulder blades was always his default option.

Hardly surprising, instead of volunteers lining up for overtime, when the mayor needed extra security, it was often mandatory and resented. If he expected anyone in his security detail to take a bullet for him, his grieving widow would be greatly disappointed.

Rumor had it, the good mayor planned to run for the congressional seat that had unexpectedly come open. The local congressman had already announced he would not be seeking re-election. With a straight face, he said it was because he wanted to spend more time with his family. Getting caught on video accepting envelopes full of cash from an undercover FBI agent might have helped him make the decision. It was better than even money the only time he would be spending time with the family soon would be in the visitor's center at a federal minimum-security prison.

Most politicians only leave office in handcuffs or when there is a chance to move up to a better position on the public trough. With this unexpected opportunity on the horizon, the last thing Mayor Jackson wanted was a high-profile murder on his watch. With the mayor's history of throwing law enforcement under the bus at the first sign of controversy, to his credit, Lt. Garrison was listening calmly and not strangling the two-faced son-of-bitch.

Standing shoulder-to-shoulder with the mayor was the president of the university, Joan Winston. She had just turned sixty and was mousy with her salt and pepper hair cropped close. She was wearing an expensive and well-cut business suit that complemented her petite figure.

She had advanced to the top of academia by spending her entire career avoiding controversy. Never once in nearly forty years had President Winston ever veered far enough from the politically correct groupthink of the facility lounge to create any problems for herself. Now, like Mayor Jackson, she was deeply concerned. The GAIA Institute was the crown jewel of the campus and a massive cash cow. Her current prestigious seven-figure indoor job with no heavy lifting and future employment were directly linked to the success or failure of the GAIA Institute. She had the look of someone terrified, that at her age, she might actually have to go out into the real world and find a job in the private sector.

Lurking behind the three, in a pompous custom-made uniform that a Third World dictator would have been embarrassed to wear, was the head of campus security, Wendell Mucker.

From his body language, it was clear Lt. Garrison had about had his fill of the mayor. Garrison was fast losing interest in the conversation as his eyes drifted, then locked on Pryor.

"About time," Garrison muttered as he turned and walked away.

"I'm not finished," the mayor shouted at Garrison's back.

Garrison gave the mayor a dismissive wave but neither slowed down nor looked back. "I'd love to chat Mr. Mayor but we've got a homicide to solve."

Both Pryor and Holden nodded as their boss joined them.

Garrison's eyes started at the top of Pryor, went to the bottom then back to the top again. "Man. You look like crap on toast."

"Or a Dot Com billionaire," Pryor answered. "Why exactly am I here?" Albert Pryor asked.

"We've got a dead research assistant in Dr. Plato Vane's lab."

"Vane?" Pryor repeated. "I should be the last one investigating this then."

"That's exactly what I said," Garrison replied. "But with your old buddy Vane having an ironclad alibi, neither the Chief nor the DA sees any conflict."

"Define ironclad?" Pryor queried.

"At the time of the murder, Vane was three thousand miles away in the Green Room of *Good Morning America* in Midtown Manhattan getting his hair fluffed and his makeup applied."

"Of course he was," Pryor answered and looked like he wanted to spit on the sidewalk but restrained himself. Instead, he turned and headed back to his truck.

"Where are you going?" Garrison demanded.

Pryor stopped and wheeled around. "Tell the chief I'm flattered but I'm still on my unpaid suspension and waiting to hear the news about my Internal Affairs inquisition." Pryor shook his head and laughed.

"Besides, I'm pretty sure Professor Vane has a restraining order out on me."

"The chief thought you might say that," Garrison replied. "He asked me to inform you that your suspension has been changed to paid probation effective immediately."

"Probation? What the hell does that mean?"

"It means: if you refuse to work this case, he'll consider it yet another act of insubordination, and he'll buy the first round at your farewell party."

Danny Holden emitted a soft whistle. "Man. That's cold."

"Yeah," Garrison added. "It would be a crying shame, considering you are only a little over a year from having your twenty in and qualifying for your full pension and all."

Lt. Garrison reached into his windbreaker pocket, pulled out a gun and badge, and offered them to Pryor.

CHAPTER 3

PRYOR EYED THE tools of his trade but didn't move to accept them. When the video of his little dustup with Plato Vane had gone viral, he had been certain his career with the department was over. Cops don't go around, with people filming, throwing one of the richest and easily the most famous man in town through a plate glass window. He was pretty sure the decision had already been made to terminate his relationship with the department and it was only a matter of time before the gnomes at internal affairs would have crossed all of the 't's and dotted the 'i's and would give him his walking papers.

Pryor had already worked his way through the five stages of grief and arrived at acceptance. He had never expected to see his badge and gun again.

Now this.

Pryor was a good detective, but Danny was every bit as good as he and there were a few fire-breathers currently working their way up the ranks with more internet savvy and less baggage. Why him? Why now? Then it hit him.

"What about my termination hearing?" Pryor asked.

"I don't have any control over that," Garrison answered.

Pryor shook his head and grunted. "Bite me," he muttered as he started to walk away.

Danny Holden grabbed him with one hand while taking the gun and badge out of Garrison's hand with the other.

"You know how bashful Albert can be lieutenant," Holden said with a chuckle. "What he meant to say was, please thank the chief for giving him a second chance and tell him he won't let you down." Holden leaned in and whispered in Pryor's ear. "Don't be a putz. You solve this one and they can't fire you."

"This is bullshit and you know it, Danny. They're just looking for a fall guy to take the heat off of them. I'm disposable."

Holden leaned in closer. "No argument, but right now, buddy, you've got nothing to lose. At least, if you take this case you might be able to save your job. You leave now and you've burned the last bridge." Holden grinned at Pryor. "In the meantime, you might get to take the high and mighty Plato Vane down a notch or two." Holden held out Pryor's gun and badge. "It is the smart play."

Pryor thought about it for a few seconds then accepted them and clipped both to his belt.

"If it makes you feel any better," Lt. Garrison said. "With your history with Vane, the president of the university and the clown show head of security are both about to have kittens at the thought of having the likes of you running loose on their campus." Garrison lowered his voice. "The University already has the mayor doing the St. Vitus Dance and the city council reaching for smelling salts and that's while the body is still warm."

"With all of them lined up against me, who had the political pull with the chief and the DA to get me assigned to this case?"

"Seriously?" Garrison asked with an amazed expression on his face. "You have to ask?"

"Crap," Holden muttered as he noticed the two women approaching. "Incoming."

Pryor turned and saw his ex-wife, Melissa Pryor Vane, and their daughter, Brooke, striding purposefully in his direction. "Oh, hell, no," Pryor muttered.

"There is only one dog in the kennel bigger than Vane in this town," Garrison said with a shrug. "And that would be your ex-daddy-in-law, Malcolm Kauthmann."

Pryor closed his eyes and shook his head.

Melissa and Albert had only been together long enough to have a child, a trial separation, a restraining order and a less than cordial divorce. In total, they were only married for eighteen months and that was longer than any of their friends and family would have thought possible.

It would have been difficult to find a more mismatched pair. Melissa came from old money and a lot of it; Pryor was blue-collar and dirt poor. Melissa had traveled the world; until he enlisted, Pryor had never been east of the Mississippi River. Melissa was a patron of the arts; Pryor had season football tickets in the nose-bleed section nowhere near mid-field.

The former Mrs. Pryor had the tall and lean figure of a runway model, which was a good thing since Melissa did most of her wardrobe shopping during fashion week in Paris. Between her Valentino original summer dress, Hermes bag, Louis Vuitton shoes and the assortment of carbon-based stones on her fingers, the value of the clothing and accessories she was currently wearing exceeded Pryor's annual take-home pay.

Their daughter, Brooke, thankfully, had gotten her good looks from her mother. But she also got her father's competitive nature and more than her share of common sense. Plus, unlike many of the other children of her one percenter friends, Brooke was not afraid to get dirty. Earlier this summer, she had helped her dad rebuild the engine of the 1958 F-150 pickup he was driving today.

Pryor was livid as he wheeled on his ex-wife. "I can't believe you had your daddy throw his weight around to get me assigned to this case."

"Oh, get over yourself," snarled the former Mrs. Albert Pryor, now Mrs. Plato Vane. "This wasn't my idea."

"Whose idea was it then?" Pryor demanded.

"I'm the one who asked grandpa, Daddy," Brooke Pryor answered.

"Why?"

"I knew Nick."

Pryor looked at Garrison and mouthed 'who's Nick?' Garrison silently mouthed 'the victim'.

Holden and Garrison exchanged glances and both of them shook their heads. First, a murder in a guy's lab with who Pryor had a history, and now, Pryor's daughter knowing the victim well enough to have her grandfather start throwing his considerable weight around.

This had FUBAR written all over it.

Pryor's eyes narrowed. "Knew him? How well did you know him?"

"We had some classes together," Brooke answered meekly.

"How did you even find out he was dead?" Pryor asked bluntly.

A sneer covered Melissa Vane's face as she put her arm around Brooke. "Would it kill you to be a father for once and not be a cop for just thirty seconds?"

Pryor, Holden and Garrison all knew that Brooke was going to need to be interviewed. Garrison nodded at Melissa and shook his head and the three detectives silently agreed the interview would probably go better if Brooke did not have her mother with her.

"Sorry. You're right," Pryor answered as he turned to his daughter. "Are you okay, Brooke?"

"No! I'm not okay!" Brooke snapped as her anger evaporated the tears in her hazel eyes. "I'm mad as hell and I want you to find the bastard who did this."

"We're going to need to talk to you some more," Pryor said gently as he eyed his ex-wife.

"I'm in class until 11:30," Brooke answered. "Then I'm free the rest of the day."

Melissa Vane glared at Pryor. "In the meantime, you might want to work on your personal hygiene." With a dismissive wave of her hand, Melissa turned and walked away.

Brooke grabbed her father and kept him from following her mother.

"Let her go, Daddy," Brooke said softly then leaned in. "We need to talk. I'll be at my apartment by noon." Brooke gave Pryor a peck on the cheek then turned to Holden. "Don't let him do anything stupid, Uncle Danny," she said as she gave Holden a hug.

"You know your dad," Holden answered as he patted the young woman on the back as he returned the hug. "Stupid is his middle name."

As she turned to walk away, Brooke gave the trio a weak wave and an even weaker smile. "Just try, okay?"

Brooke brushed past the head of campus security, Wendell Mucker, who gave her backside an admiring glance as she passed by.

Pryor started to take a step toward Mucker but Holden stopped him.

"Easy, big fella," Holden said softly. "You've got enough on your plate already. Besides." Holden glanced in the direction of Lt. Garrison. "Lou hates this guy."

Wendell Mucker was big, nearly three hundred pounds and, given the chance, he liked to throw every ounce of it around. He had close-set, beady brown eyes like a predator near the middle of the food chain. He always seemed to be sizing people up to see which side of the line they belonged on. Were they someone he could eat for lunch or someone who might devour him?

Mucker had a history with Lt. Garrison and had come out on the short end. Now his old enemy was on his turf. Mucker was confident this time he would come out on top.

"Lieutenant," Mucker said in a voice that seemed about an octave too high for a man of his size, "we need to discuss how we're going to proceed with this investigation."

Lt. Garrison's eyes flashed with anger and he made no attempt to conceal his contempt for Mucker. "First off, there is no 'we' in this investigation, Wendell."

Mucker flinched at the sound of his seldom used first name.

Lt. Garrison was just getting warmed up.

"Detective Pryor will be the lead investigator and if he tells you to go piss on that tree, the next sound I expect to hear will be your zipper."

Mucker was momentarily stunned by this unexpected assault, especially while on his own turf. "How dare you speak to me like that?"

"Half the people who work for you were guys I personally ran off the force because they were drunks, crooks, or a little too quick with the nightstick," Garrison answered as he glared at Mucker. "And as I recall, Wendell, you were all three." Garrison drove his index finger hard enough into Mucker's chest he had to take a step back. "Detective Pryor doesn't need a bunch of cop wannabes in pussy-boy uniforms getting in the way of his investigation."

"The mayor and the president of the university assured me...," Mucker sputtered.

"Well, then," Garrison said, cutting him off mid-sentence. "I would recommend you take your concerns up with them."

"I intend to," Mucker answered just before he stormed away.

"Damn," Pryor said. "That may have been the sexiest thing I've ever seen you do. You know, I've never kissed a grown man before."

"You're not going to start now without dinner and a movie and a note from my wife." Garrison turned serious. "You had better wrap this up fast, Albert," Garrison said, as he nodded in the direction of a television van, with smiling photos of the various personalities painted on the side, rolling to a stop near the rookie Pryor had manhandled earlier. "This is going to get ugly, fast."

"Yes, sir," Pryor answered glumly.

"You want the good news or the bad news?" Garrison asked.

"I could use some good news," Pryor answered.

"I'm going to have Danny take the point on handling the press."

Danny Holden took a small bow. "Our investigation is ongoing and at a sensitive juncture so I will not be able to take any questions at this time."

"That's my boy," Garrison said before turning to Pryor. "I don't want you within a hundred miles of a reporter and," Garrison looked at Pryor's appearance and shook his head before continuing, "I certainly don't want you anywhere near a camera."

"No problem," Pryor answered. "What's the bad news?"

"I've assigned you a new partner."

"No. No. No, no, no," Pryor protested. "I don't have time to break in somebody new. Where's Ruiz?"

"She has already been reassigned," Garrison answered.

"She was distraught when she thought you might not be coming back," Holden said as he patted Pryor on the back.

Pryor glared at Holden. "I heard about the party she threw." Pryor turned his attention back to Garrison. "So who have you assigned to me?"

"You remember Max Cummings?" Garrison asked.

"Reload?" Pryor answered. "He was my training officer a lifetime ago but he's been retired for what? Ten, fifteen years?"

"I know. I know," Garrison answered. "His grandson has been out of the academy for about nine months and he's a house of fire..."

"What?" Pryor shouted loud enough that heads turned in their direction. "You want to partner me up with a rookie who is still in his probationary period on a high-profile homicide? Are you nuts?"

"Look, Albert," Garrison said. "You may be able to pull the transmission and engine on a car, but you're a complete idiot when it comes to electronics. Give the kid a chance. He might surprise you."

"I can't believe you're doing this," Pryor replied.

Wilson Garrison just shrugged. "You seem to be under the misconception that I have any say in any of this. This is coming straight from the top."

"The chief?"

Garrison motioned higher with his thumb.

"The DA?"

Garrison motioned higher.

"Son-of-bitch," Pryor muttered. "Why would Kauthmann care?"

"Brooke may think she got you involved by batting her eyes at your ex-father-in-law but that's not the case. Apparently, he has a ton of cash invested in the GAIA institute. Old man Kauthmann wants this solved quickly to protect his investment."

"I'm not the only detective on the force."

"True," Garrison answered with a dismissive wave of his hand. "With Vane alibied out, Kauthmann wants you because everybody knows you're an asshole who will push the envelope if necessary and actually seems to enjoy pissing off rich and powerful people."

"He would have first-hand knowledge," Pryor said with a sigh. He scratched the stubble on his face. "Still, it's nice to be appreciated."

Garrison pointed to a keycard box mounted on the wall by the entrance to the GAIA Institute entrance. "Whoever did this had access to the lab which makes them nerds," Garrison said then continued. "This Cummings kid will speak their language. Plus, he's some kind of technical wizard."

"So where is this genius?" Pryor asked.

"He's already at the crime scene." Pryor pulled a face as he looked around. Garrison thought Pryor was concerned with a rookie tromping all over potential evidence. "Don't worry, Albert," Lt. Garrison quickly added. "He's housebroken and isn't going to screw anything up."

"I wasn't worried about that." Pryor pointed in the direction of the coroner wagon and three different CSI vehicles then at the building surrounded by police tape. Through the glass he could see a few police officers milling around inside but that was it. "That building is maybe eight hundred square feet and they've got all hands on deck from the crime lab. Where the hell is everybody?" Pryor asked.

"Good lord, Albert," Holden said. "Don't you ever read a newspaper?"

"Sports and comics," Pryor answered. "But I certainly don't bother with the stories about my ex-wife's celebrity husband."

"Vane insisted his computers needed to be underground," Garrison said.

"Why?"

"It was some green energy bullshit," Garrison answered. "His lab is about four hundred feet below where we're standing." Garrison pointed toward the entrance of the GAIA Institute and started walking. "Come on," he said, "I'll introduce you to your new partner."

CHAPTER 4

BEFORE THEY REACHED the entrance to the GAIA Institute, they all turned when they heard a commotion at the barrier leading to the parking lot. A pushy local on-air talent, with visions of the big time twinkling in his eyes, was giving young Officer Polling a tough time. His cameraman was preserving the encounter on video for posterity. To his credit, the rookie wasn't backing down.

Pryor nodded his approval.

"I'm on it," Danny Holden said. As Holden turned to walk away, he looked back over his shoulder and said. "We're probably going to need more uniforms until they remove the body. Since they know we're reluctant to shoot them when the cameras are rolling, those press clowns can be real assholes when they think they have us outnumbered."

"Okay," Lt. Garrison said as he fished his cellphone out of his pocket and hit a speed dial button. "Frank? Get me some more warm bodies down here pronto. The press is starting to show up." Garrison returned his phone to his pocket as he admired the turquoise mountain bike with a pair of heavy U Locks with 'Kryptonite' written on it. One of the locks passed through the rear tire and frame and was attached to a bike rack near the door. A second lock secured the front tire to the bike rack.

"Sweet," said Garrison.

Al Pryor pointed to the pair of locks. "Two locks is a little overkill for a bike, don't you think?"

"Bike?" Garrison shook his head. "That, my friend, is the Yeti SB140 GX Eagle. I've had my eye on one of these bad boys but with one kid in college and another only a year out, there is no way I could afford one."

Pryor looked at the bike with new respect. "How much does that thing cost?"

"North of six grand."

"Yeah, right," Pryor answered in disbelief as he pulled the door to the GAIA Institute open.

The lobby of the compact and ultra-sleek building had a two-man security desk in front of a pair of elevators.

"Is this the only way in or out?" Pryor asked.

Garrison pointed to the rear corner of the room and steel fire door with an exit sign over it. "There's a staircase which only has a door on this level and the lab level."

"The elevators?"

"Like the stairs, they only stop on this floor and the lab. When the security team is here, they have total control of the access."

"And when they're not here?" Pryor asked.

Garrison pointed to a small box between the elevators. "You need a swipe card and the entry code."

"A place like this doesn't have a nightwatchman?"

Garrison shrugged. "Apparently everything is automated and other than computer data, there isn't much worth stealing."

Albert Pryor slowly took in the rest of the room and concluded it was pretty much a shrine to the esteemed Plato Vane. On one wall was a poster size blowup of a magazine cover with Vane staring intently into the camera with his hand resting on an oversized globe. The caption proclaimed him The Earthquake Whisperer. The rest of the walls were littered with pictures of Vane with politicians and celebrities. Pryor's beaming ex-wife was in about half of them.

Pryor motioned to the collection of video cameras in positions along the wall. "Video?"

"Tons of it," Garrison answered with a sigh.

"Any blind spots?"

"None that immediately jumped up," Garrison answered. "I have the tech guys reviewing it now."

"Only one way in or out and no way to avoid being captured on video. We might have this one solved before lunch."

"Yeah. About that," Garrison answered. "According to the electronic login and from a quick review of the raw video, our victim was the only one to come in last night and no one else until…" Garrison checked his notes, "an Okmar Patel came in about two hours ago and found the body."

"Where is Mr. Patel?"

"Luke Nash is interviewing him at the moment."

"Excellent. So where is my body?" Pryor asked.

Garrison motioned toward one of the uniformed officers by the elevator who swiped a card then pressed a six-digit code. The elevator on the right immediately swished open. Pryor and Garrison entered the elevator where the control panel only had two options: Lobby or Lab. Garrison pushed the 'Lab' and the elevator door closed and they began their descent.

At the lab level, Pryor and Garrison exited the elevator and made their way down a corridor. They were passed by a three-foot-tall robotic device with several appendages, including one similar to a human hand. When it approached a door marked 'Computer Room', the door sensed the device coming and automatically swished open.

"What the hell is that?" Pryor demanded.

"My guess is a Roomba on steroids," Garrison answered, "I think they use them for maintenance or something. The place is full of them."

"Good lord," Pryor muttered.

After they had passed the door to the computer room, they could see the real-life R2D2 through an oversized picture window. Through the glass, they could see massive amounts of computing power in action. There were rows after rows of racks and cables. They watched as the mini-robot that had passed them was changing out a hard drive. The robot replaced the old drive with a new one. Then it moved to a black box, about the size of a breadbox, with a warning label identifying it as a 'Degausser'. The robot placed the drive in the box and pressed a button. After a few seconds, the robot removed the hard drive from the box and crushed it with one of its appendages.

"Okay," Garrison said. "That was too weird for me."

"What the hell does 'Degausser' mean?" Pryor asked.

"Don't hold me to it, but I think it means demagnetize."

"Okay," Pryor said as he motioned for Garrison to continue.

"It completely erases all of the data on the drive so it can never be restored."

"Ah. Good to know."

Pryor and Garrison continued down the hall in the direction of a fish bowl conference room where they could see a college-aged student with dark skin and even darker hair with his back to them fidgeting nervously. Across the table from him were Detective Luke Nash and his new partner, Pryor's ex-partner, Detective Maria Ruiz.

Ruiz, a petite and intense Hispanic woman, just short of turning thirty, saw Pryor approaching and her large brown eyes grew even larger. Pryor was no lip reader but he was pretty sure, as his ex-partner closed her eyes and shook her head, she muttered 'oh crap'.

Pryor glanced at Garrison. "A heads-up would have been nice."

Garrison shrugged. "Ruiz is the least of your problems at the moment."

"Fair point," Pryor answered.

Garrison continued. "That's Okmar Patel. He's the one who found the body and he also happens to be our victim's roommate."

"Interesting coincidence."

"My thought, too," Garrison said.

Through the glass, Detective Luke Nash saw Pryor and Garrison approaching, excused himself, and joined them in the hallway.

Nash had briefly been Pryor's partner after Holden and he had gone their separate ways. Nash was a good detective and an even better guy. Pryor's glowing recommendation had been the deciding point for the upper brass to promote Nash to lead detective. Being fairly young for a lead, only thirty-five, and with an unflappable temperament, everyone expected Nash to take Lt. Garrison's spot if he ever got promoted or retired.

Nash had an ear-to-ear grin on his ruddy face as he approached Lt. Garrison. "Please tell me this means our senior homicide detective is back on duty."

"Our senior homicide detective is back on duty."

"Now tell me you're making Albert the lead detective on this case."

"I'm making Albert the lead detective on this case."

"Yes!" Luke Nash did a happy dance then patted Pryor on the shoulder.

Pryor grunted. "No need to be so damn pleased."

Nash continued to smile. "Better you than me on this hot mess."

Pryor pointed in the direction of Okmar Patel. "Is he a candidate?"

"Naw," Nash answered. "We have an exact time of death and unless he has an invisibility cloak he wasn't here. Plus, he had his head between his knees and was breathing into a paper bag to keep from hyperventilating when I got here." Nash glanced at Patel. "But, he clearly knows more than he's saying."

"What's he saying?" Pryor asked.

"He had no idea why his roommate was here. He didn't hear him leave. Blah, blah, blah."

"You think you can sweat the truth out of him?" Lt. Garrison asked.

"Is Christmas going to be in December this year?" Nash answered with a laugh. "I think if I slapped the cuffs on him he'd need a change of undies."

"Great," Garrison said. "Take him downtown and put the fear of God in him."

Luke Nash winked at Pryor. "I've got fifty bucks that says in four hours I'll know everything about him including what porn site he was on the last time he beat off."

Pryor glanced at Patel and shook his head. "Nope," he answered.

"Two to one?"

"Given how much heat is coming down from upstairs," Pryor replied, "I'll give you three to one if you DON'T break this guy in four hours, you'll be assigned to the traffic division by this time tomorrow."

Garrison nodded his agreement.

Nash laughed and pointed toward Pryor. "Like I said. Better you than me."

As Nash turned to reenter the conference room, his smile vanished and was replaced with a scowl. Pryor and Garrison watched through the glass as Nash motioned for Patel to stand up.

"On your feet," Nash said harshly. "We're going to continue our conversation at police headquarters."

Okmar Patel was slow to react as he processed what Nash had just said. As he felt Nash's hand on his arm, jerking him to his feet, his knees nearly buckled. "Oh, God," he muttered as he reached for his paper bag and started breathing into it again.

"By the way," Nash asked bluntly. "What was your immigration status?"

"I have an F-1 student visa and…" Patel panicked. "Wait. Did you ask: what <u>was</u> my immigration status?"

"Yeah," Nash answered casually. "While America welcomes the wretched refuse of our teeming shore, we really don't care much for people who withhold information from the police."

"Especially during a homicide investigation," Maria Ruiz added.

Nash gave Patel an encouraging shove in the back to get him moving. "That's pretty much a guaranteed ticket home for you."

"After a couple of years in prison," Maria Ruiz added in a matter-of-fact tone.

"That's a given at this point," Nash added.

"A cute little guy like you will be real popular on the cellblock," Ruiz said as she sized Patel up. "We're pretty close to the same size. Would you like me to give you a few of my old dresses?"

Patel went ashen and looked on the verge of bursting into tears.

Pryor nodded his approval and leaned into Garrison. "Damn. She's picked up all of Luke's best moves already."

"Agreed."

Maria Ruiz was a step behind Nash when she said to her new partner, "Give me a minute, Luke."

Nash, being a good detective, had been expecting this. He waved over his shoulder without looking back. "I'll meet you upstairs." Then added. "Are the handcuffs in the car?"

Patel groaned, and Pryor and Garrison chuckled.

Ruiz didn't.

Her eyes were locked on Pryor. "Can we talk?"

Pryor shook his head. "Not necessary, Maria."

"But," Maria Ruiz started but stopped when Pryor held up his hand.

"You made the right call. I would have done exactly the same thing you did. At this point in your career, Nash is the perfect partner for you."

"Thanks, Albert," she said as if she had a weight lifted off her.

"Of course," Pryor said with a wicked gleam in his eye. "Getting traded to the B Team means you won't get any of the glory when I solve this case."

Ruiz nodded, slugged Pryor softly in the shoulder then took off in a trot to catch up with Nash before he got to the elevator.

"Damn, Albert," Garrison said. "That was not like you at all."

"What do you mean?" Pryor asked.

"That was nice."

"Maria is a good cop and in a couple of years, after Danny and I are gone, she's going to be the best detective on the force."

"That's the way I see it, too," Garrison said as he motioned toward a door marked 'Main Lab.'

Pryor and Garrison entered the main lab, where it was organized chaos. Considering the high-profile of this case, there was fingerprint powder on every surface. An army of technicians was milling around and every few seconds a camera flash would go off. Along the far wall, there was a station where the robots could roll up and recharge themselves. The station could service a dozen of the robots at the same time, but currently, only three of the bays were occupied.

"Those things are creepy," Pryor said.

"Tell me about it," Garrison agreed.

The body of Nick Blake was still lying on the floor with the Coroner leaning over the corpse. For a gunshot homicide, the body was in remarkably good shape. Other than a red hole in the front of Nick Blake's shirt, it would have been easy to think he was just taking a nap.

Dr. Louis Cutter had started his career as the County Coroner roughly the same time Albert Pryor had moved over to homicide. They had worked more cases together than either wished to remember. Cutter was in his mid-fifties, a bit plump and office-soft. His face looked like it had been arranged in the dark from a box of mismatched pieces. His eyes were too close together and one was slightly lower than the other. His nose was off center and his teeth were crooked. With his short cropped hair and oversized protruding ears, his head looked like a car going down the street with its doors open.

While he was far from pretty, Pryor had always marveled at his meticulous attention to detail and annoyingly methodical step-by-step procedure for dealing with a corpse. He was never going to be rushed and he would never speculate about anything until after he had spent a few close and personal hours with the body on his table.

"Look who's back from the dead," Dr. Cutter said as he glanced up and saw Pryor.

"What we got, Louie?" Pryor asked.

Dr. Cutter glanced up at Lt. Garrison who nodded his approval. "It appears we have a single .357 magnum gunshot to the center of the chest."

Pryor made a face. "That's not like you, calling the caliber so early."

Cutter pointed to his assistant who was holding up an evidence bag with a spent .357 casing. "I'm no detective, but I took that as a clue."

"Ahh," Pryor said as he took the evidence bag and examined the contents.

"Judging by the size of the entry wound and lack of an exit wound," Cutter stated then continued, "I'd say it was probably either a jacketed soft point or a hollow-point. With the small amount of blood on the floor, and lividity, my guess is it was a direct hit that stopped his heart instantly. I'll know more when I get him on the table."

"Time of death?"

"3:10 a.m.," Cutter stated with conviction.

"Again," Pryor said as he pulled back, "that's not like you. How can you be so sure?"

"Based on liver temperature," Dr. Cutter said with a grin, "and the timestamp of the video of him being shot at 3:10 a.m., I'm pretty confident. I'll know more…"

"When you get him on the table."

Dr. Cutter chuckled then nodded in the direction of the young man on his hands and knees with his face in a recycling bin. "Your new kid is an odd one."

"Oh, lord," Pryor muttered as he glared at Lt. Garrison then pointed at the body of Nick Blake. "If a crime scene this neat and tidy sends him looking for something to puke in, what's he going to do at something messy or ripe?"

"Or a floater that's been in the water for a few weeks?" Cutter added.

Lt. Garrison shook his head. "Officer Cummings. What are you doing?"

Kevin Cummings jumped to his feet. His color was good and he didn't look like he had been throwing up. He handed the recycle bin to one of the Crime Scene Techs. "Have the contents checked for gunshot residue."

The tech looked in the container and its shredded contents with a puzzled expression on his face. He glanced at Lt. Garrison who nodded his approval.

The police department required all new recruits to be at least eighteen years old and Pryor would have wanted to see a certified birth certificate and photo ID before letting Kevin Cummings in the doors of the police academy. With his broad shoulders and his narrow waist, he had the long, lean athletic look of a high school middle distance runner or a swimmer who would fill out later at college. Well-muscled, and well-tanned, he did not appear to have an ounce of fat on his six-three frame.

"Why should we check a recycle bin for GSR?" Pryor asked.

"I think that bin contains the murder weapon," Cummings answered. "Or at least what's left of it."

"Excuse me?" Pryor said, trying hard to keep the skepticism out of his voice and off his face but missing both badly.

"According to the computer logs and external video, no one came in or out of this lab after our victim entered until the body was discovered this morning," Cummings answered.

"Okay. So?" Pryor asked.

"So," Cummings answered, "we sort of have a locked room mystery."

Pryor glanced in the direction of Lt. Garrison and rolled his eyes.

"Let's hear him out," Garrison said.

"We found an empty shell casing but a complete search of the lab could not locate the weapon that fired the fatal shot. Sherlock Holmes observed: *Once you eliminate the impossible, whatever remains, no matter how improbable, must be the truth*," Cummings said. "The only logical answer is the killer manufactured his own gun then destroyed it after using it."

Wilson Garrison was grinning from ear to ear. Pryor rolled his eyes again.

"Manufacturing a weapon and then destroying it sounds pretty improbable to me," Pryor said.

"I take it you've never used a 3D printer," Cummings said.

"I've never even seen one," Pryor replied.

Kevin Cummings pointed to a big square machine then waved his hands above his head. "That distinctive sweet oily smell that is in the room comes from the PLA…"

"What the hell is PLA?" Pryor asked as he felt his patience fast approaching a breaking point.

"Sorry," Kevin Cummings said. "Polylactic acid. That's what the 3D printer used to make the gun."

"And you know this how?"

"The heat of the bullet passing through the barrel would have excited the PLA, which is made with either corn starch or sugar cane. That's why the sweet smell is so intense in here. Clearly, the killer manufactured a gun with the printer and ran it through the shredder after firing it."

Pryor and Garrison turned when they heard a tech behind them mutter, "Well I'll be damned."

"What?" Pryor demanded.

"The contents of the bin field tests positive for GSR," the tech answered. "And a whole lot of it."

Pryor had a stunned expression on his face at this unexpected turn of events.

Lt. Garrison patted Pryor on the back. "I told you," Garrison said. "You're going to love this kid." Garrison checked his watch. "Cummings, Pryor. Pryor, Cummings. I'm heading back to the precinct to get a task force set up." Garrison glanced at Pryor as he turned to leave. "Albert, for God's sake, get yourself cleaned up and leave the press to Danny and me."

Pryor snapped off a sorry excuse for a salute. "Yes, sir."

"You two play nice." Garrison turned to Pryor. "It's good to have you back," Garrison said, then added, "I think."

Kevin Cummings extended his hand and Pryor accepted it.

In Pryor's mind, you could tell a lot about a person when they shook your hand. Kevin Cummings checked off all of the good boxes. His grip was firm, but he was not trying to prove a point by squeezing too hard, and he could look you straight in the eye. With his youth and lack of experience, Pryor still had his doubts. But after figuring out the 3D gun thing, combined with his family lineage, he was already starting to like the kid.

"My grandfather told me some stories about you."

"I could tell you a few about him, too," Pryor said. "How is Max?"

"Early stages of Alzheimer's."

"Damn," Pryor said. "I'm sorry to hear that. How's he holding up?"

Cummings shrugged. "He has good days and bad days. He can usually remember stuff that happened 20 years ago clear as a bell but can't tell you what he had for lunch." Cummings's eyes locked on Pryor's. "He would love to see you."

"How's Grace?" Pryor asked.

"You know my grandma," Cummings said with a slight hint of pride. "She's a tough old bird."

"I'll stop by," Pryor said and Cummings knew he meant it. "There is just one problem with your locked room theory, Sherlock."

"What's that?"

"If the gun is still locked in the room, why isn't our shooter still in here too?"

CHAPTER 5

"THAT IS AN excellent question," Kevin Cummings stated. "Another couple of good questions. Our victim knew the elaborate security protocols Vane has in place."

"Meaning?" Pryor asked.

"The mainframe is damn near hack-proof from the outside."

"So he needed to be in the building and he didn't want anyone to know he was here." Pryor nodded. "Which explains why our victim was here at 3 a.m."

"The big questions are," Cummings added, "what was he looking for and what did he find that got him killed?"

"You think he found something?" Pryor asked.

"I know he did. Look at this." Kevin Cummings jumped behind the keyboard at a workstation and the surveillance video from the lab appeared on the screen. "According to the elevator log, he arrived at 1:04 a.m."

In fast forward the video showed an obviously nervous Nick Blake entering the complex, coming down in the elevator and along the hallway and entering the lab. He arrived at the workstation where he was murdered and the camera continued to roll.

"It was nice of the university to give you this video so quickly," Pryor said as his eyes stayed fixed to the scene.

"About that," Cummings said as he hit a button that accelerated the video to the moments just before he was killed. In less than ten seconds they watched Nick Blake consume four Red Bulls and smoke six cigarettes. "Sometimes it is easier to ask forgiveness than permission."

Pryor chuckled. "That's what Max used to always say." Pryor leaned in closer as Cummings slowed the video down to closer to normal speed as it approached the money shot. "So let me guess, you hacked the university's security network?"

"Pretty much," Kevin Cummings answered.

"Will they be able to trace the hack back to you?" Pryor asked.

"What hack?" Cummings asked. "If I get any blowback, my story is that this was already up on this monitor when I got here and we suspected the killer may have hacked into the system to try and cover the crime." Cummings glanced up at Pryor. "You okay with that?"

"If it helps crack the case, I'm more than okay with it."

"Excellent," Cummings answered as the replay slowed to normal speed. "Here we go."

The pair watched as Blake tossed the Red Bull can in the general direction of the recycle bin.

"I'm guessing he wasn't here on an athletic scholarship," Pryor said.

Cummings hit the pause button. "Check out his body language." He hit play. They watched as Blake reread the screen to be sure he was seeing it correctly, then Blake muttered, "Eureka."

"Pause it," Pryor said and glanced at Cummings. "Is there any angle where we can actually see what he is seeing on his screen?"

"I tried every camera angle available but unfortunately no," Cummings answered. "Right after he found what he was looking for, he was murdered." Cummings hit play.

The pair watched as Blake bristled and tensed when he heard a sound at the far end of the room and they heard him ask, "Hello? Is somebody there?" They saw him relax and say, "Oh, it's only you." Then they heard the shot ring out and watched as he took the round in the chest and fell backwards to the floor.

"Okay," Pryor said. "Show me the video of the killer and we can all go home."

"There isn't any."

"Why?" Pryor asked. "Was he in a blind spot or something?"

"That's just it," Cummings said. "With the multiple cameras in the lab, there are no blind spots."

"Then why don't we have a video of the killer?"

"Let me rephrase that," Cummings answered as he rewound the video back a few seconds. "Where is our victim looking?"

Pryor looked at the screen and followed the trajectory of Nick Blake's eyes. "I'll be damned," Pryor muttered. "He was looking down."

"Exactly," Cummings answered. "The desks, oversized monitors and partitions create multiple blind spots below three feet."

"Are you saying our killer crawled in here undetected, killed Blake then crawled out again?"

"No," Cummings answered flatly. "There are no obstructions or desks in the hallway. Even if he were crawling, the camera would have picked him up."

"So how did he get in and out?"

"No idea," Cummings answered with a shrug. "Logically, our killer should still be hiding under a desk in here somewhere."

Pryor scratched the stubble on his cheek and made a face. "At least we know he knew his killer and didn't consider him a threat. That will move his roommate up on the list."

Kevin Cummings laughed. "Who? Okmar Patel?"

"You know Patel?" Pryor asked.

"Yeah," Cummings answered. "We've had a few classes together. He hardly strikes me as the master killer type who could sneak out of here after shooting someone then calmly walk back in a few hours later to discover the body."

"I agree," Pryor answered. "But Detective Nash thinks he's not telling us everything he knows so he's taking him downtown to sweat him a little."

"Sweat him?"

"Luke Nash is probably our best interrogator," Pryor stated. "He likes to let his suspects stew for an hour alone in the interrogation room before he starts the interview, to soften them up. It works great."

Kevin Cummings made a face but it quickly vanished. "Here's another good question. Since the door logs say our victim was the last one in, it stands to reason the killer was already in the room when he arrived but he didn't notice him when he walked in?"

"How does that make any sense?" Pryor asked.

"It doesn't, unless the killer knew he was coming and hid or someone changed the door log," Cummings answered.

"How hard would it be to change the logs?"

Cummings puffed out his cheeks and thought about it for a moment before answering. "Vane is a real Nazi about security with multiple redundancies and offsite real time back-ups of damn near anything that happens in here. With that said, if our killer had full admin rights, it would be difficult to do it without leaving footprints, but not impossible."

"Couldn't someone hack in?"

"No," Cummings stated firmly. "None of Vane's critical systems are online. You need to be in this building to access them."

"Ahh," Pryor said. "Which would explain why our victim was here in the lab instead of doing his mischief from the safety and comfort of his living room." Pryor nodded. "That should narrow down our list of suspects."

"It might not narrow it down as much as you think." Kevin Cummings's fingers flew across the keyboard in front of him. "This is a huge operation," Cummings said as he tapped the computer monitor when the list came up on the screen. "There are currently twenty-two full and part-time paid staff and a like number of interns and grad students with touchpad access to the facility." Cummings turned and faced Pryor. "They're all computer nerds and would have the skill set to hack the system."

"What about the full admin rights?"

Cummings shrugged. "You could watch someone login over their shoulder and not be seen."

"Is that what you did?" Pryor asked.

"No, I..." Cummings stopped and chuckled. "Good one."

"If someone did have the full admin rights to the system." Pryor leaned in and stared at the screen. "Can they make a list of everyone with touchpad access for the past two years?"

"Two years? Ah," Cummings said as he caught up. "Disgruntled former employees." Kevin Cummings's fingers flew across the keyboard, barely touching the keys. "That's two hundred and twelve people."

"Email the list to Lt. Garrison. He can have the task force people start running down alibis."

Before Cummings attached the list to the email, he glanced at Pryor. "Including this one?" Cummings asked as he tapped the screen.

Highlighted was the name "Brooke Pryor."

Pryor shook his head. "No, I already have plans to talk to my daughter after she finishes her morning classes."

With a few lightning-quick keystrokes, her name vanished from the list and it was sent to Lt. Garrison. "Okay," Cummings said. "The lieutenant should have it right now."

"Not that it is going to help much," Pryor said with a yawn.

"Why not?"

"Where were you between 2 a.m. and 4 a.m. this morning?" Pryor asked.

"Oh," Cummings answered as he nodded he understood. "Most of them were in bed, and with them being mostly single college computer nerds, they were likely alone and not snugged up with someone who could give them an alibi."

"Even if they were sleeping with someone, that alibi wouldn't be worth a damn since their partner could be covering for them or they could have snuck out," Pryor said. "So it is unlikely many of the two hundred and twelve will have an airtight alibi."

"Also," Cummings added, "if our killer worked here, his fingerprints could be easily explained away."

Pryor eyed Cummings. The kid had potential.

"Do you have anything else?" Pryor asked.

"The next twenty minutes are totally wiped on all cameras and all angles in the building."

"Why didn't the killer wipe the video of the murder?"

"Wiped was the wrong word," Cummings said. "With Vane's system, once a video is made, it is stored in multiple places, including off-site, and is damn near impossible to delete."

"But," Pryor said. "If you shut down the cameras, there is nothing to erase."

"Bingo."

"Why only twenty minutes?" Pryor asked.

"That would give the killer time to dispose of the gun and hide."

"Hide?" Pryor said with a shocked expression on his face. "Do you think the killer is still here in the facility somewhere?"

Cummings shrugged. "I've accessed the cameras on the exterior of the building, which were not disabled, and no one came out after the murder. Also, no one used the elevator and if they had opened the door to the stairs, an alarm would have gone off."

"Dammit!" Pryor shouted as he reached for his cell phone. "You didn't think to mention that sooner!"

"I did," Cummings answered defensively. "By the time I got here, I was told the uniforms had already done a sweep of the building and it was clear and no one seemed interested in listening to what I had to say."

Pryor couldn't get a signal on his cell phone. "Dammit."

"We're too far underground," Cummings said. "Who are you calling?"

"Garrison," Pryor said abruptly. "I want to get K-9 down here."

"I really don't think that's necessary," Cummings said.

"I don't give a crap what you think," Pryor said as he jammed his phone back into his pocket then put his two pinky fingers to his lips and produced a whistle loud enough to bring all activity in the lab to a halt.

"This building is now on a complete lockdown," Pryor shouted. "No one, and I mean no one, is to leave until they have been cleared. Understood!" Pryor glared and pointed a finger in the direction of a small knot of uniforms near the coffee machine. "And the next time my partner tells you to re-sweep an area, the only words that will come out of your mouth are 'yes and sir' or your sorry asses will be walking a third-shift beat."

Pryor rubbed his forehead and made a face. "Idiots," he muttered under his breath.

CHAPTER 6

L T. GARRISON WAS livid. "I want a name, Cummings," Garrison barked, his voice loud enough to bounce his words off the walls in the nearly deserted conference room. Only four people were attending this gathering. Pryor, Cummings, Lt. Garrison, and the Watch Commander, Frank Manheim, who supervised all of the uniformed officers at the scene.

"I didn't get a name, sir," Cummings said softly.

"Well then," Garrison ordered. "Then let's go back into the lab and you can point him out."

Cummings didn't have to review the troops. Manheim, a twenty-eight-year veteran with the last six as Watch Commander, was standing next to Garrison and was the one who had blown him off. Over six three and in an impressive well-cut and freshly ironed uniform, he looked like a police recruitment poster boy.

Manheim was relaxed and calm, and didn't seem overly concerned. In fact, he seemed to be amused. He had played this game before. If Cummings snitched, he wouldn't deny it but would say he was making a thousand decisions on a high-profile case and he didn't even remember talking to him. He knew the brass would buy his story and nothing would come of this. For him, the big question was what would Cummings say and do. Like everyone else, he knew the lineage and it would be interesting to see how much of his grandfather the rookie had in him.

"It was entirely my fault, sir," Cummings said.

"How the hell do you figure that?" Garrison demanded.

"I failed to identify myself as Detective Pryor's newly assigned partner. Plus," Cummings pointed to the badge clipped to his belt, "not only do I lack a detective's gold shield, since I am still in my

35

one-year probationary period, I have my rookie shield. Considering my rank and youth, there was no reason in the world for any of these officers to take me seriously. In fact, it would have been a breach of the chain of command if they had complied with my request. Sir."

"Is that right," Garrison said as his tone softened. "And why didn't you mention you were working with Detective Pryor?"

"I wasn't certain that I was."

"Meaning?"

"At that point in time," Cummings said as he nodded in Pryor's direction, "I didn't feel it was my place to toss Detective Pryor's name around especially since you had indicated there was a good possibility he might not even be working the case."

All heads turned when a young police officer with a handsome German shepherd in a K-9 vest trotting behind him entered the room. "We've finished the sweep, lieutenant."

"And?" Garrison said.

"Other than Bruno not thinking much of one of the little robots, the area is clean."

"Did you find anything suspicious?" Pryor asked.

"There was a locked door at the rear of one of the maintenance rooms we couldn't access and we didn't breach it."

"Why not?" Garrison demanded.

"For the same reason we didn't, lieutenant," WC Manheim said. "It has a steel bar locked in place on the inside by a heavy padlock."

"If anyone had gone out that door," the K-9 handler added, "they would not have been able to relock it."

Garrison shook his head and turned to the Watch Commander. "We'll just mark this down as a miscommunication, Frank, and it goes no further."

"Yes, sir," the Watch Commander answered crisply.

Garrison wheeled on Pryor. "Don't you have a murder to solve?"

"Yes, sir," Pryor answered quickly.

"Then get to it," Garrison barked as he walked away.

Pryor leaned into Cummings as they headed back into the lab. "Nicely played." Pryor nodded at the Watch Commander who was briefing his men on the outcome of the meeting. A few of them were craning their necks to get a better look at Kevin Cummings.

Cummings nodded in the direction of the Watch Commander. "Like my grandpa always said, never piss off the guy…"

"Who makes out your work schedule," Pryor finished.

They both laughed.

"You made some friends today."

"I'm going to need them," Cummings said matter-of-factly.

"How so?" Pryor asked.

"The way I see it, I'm in a lose/lose situation."

"How so?"

"I know this is a temporary assignment and so does everybody else. After this case is over, and until I have the five years of seniority normally required to take the detective exam, I'm going to have a target on my back. Every ambitious cop on the force will be taking potshots at me and trying to bring me down a notch." Cummings sighed and shook his head. "Even if we solve this case -- a pretty big if -- there is no way in hell the department is giving a gold shield to a guy less than a year out of the academy and six months short of the legal drinking age."

"If you felt that way, why did you take the assignment?"

"I initially turned it down but Lt. Garrison played dirty."

Pryor laughed. "He called your grandfather."

"Worse," Cummings answered.

Pryor burst out laughing. "He called your grandmother?"

"Yup."

Pryor puffed his cheeks out and shook his head. "Damn. That's wrong." Pryor grinned at Cummings. "Do you know who was the least experienced homicide detective in the history of the department?" he asked.

Cummings shook his head.

"You're looking at him."

"How old were you?"

"Because of my military experience, I was older than you," Pryor answered then added. "But I was less than two years out of the academy."

"How did you do it?"

"I was riding with your grandfather one night and he pulled over at a convenience store so he could get a cup of coffee. He stumbled in on an armed robbery in progress. A stupid and scared kid with a gun.

There were three customers and the owner in the store and as soon as he saw Reload, he took them all hostage. As your grandfather tried to talk the kid down, I snuck in a backdoor and found some cat laser pointers."

"Laser pointers?"

"Yeah," Pryor answered with a chuckle. "I hid behind a shelf and put a couple of dots on the middle of the kid's chest. Your grandfather saw them and told the kid to look down. When he did, Reload told him the dots were sniper laser sights. He then told the kid they were locked and loaded and if he didn't drop his gun they'd shoot him." Pryor chuckled again. "The kid not only dropped his gun, he peed his pants."

"Yeah, right."

"I'm serious," Pryor said. "After your grandfather got finished telling the story and writing up the report, I got a medal and my choice of assignments. I've been in homicide ever since." Pryor shook his head and laughed. "Knowing that, Grace probably figures if we solve this case, you might get your gold shield."

"I hope she is right," Cummings answered.

"Your senior officer's recommendation would be mission-critical to get your gold shield." Pryor eyed Cummings hard. "Anything you would like to share?"

"What do you mean?"

"When I got here, your gloves were dirty with slight tears in them like you were doing some quick salvage work around sheet metal." Pryor's eyes narrowed as he pointed toward Cummings's windbreaker. "And you've got something fairly heavy about the size of a deck of playing cards in your left coat pocket."

"Damn," Cummings said as he looked for a quiet spot away from prying eyes and ears. There wasn't any place any better than where they were so Cummings leaned in and lowered his voice. "I've sort of got the computer our victim was working on when he was killed."

"Sort of?" Pryor asked.

Kevin Cummings pointed to a wrecked mess in the general shape and size of a computer on the floor behind where the body had been before Dr. Cutter had it transported back to his office. "The killer knew he didn't have time to format the drive properly and didn't have the access to the server room to degauss it…" Cummings glanced at Pryor to see if he was still keeping up.

"Disks store magnetic information," Pryor said. "When a disk is degaussed, it is wiped completely clean and makes it impossible to recover anything on the drive."

"Okay," Cummings said. "That was unexpected."

"I saw the one in the server room in operation on my way in and I asked about it. While I'm not smart, I'm trainable."

"Good to know," Cummings said.

Pryor pointed to a battered mess on the floor. "Since our killer couldn't format it or degauss it, he beat the crap out of it instead."

"So how does that help us?" Pryor asked.

Kevin Cummings lowered his voice even more. "My grandfather told me you would sometimes overlook a few minor infractions if it helped to catch a murderer."

Pryor shrugged. "There's crime and then there's crime. I've never arrested anyone for littering that helped me put a killer behind bars if that's what you're asking."

"That's exactly what I'm asking," Cummings answered with a smile. "I know somebody who might be able to salvage some of the information on the disk." Cummings's eyes twinkled. "Maybe even what Nick Blake was looking at that was worth killing him."

Cummings pulled a battered hard drive out of his pocket and showed it to Pryor. It was warped and bent.

Pryor eyed the damaged drive and wasn't convinced. "That thing is pretty beaten up."

"True," Cummings said. "But I'm guessing the killer wasn't carrying around magnets so there could still be some salvageable data on it. If the plates on the inside of the drive aren't too badly damaged, we might be able to get something off of them."

"And this is beyond the skill set of our tech people?"

"Yeah," Cummings answered. "Light years beyond. You can probably count on one hand the number of people outside of one of the national security agencies who could pull the data and make sense of it. I don't even come close to making the short list."

"The person you want to give it to is on the list?"

Cummings nodded. "Probably right at the top."

"We use outside contractors all the time for stuff like this. Where's the problem? Is he too expensive for the department's budget?"

Kevin Cummings looked around again before speaking. "There is a better than even money chance the FBI is currently looking for my friend."

"Why are the Feds interested in this guy?" Pryor asked.

"Have you ever heard of BONK?"

"You mean like that hacker character who posted a list of the kinky porn sites the mayor likes to visit?"

"Exactly," Cummings answered. "BONK doesn't steal anything of material value but just likes to bonk self-absorbed jerks and hold them up to public ridicule."

"I like him already," Pryor said with a chuckle. "You want to give him the hard drive?"

"Yeah," Cummings said as he lowered his voice even further and leaned in even closer. "But that would open up a whole bunch of chain of custody issues and make anything we find inadmissible in court."

"So your guy doesn't want anything to do with Five-O and our crime lab can't handle this?"

"Our crime lab is run by a sixty-year-old career bureaucrat who still uses a flip phone and can't figure out how to attach a pdf to an email."

"Huh," Pryor said. "I heard our tech guys are pretty good."

Cummings started laughing so hard he almost choked. When he regained his composure, he said, "I bet you heard that from one of our tech guys or one of the dinosaurs in the department. Just because someone can track down an IP address doesn't make them a tech wizard." Cummings shook his head. "They call me all the time for help."

Pryor blinked a few times but didn't answer. Cummings – and by extension, Lt. Garrison – was correct. He knew nothing about the new technology. He had no baseline to judge what was good or lousy tech work.

"Educate me," Pryor said softly.

"Our tech guys are fine for routine police work. But if they were elite, they would be making twice as much in the local private sector or twenty times as much in Silicon Valley." Cummings let that sink in before continuing. "If we go around them and they find out, we might step on a few toes at the police lab."

"I've never worried about stepping on a few toes if it gets a murderer off of the street."

Kevin Cummings nodded his approval. "That's what my grandfather said you would say."

"So how did you get the hard drive out of the computer without CSI noticing?"

"While they were busy with the body, I might have removed it and inadvertently put it in my pocket instead of with the other evidence."

"These things happen sometimes," Pryor said, sympathetically. "One question. If I had come across as a stickler for the rule book, would you have given your buddy the hard drive without telling me?"

"If I thought it would help find the killer and not corrupt the case, absolutely."

Pryor chuckled. "You are definitely related to Reload. How do you think the killer got out?"

"What you see is just a tiny fraction of the total space."

"I don't understand," Pryor said.

"The only drilling they did was for the elevators. The rest is an ancient tunnel system cut by an underground river eons ago." Cummings could see Pryor wasn't tracking so he clambered up on one of the desks and pushed aside one of the ceiling tiles. "Do you have a flashlight?"

"Always," Pryor answered as he joined Cummings on the desk. He fished his small Maglite out of his pocket and flipped it on before sticking his head through the opening in the false ceiling. He was stunned by what he saw. It was at least another fifteen feet to the rock ceiling and the river cut tunnel went on well after his flashlight beam had reached its limits.

"This place is massive with service tunnels and hidey-holes all over the place," Cummings said. "There are two options. Our killer could lay low in the tunnels until after we leave. Then just mingle with the crowd during a shift change and walk out later. Or, there are multiple access points to the surface if you know where to find them. Either he is long gone or so well hidden he would never be found."

Pryor jumped down off the desk and glared at Cummings. "And you didn't think to mention this earlier."

"Hell!" Cummings answered with a chuckle. "It was you who threw a hissy fit and had the place re-searched before I could tell you about the tunnels. I knew, if our killer knew about the tunnels, we would have no chance of ever finding him down here. It would be a complete waste of manpower and resources to even try."

"That's not your decision to make, Officer Cummings," Pryor snapped. "Old school police work is often a waste of time but you need to check off all of the boxes or a case that looks airtight gets blown up in court." Pryor glared at Cummings. "When you have a high-profile case like this, use your resources and cover your ass."

CHAPTER 7

"FINE," CUMMINGS SAID with a dismissive wave of his hand. "The campus geology department has mapped over thirty miles of tunnels and passageways and they don't think they've even scratched the surface." Cummings shook his head. "If you want to try to search a place half the size of the entire county with multiple exit points, for a guy who is probably long gone by now, be my guest." Cummings shook his head again. "Just leave my name out of it."

Pryor stewed over this new information for a moment. "You're familiar with the layout?"

"I worked here for three months and did some exploring," Cummings answered.

"Hold on," Pryor said with a startled expression on his face. "You worked for Vane?"

"Pretty much everyone in the Computer Science department works for him for a while as a code monkey doing grunt work. He gets free labor and we got a nice addition to our resume."

Pryor shook his head. "That was how you were able to hack the systems so easily. You'd done it before."

"Allegedly," Cummings corrected, "but never proven."

"Since you know the place, you can give me the nickel tour," Pryor said. "After that, I'll need to run home and get cleaned up before we visit our victim's residence."

"On your way in you walked past the computer room, the rest of the finished spaces are just individual offices and storage. Nothing much to see."

"I want to see Vane's office."

Cummings pointed down a hallway.

"So what's the big deal about this place?" Pryor asked.

"This is a massive data center that rivals anything Google or Amazon might build and its only function is to compile data for Dr. Vane's earthquake research."

"I get that," Pryor said. "But why underground?"

"Computers generate heat. The single largest overhead cost for the data center is providing enough air-conditioning to keep the computers cool. Because we're in a cave, the ambient air temperature down here is fifty-eight degrees Fahrenheit. Instead of tons and tons of air-conditioning compressors, all you need are a couple of fans to blow the hot air created by the servers through the miles and miles of cooling tunnels and back into the room."

They arrived at a door marked 'Plato Vane, PhD' but it was locked. Kevin Cummings pulled out his smartphone then swiped the screen of the phone over the sensor pad and a faint 'click' was heard as the door unlocked.

Pryor raised his eyebrows and shot Cummings a look.

"Don't ask."

"I wouldn't think of it," Pryor answered.

As they entered the room, the overhead lights automatically clicked on. Vane's office was a smaller version of the ground floor shrine in the lobby. On the corner of his massive desk was a framed copy of a Time magazine cover with him grinning into the camera. The headline read, "Earthquake Whisperer Is Right Again".

Albert Pryor pointed to the cover. "How do you think he successfully predicts earthquakes?"

Kevin Cummings shrugged. "I have no idea. Frankly, even after working here, it doesn't make any sense."

"Why?"

Cummings pointed to a map on the wall showing the Pacific Ocean and the places where Dr. Vane had sites installed. Operational locations include the West Coast of the continental USA, Alaska, Hawaii, Japan and Indonesia. "He has drilled probes deep into the earth around earthquake fault lines all over the Pacific Rim that send out harmonic waves that bounce back to sensors his computers read and analyze."

"Like radar?"

Cummings shook his head. "More like sonar on steroids. He uses different sound wave frequencies and complex harmonics and bounces them around underground. The computers are constantly crunching the data, then bang, for no rhyme or reason that I could figure out, it spits out his next prediction."

Pryor pulled on a fresh pair of crime scene gloves before moving around to the other side of Vane's desk and opening the top drawer. He discovered a Smith and Wesson .357 chrome model 66 revolver with a 2.8-inch barrel. "My, my. What have we here?" He gently picked up the weapon by the barrel to not smudge any potential fingerprints on the grip or trigger. He carefully pushed the chamber release button on the left side and it flipped open. "Either Vane liked to have an empty chamber so he didn't blow his own foot off or there's a bullet missing."

Pryor brought the .357 up to his nose. "It hasn't been fired recently." He looked at the weapon even closer. "Hell, it doesn't look like it has ever been fired." Pryor dropped the gun into an evidence bag and stuck it into his pocket. "We'll leave the door open and have the crime scene posse process this room."

"When you have a high-profile case like this, use your resources and cover your ass." Cummings grinned in Pryor's direction. "See. I'm trainable too."

"Don't get cocky, kid," Pryor said. "I've been on the force for nineteen years and I've never seen a higher profile case than this one." Pryor tried a file cabinet but it was locked. "Just remember, the quickest ticket from homicide detective to passing out parking citations is to cut a corner or be lazy and have it blow up in your face in court. It makes the DA look bad, the department look bad and you look bad. The higher the profile of the case, the higher the chances of a minor screw-up turning into a major embarrassment."

"Sounds like the voice of experience."

Pryor shook his head. "Your grandfather pounded that into me from day one. There is no use arresting anyone if you can't put them away."

Cummings nodded as he processed this nugget of wisdom. When he saw a uniform walk by the partially open door, he whistled.

The Watch Commander turned around and stuck his head into Vane's office. "Yeah?"

"Could you ask the Crime Scene team to process this room?"

The Watch Commander gave Cummings an odd look then glanced in Pryor's direction. Pryor held up the evidence bag with the .357. The Watch Commander nodded at Pryor before turning his attention to Cummings. "Will do." He grinned at Cummings. "Detective."

Meanwhile, Cummings tried to get into Vane's computer with no luck.

"With all your computer skills, how did you ever end up as a cop?" Pryor asked.

Kevin Cummings shrugged. "I'm good with computers but I don't like being tethered to a desk. Besides, I can't keep up with the average bright 8th grader anymore." Cummings shrugged again. "Plus, I decided I wanted to make a real difference."

"That's a new one," Pryor said with a chuckle. "Why do you think cops make a difference?"

Kevin Cummings gave his senior partner an incredulous look.

"We take the bad people off of the streets and make it safer for the good guys. How can that not be more important than only eating locally grown organic vegetables or spending a Saturday at some protest march that won't change a damn thing?"

Pryor nodded his approval then pointed to a section of the wall which showed a massive project in Hawaii. "What the hell is that?"

Kevin Cummings followed Pryor's eyes to the display. "That's the new Hawaii superstation which is due to come online in the next few days. When that happens, Vane is claiming he will be able to predict every earthquake larger than 4.0 on the Richter scale from San Francisco to Tokyo and Fairbanks to Melbourne."

"Do you believe him?"

Kevin Cummings shrugged. "The new lab is going to be almost dead center in the Ring of Fire."

"You mean like the Johnny Cash song?"

"Who?"

"Good lord," Pryor said as he shook his head. "Never mind. Go on."

Kevin Cummings motioned toward the map on Vane's wall. "This rim around the ring of fire contains some of the most unstable geography on the planet. It has active and dormant volcanoes, earthquake fault lines with a good hunk of the world's population living right on top of them." Cummings paused to be sure Pryor was keeping up. Satisfied, he continued. "Vane claims if he had had the Hawaii facility online in 2012 he would have been able to predict the earthquake and tsunami that caused the Fukushima Daiichi nuclear disaster."

Pryor shook his head skeptically. "Yeah, but do you believe him?"

"The Japanese government believes him," Cummings answered. "They provided over $2 billion in financing for the project."

"You sound like you have your doubts."

Cummings gathered his thoughts for a few seconds while drawing in air and puffing out his cheeks. He slowly let the air out, then said, "The few times I've spoken to him I wasn't impressed. I suppose he's bright enough, but this is NASA moon launch or the Manhattan Project, that built the first atomic bomb, level science with a lot of moving parts. For one guy to pull it off is tough to buy. But, with his track record, it would take long odds to get me to bet against him."

"What do you think of his theory on world overpopulation?"

"He's pretty much like all academics."

Pryor pulled back then asked, "What the hell does that mean?"

"He's a pompous, womanizing, self-righteous asshole. But, I doubt he really believes the world would be a better place if we killed off a few billion people."

"Then, why does he say it?" Pryor asked.

"I think he's just trying to be more outrageous than some of the other alarmists and wants to keep the limelight shining on him. Plus, the more press he gets, the more funding he gets." Cummings grinned. "I'll tell you this, there were more cheers than tears on campus when you kicked his ass."

"I didn't kick his ass," Pryor corrected.

"I've seen the video on YouTube. You threw him through a plate glass window." Kevin Cummings chuckled and shook his head. "If that doesn't count as kicking someone's ass, I'm not sure I know what does." Cummings gave Pryor a quizzical look. "Why didn't he press charges?"

Pryor glared at his new partner. "Ask him."

Cummings gave Pryor a hard look. "Why did you do it?"

"Good lord, Garrison has me riding with Oprah."

"Touchy, touchy," Cummings answered with a quick bark of a laugh then continued. "So. What's next?"

"How did you get here?"

"The Lieutenant rolled me out of bed and since I only live a few miles from here I rode my mountain bike."

Pryor's mouth fell open. "Bike? Seriously?" He shook his head. "You rode your bike to a crime scene?"

"Anytime you want to wager who can get across town faster during rush hour traffic," Cummings answered with a confident grin. "You just let me know. Odds are available."

"Right," Pryor answered. "Unless your bike is built for two, you'll ride with me."

"Tell me you're driving the Barracuda," Cummings said, as he turned and headed toward the door.

"You know about the Barracuda?"

"Yeah. Brooke talks about it a lot."

Pryor grabbed Cummings's arm and spun him around. "Hold on. You know my daughter?"

"Yeah. We went to high school together."

Pryor shook his head in disbelief. "I've met your parents. How could they swing thirty-five grand a year for Churchill Academy?"

Cummings grinned and his eyes twinkled. "I got a scholarship."

"Really?"

"Yeah. I studied football in the fall, basketball in the winter and soccer in the spring."

Pryor said, "Ah. One of those academic scholarships the state athletic director frowns upon."

"I was going to play the sports anyway." Kevin Cummings shrugged. "There were lots of benefits of going to a place like Churchill."

Pryor shook his head and they turned to leave.

As they headed back down the corridor to the elevator, Pryor asked, "Is there anybody involved in this case you don't know?"

"What can I say? This is a small town with a limited supply of computer geeks."

When the duo emerged from the building, the sun was higher in the sky. Most of the police cars had left as soon as the body was loaded into the coroner's van and, without much to see, most of the students had drifted off to class. The handful of uniforms and civilians still milling around weren't a big enough attraction for the enterprising food truck and it had moved on to a more promising location.

Kevin Cummings's mountain bike was the one Lt. Garrison had admired earlier. Cummings bent down and began removing the multiple locks that were securing his bike to the bike rack.

"Those are some heavy-duty locks," Pryor said as he eyed the hardware.

"I paid more for my bike than I did for my car."

"Seriously?"

Cummings finished unlocking the bike and put the locks in a saddlebag behind the seat. Since he was walking with his new partner, he tossed the bike over his shoulder and followed Pryor toward the parking lot. When they reached the restored pickup, Kevin Cummings stopped short.

"I don't know a lot about cars but I'm pretty sure this isn't a Barracuda."

Pryor shook his head. "You're going to make detective in no time." As Cummings started to put the bike in the pickup, Pryor shook a warning finger in his direction. "Watch the paint job," he said as he pulled a tarp out of a toolbox and laid it on the bed of the truck. Under the watchful eye of Pryor, Cummings gently laid his bike on the tarp.

"Happy?" Cummings asked sarcastically.

"Never that I can remember," Pryor answered as he opened the driver's side door and climbed into the old Ford. As they rolled past the barricade and out of the parking lot Cummings started to ask a question but stopped when he saw Pryor raise his hand to stop him.

"I need a shower, another cup of coffee and I need to think."

Cummings made a face and shrugged. As he looked around the restored interior of the truck, he started to reach for the radio but Pryor slapped his hand away. "Don't touch anything."

Cummings gave up, leaned back in his seat and spent the next five minutes sitting still and quiet as Pryor navigated the way to his house,.

Albert Pryor's house was a small and snug Cape Cod with clapboard siding and dormer windows on the second level. Sitting on a flat three acres plus, the yard had grass only; no flowerbeds and no shrubs. While well-groomed, the lack of landscaping meant the yard was very low maintenance. The house sat well back from the road with a poker straight asphalt driveway leading even further back to a garage larger than the house. The building had four massive overhead doors, each large enough and wide enough to accommodate a Kenworth tractor.

On the front porch of the house, an enormous German shepherd lifted his head as he heard the truck approaching. After a yawn and a stretch, the big dog headed off the porch and trotted in the direction of the garage.

Pryor flipped down the visor and hit a button on a remote control device. Instantly, the overhead door on the far left-hand side began to open. He pushed another button on the remote and the door next to it opened as well. Cummings craned his neck and saw an assortment of heavy-duty tools and multiple cars in various states of being restored. In the spot at the far end was a fully restored 1971 Barracuda convertible.

As the pickup rolled to a stop the big dog was standing next to the passenger side door staring hard at Cummings.

Pryor said, "Sit and stay."

The dog didn't sit and continued to stare menacingly at Cummings.

Kevin Cummings said, "Your dog isn't very obedient."

Pryor shot Cummings a glare. "I wasn't talking to him."

Cummings, staying put, twisted his head so he could use the truck's rearview mirror. As he watched Pryor enter the back door of his house, he pulled his phone out of his pocket and hit the first button on his speed dial.

"It's me," he said as glanced around to be sure he was still alone. "They've taken Okmar in for questioning. If he starts talking, we could all be in serious trouble."

CHAPTER 8

ALL SHOWERED AND shaved, wearing a dark blue windbreaker to conceal the badge and gun clipped to his belt, Pryor came out the backdoor of his house.

"Son of a…" he muttered when he saw the hood of the Barracuda up and Kevin Cummings leaning in and examining the engine.

Pryor picked up his pace as he headed down the well-used gravel path leading from the house to the garage. As he walked through the garage door Pryor glared at the German shepherd. "You're some watchdog." The big dog turned his head to avoid Pryor's eyes.

"Blame me, not Blitz," Cummings said as he gave the big dog a much appreciated scratch on the ear.

"Wait a minute," Pryor said as his head snapped in the direction of Kevin Cummings. "How do you know my dog's name?"

Cummings laughed. "While I haven't seen him in years, when I was a kid, my grandfather still had some buddies at K-9. He used to let me wear the pads and have the dogs practice attacking me. I've knew Blitzkrieg when he was a trainee." Cummings gave Blitz another much appreciated ear scratch. "It was really nice of you to take him in after he retired." Kevin Cummings pointed at the Barracuda. "Brooke told me you put some kind of 'semi' engine in this thing."

Pryor closed his eyes and shook his head. "Hemi. A four twenty-six Hemi."

"What the hell is that?" Cummings asked.

Pryor shook his head again. "Just get in."

When Pryor pulled Blitz's vest off the peg on the wall, the big dog trotted over and sat down. The vest was dayglow orange with 'K-9 (Retired)' printed on it so it was readable on either side of the dog's big

51

chest. After it was clicked in place, Blitz bounded into the backseat of the Barracuda without waiting for Pryor to open the door.

"We're taking him?" Cummings asked in disbelief.

"You're a smart boy. You'll figure it out," Pryor answered as he fired up the Barracuda and it rumbled with the unmistakable growl of a vintage muscle car.

Cummings's eyes grew large as he reached for his seat belt and fastened himself in. "How fast will this thing go?"

The Barracuda had been backed into the garage. Pryor pulled a few feet outside of the garage and hit a button on a remote clipped to the sun visor. The big overhead doors closed behind him. He let the Barracuda idle at the end of the long, straight and flat driveway which was nearly a half-mile long. With a smirk on his face, he pulled a hundred-dollar bill out of his front pocket and clipped it under a magnetic hula dancer on the dashboard.

Blitz, knowing what was coming next, whimpered and laid down on the backseat with his head under his paws.

"After I count to three," Pryor said. "If you can grab that hundred-dollar bill before I get to the street, it's yours."

Cummings gave Pryor a sideways glance. "What's the catch?"

"No catch," Pryor said. "One. Two." Just before reaching three, Pryor slapped the Barracuda into first and floored it. The rear tires put up a cloud of blue smoke as the car roared down the asphalt.

"Three."

The sudden acceleration pressed Cummings back in his seat and he had no chance to grab the cash.

Pryor slowed down before reaching the street but Cummings, his face ashen, was too stunned to move. Pryor unclipped the bill and tucked it back in his pocket.

"Maybelline is also equipped with grill lights and a siren," Pryor said as he pulled out onto the empty suburban street. "Whenever you want to have our little competition about who can get across town faster, you let me know."

CHAPTER 9

POLICE HEADQUARTERS WAS in an aging nondescript building that wasn't going to win any architectural awards even when it was new. And it was a long way from being new. Four stories high, it took up about half of a city block with the rest of the block official parking. The entire parking lot was surrounded by a heavy chain-link fence with razor wire on top. The top floor of headquarters, affectionately known as the 'Penthouse', was where the chief and other ranking officers had their offices. The third floor contained the homicide and major crimes divisions, a pair of interrogation rooms and four holding cells.

Putting the holding cells near the top floor instead of in the basement had been a master stroke. Instead of being out of sight and out of mind in the basement, the only door leading to the cages always was in a clear view of anywhere from ten to thirty cops in the bullpen. The door and walls were thick enough that even the rowdiest drunks or belligerent homeless person screaming nonsense couldn't be heard in the main squad room. In the thirty-two years the building had been in use, they had never had an escape from one of the holding cells.

Detective Luke Nash entered the station with a fresh cup of Starbucks coffee in his hand. The writing on the paper cup was roughly novel-length. Above his hand and the liner sleeve you could see, *Half Caf, No Foam.* The rest of the instructions were obscured by the brown cardboard he had slipped on his cup after it was delivered. Nash was picky about his coffee and he kept a private stash of organic, fair-trade dark Sumatra locked in his drawer on the rare days he was tethered to his desk all day. He turned to his partner, Maria Ruiz, who was also carrying a small Starbucks to go paper cup. She wasn't a coffee snob like her partner, so hers was plain black.

"The kid has been alone in the box long enough; he probably needs another paper bag to breathe into by now," Nash said as he took a sip of his beverage. Simply calling it coffee didn't seem right.

Ruiz nodded her agreement.

They arrived at the one-way glass window overlooking interrogation room Number One and saw that it was empty. "What the hell!" Nash barked as he wheeled and headed in the direction of a grizzled old desk sergeant who was busy filling out some paperwork. When he saw who was managing the desk, Nash shook his head. "O'Malley," Nash muttered. "I should have known."

"He may just be in the bathroom," Ruiz offered half-heartedly.

There was always some tension between plain clothes detectives and uniformed officers. With Detective Luke Nash and Sergeant Frank O'Malley, it often erupted into open warfare. Nash thought O'Malley was an annoying paper pusher with zero sense of urgency who only operated at two speeds. Slow and slower. O'Malley, after nearly twenty years as the gatekeeper of the third floor, thought Nash was a lazy waste of a gold shield who tended to cut corners and was sloppy with his paperwork.

Sadly, they both were probably right.

"You were supposed to be keeping an eye on my witness," Nash barked at O'Malley. "Where is he?"

The sergeant put his pen down and looked first at Nash then his cup of coffee. He shook his head and picked his pen back up. O'Malley's eyes locked on Nash and he said caustically, "Since the precinct's coffee isn't good enough for you and you were on one of your famous coffee runs, you missed seeing two big-time lawyers walking him out of here about ten minutes ago."

"On whose authority?" Nash demanded.

"Lt. Garrison said to kick him loose, so I kicked him loose." The sergeant turned his attention back to his paperwork. "If you've got a problem with that, I recommend you take it up with Lou."

CHAPTER 10

EADS TURNED AT the sound of the throaty rumble of the Barracuda's engine as it rolled to the curb in a sketchy part of town. The deceased Nick Blake had lived in the first ring neighborhood closest to the college campus. Most of the buildings were old and minimally maintained. Nearly every building within sight was three or four stories with retail shops on the ground level and apartments on the upper floors. Apparently, both the building owners and the retail renters viewed these places as nothing more than cash cows and things like fresh paint and regular cleaning were considered detrimental to the cash flow. The residents were a mix of a few low-income, blue-collar families but this close to campus, it was mostly students. The farther you moved from campus, the student to civilian ratio dropped. A stone's throw from the main campus, the neighborhood was fairly safe during daylight hours but after sundown, it was best to travel in a group and not solo.

"Blitz," Albert Pryor said.

The big dog's ears perked up.

"Guard the car."

The dog's demeanor immediately changed from big and lovable to threatening. Blitz was now sitting in the backseat at full attention with his ears up and his head slowly rotating, looking for any potential source of danger. His presence did not go unnoticed. Some of the locals suddenly found the urge to head in a different direction or cross the street to avoid walking past the glaring beast.

A college-aged kid who, considering his wardrobe and haircut, probably was a trust funder, started to approach the Barracuda. Wearing five hundred dollar sneakers, designer blue jeans and a four hundred dollar North Face windbreaker, he was making no attempt to look like the common man. He had the look of a guy more interested in impressing the ladies at the local coffee shop or bar than his neighbors. He walked with a confident, bordering on cocky, stride in the direction of the meticulously restored muscle car.

"Sweet ride," he said before stopping short when Blitz growled and showed his teeth. Startled that Blitz did not share his level of self-importance, he pulled back. "That thing should be on a leash."

"College boy?" Pryor asked.

"Yeah."

"Try reading the vest." Pryor casually let his windbreaker flip open as he got out of the car so the college kid could see his badge and gun. "I would highly recommend you do not put your hands on or near this vehicle."

The student started to say something but thought better of it as his eyes locked on Blitz. The big dog gave him a cold, dark stare and licked his chops like he was anticipating a nice snack. The student scurried away.

"Ah," Kevin Cummings said as he nodded his approval. "I'm guessing Blitz would be a better deterrent than a few bike chains."

"Natural born detective," Pryor said sarcastically as he rounded the Barracuda and headed to the curb.

Cummings joined him on the sidewalk and pointed in the direction of a weather-beaten door with faded and flaking green paint in a small alcove between a dry cleaner and a coffee shop. "That's it right there."

"You've been here before?" Pryor asked.

"Yeah," Cummings answered. The door's lock wasn't working and the hinges groaned and complained when Cummings pushed it open. The entry was poorly lit by a single 40 watt bare bulb. The smell of fish and cabbage hung in the air.

"Nick's place is on the second floor," Cummings said as he waited to see if he should take the lead or not.

Since he was familiar with the building, Pryor indicated Cummings should take point and then followed his partner up the stairs.

When they reached the top of the stairs, they could see the door to Nick Blake's apartment was slightly ajar. As they moved closer, they could hear activity inside.

Both cops pulled out their department issued Glock 17's.

Pryor nudged the door with the barrel of his Glock but stopped when he saw someone in a hoodie with their back to him typing on a computer. Pryor pointed to his eyes then held up one finger. Cummings nodded. Even though Cummings had never served in the military, basic hand signals had been pounded into him at the police academy. Next, Pryor silently indicated he would go left and Cummings should go right. Cummings, with his Glock drawn, knew this was no time for questions or missed communication. The only call worse for a cop than entering a room with an unknown number of suspects, was a domestic violence call. On a domestic disturbance run, there was always a chance you'd die on some deranged wife-beater's front porch while you had your gun in its holster and your finger on the doorbell button.

Pryor charged in. Cummings was half a beat behind.

"Freeze!" Pryor shouted as he leveled his weapon on the person in the hoodie. "Put your hands where I can see them!"

While this was happening, seeing his partner had the known suspect under control, Cummings began clearing the room looking for any other potential threats. He stopped when he heard a familiar voice.

"About time you got here."

Pryor lowered his weapon. "Brooke?"

Pryor's daughter, Brooke, swiveled around in her chair. She was wearing a t-shirt that said:

51% Angel
49% Bitch
(Margin of error, +/- 3.5%)

She had a silly grin on her face. "FYI. If you're in stealth mode, don't drive the Barracuda. I heard you coming a block away."

Pryor holstered his weapon and Cummings did the same. "How did you get in here?"

Brooke laughed. "Duh, with my key."

"Why do you have a key to a dead man's apartment?" Pryor demanded.

"You're the detective," she said with a laugh. "You'll figure it out."

Kevin Cummings reached into his pocket and handed Brooke the hard drive. "Here's the drive I sent you the text about."

"Hold on," Pryor demanded. "Brooke is your guy?"

Kevin Cummings replied, "I only called her my friend. You're the one who kept calling her my guy."

"Such a sexist," Brooke muttered. "He thinks only males have opposable thumbs." Brooke put on a pair of white cotton gloves before opening the evidence bag. Next, she pulled a set of jeweler's tools out of her pocket and started disassembling the drive.

"Brooke inherited your mechanical skills. She can…"

Pryor wheeled on Kevin Cummings and slammed him against the wall. "You've been leading me around by my nose all morning. You're that BONK character the FBI is looking for and you made my daughter an accomplice!"

"Jeez, relax, Dad," Brooke said with a dismissive tone without taking her eyes off the hard drive. "The FBI is looking for one hacker when BONK is really a combination of four people with different skill sets." Brooke held up one finger and smiled at Cummings. "Wait for it."

"Son of a bitch," Pryor shouted as he maintained his grip on Cummings. "B is for Brooke. O is for Okmar. N is for the dead guy Nick. I have a pretty good guess who K might be."

"And there it is." She glanced over her shoulder and checked the time on the computer monitor. "And since he got it before noon, the bet doubles." Brooke held out her hand in Kevin Cummings's direction. "You owe me forty bucks."

Pryor slammed Cummings into the wall again, this time with more authority. "How well do you know my daughter and what kind of nonsense have you gotten her involved in?"

"Chill, Mr. Macho. Kevin didn't recruit me for any nefarious acts." Brooke laughed. "I recruited him."

Pryor released his grip on Kevin Cummings and wheeled on his daughter. "You did what?!"

Brooke fluttered her eyes and cocked her head. "I just love these little father/daughter bonding moments, don't you?"

Pryor sighed and shook his head. "Let's start from the beginning."

"Oh, goodie," Brooke said. "This should be fun."

"Were you dating Nick Blake?" Pryor demanded.

"First off, he was hideous," Brooke answered with a quick laugh. "And second, Nick never looked up from his keyboard long enough to even notice that I was a girl."

"Then why do you have a key to his apartment?"

"Because…," Cummings started to answer but a warning finger pointed in his direction by Pryor stopped him mid-sentence.

"I'll be getting back to you in a minute," Pryor said as he turned his attention back to his daughter. "If you weren't dating him, why do you have a key to a murder victim's apartment?"

"Really?" Brooke asked in disbelief.

Pryor looked around the room and even he was impressed by the computer firepower. He closed his eyes and rubbed his forehead like he was trying to forestall a migraine.

"Crap."

"That's my daddy," Brooke said proudly. "Welcome to the secret world headquarters of BONK, Inc."

Albert Pryor took a few moments to gather his thoughts before glancing at his partner, who was doing everything possible to make himself invisible. He turned back to Brooke. "Are you dating Kevin?"

Brooke made a horrified face. "Eeew. No."

Kevin Cummings took a step back. "Eeew? What do you mean, eeew?"

"Okay. Sure we hooked up in high school…"

"Hooked up?" Cummings protested. "You make it sound like a hot weekend! We dated for nearly two years."

"You did what?" Pryor demanded as he resisted the urge to draw his Glock back out of its holster.

Brooke gave her father a dismissive wave of her hand. "What, are you twelve? Do you think all of the bored rich girls at Churchill Academy spend their time thumbing through magazines looking for the perfect debutant dress and pining for Mr. Right?" She shook her head. "Kevin was on everybody's bucket list, including most of the female staff."

Pryor glared at Cummings who just shrugged.

"Like I said. There were a lot of benefits to attending Churchill Academy." Cummings turned his attention back to Brooke. "I thought we had a great time while we were dating."

"Hey, don't get me wrong, you were great in bed and everything." She ignored her father's growl and continued. "But, you're just too much like my daddy for it to ever work."

Pryor started to speak but was too flummoxed by his daughter to form words.

"Like your dad?" Cummings said in disbelief. "Is that a compliment or an insult?"

"Probably a bit of both," Brooke answered. "I'm just not going to make the same mistake my mother made."

"What the hell does that mean?" Pryor demanded.

Brooke just laughed and shook her head. "Look, pops, I'm a bright girl who is good at math and can read a calendar. I was born five months and eight days after you and Mom got married. So unless four month premature babies routinely weigh eight pounds and three ounces at birth, Mom went down the aisle with a bun in the oven."

"You have no idea what you're talking about," Pryor said without much conviction.

"Don't get me wrong," Brooke said. "I'm not complaining. In fact, I've always been grateful I got Mom's looks and your brains instead of the other way around."

"Meaning?"

"Meaning," Brooke answered. "In this day and age, with the plethora of birth control options available, a woman has to be incredibly stupid to get pregnant." Brooke shrugged. "Mom has always been a looker but never the brightest bulb in the basket. She was stupid and got knocked up. But, you were willing to man up and marry her. All in all, this speaks better about you than her."

"You have no idea what you're talking about," Pryor repeated with even less conviction this time.

"Really?" Brooke said. "Here's what I think happened." She lowered her chin and gave her father a knowing look. "Feel free to jump in and correct me at any time." She waited for any objections by her father and when none came she cleared her throat and continued. "Mom meets this rugged, no-nonsense John Wayne type." Brooke glanced in the direction of Kevin. "My guess is you were probably working security at one of Grandpa's doodads. You intrigued her since you're very different than the pampered metrosexual, gender-fluid high society types she's always dated. Looking for a bit of rough, she spends a torrid weekend with you. Then a few weeks later, surprise, surprise. A little bundle of joy, with that being me, is on the way. How am I doing so far?"

Pryor growled but didn't answer.

"Mom wants to get rid of her little personal problem and asks Grandpa to fund her abortion. But Grandpa, being a good Catholic and knowing my mom, figures this might be his only shot at a grandchild, and he wouldn't hear of it." Brooke's eyes locked on her father. "What did Grandpa threaten her with?"

Pryor drew in a deep breath through his nose, held it briefly then let it out with a snort. So far, his annoying daughter had been spot on in her analysis and now that she was past voting age, it was time to let all of the skeletons out of the family closet. "Either have the baby or she could start looking for a job because he was cutting off her allowance, cutting up her credit cards and he would disinherit her."

"Ouch!" Brooke winced. "What did Grandpa threaten you with?"

"He didn't have to threaten me."

"Oh, that's right; he bribed you instead."

"Bribed?"

Brooke gave her father another dismissive wave. "I hacked Grandpa's computer and saw where he paid for your snug little house and fancy garage."

"He paid for it, all right. But it wasn't a bribe to marry your mother."

"Really? What was it for?"

"Your grandfather paid me to divorce your mother."

CHAPTER 11

BROOKE WAS STUNNED. "Whoa. I didn't see that one coming. What happened?"

"Your mother and I were making each other miserable and you were in the line of fire." Pryor drew in another deep breath through his nose as he decided whether or not to continue.

Brooke read him perfectly. "In for a penny, in for a pound."

"Yeah," Pryor said. "Your grandfather might have made your mother stick it out with me, but…" He hesitated.

"But, what?" Brooke demanded.

"I was a huge disappointment to your grandfather."

A light clicked on in Brooke's eyes. "Ohhh!"

"Oh, what?" Kevin Cummings asked with a confused expression on his face.

Brooke turned to Kevin. "Grandpa was greasing the skids for my daddy to eventually be the chief of police or even higher. But," Brooke nodded in her father's direction. "He had no ambition to be anything other than a homicide detective." She turned her attention back to her father. "So, why the bribe?"

"I wouldn't call it a bribe," Pryor answered. "I would have gladly divorced your mom in a heartbeat but your grandfather, the good Catholic, didn't want a divorce, he wanted an annulment."

Brooke slapped her forehead. "I get it! So by you not fighting the annulment, mom was able to have the social event of the year with a big Catholic church wedding when she married Plato."

"What your grandfather gave me was table scraps compared to what he had to give to the archdiocese to get them to sign off on the annulment. It's hard to square that a marriage never existed when there is a smart-mouthed rug-rat underfoot." Pryor glared at his daughter. "With that being you."

This time it was Brooke's turn to growl.

"Okay. Okay," Cummings said as he grabbed Brooke's arm and turned her in his direction. "Let's get back to the two of us. I've asked you out at least a dozen times in the past few years and you've blown me off every time." Shaking his head in disgust, he continued, "and now I find out it is because you have daddy issues?"

Brooke started laughing so hard she got tears in her eyes. "Don't be silly, Kevin," she said, as she regained her composure and rubbed his cheek. "I don't have daddy issues with you. I have friends' issues."

"What? You just want to be my friend?"

"No," Brooke answered with a chuckle. "My issue with you is you've had sex with all of my friends."

"Who is being twelve now?" Cummings asked.

"I'm not going to date a guy, then have everyone I know wanting to compare notes."

Pryor closed his eyes and rubbed his forehead again. "Will somebody please shoot me?"

All heads turned when Okmar Patel entered the apartment.

CHAPTER 12

P ATEL WAS FIRST relieved when he saw Kevin and Brooke but panicked when he saw Pryor. "My lawyer said I don't have to talk to you," he sputtered.

"Lawyer?" Pryor muttered. "How did they even know you had been taken…"

Brooke glanced in Cummings's direction. "Wait for it."

Pryor wheeled on Kevin Cummings again. "You called to get Patel a lawyer while I was in the shower."

"Oh," Brooke said with a disappointed groan. "So close."

"Son-of-a-bitch," Pryor said as he caught up. "You called Brooke and she called her grandfather who called the lawyer."

"That's my daddy!"

"You are a real piece of work, Brooke," Pryor said as he glared at his only child. "Not only did you get your grandfather to pull strings to get me on this case; you got Cummings here assigned as my new partner so you would know exactly what was going on in the investigation."

Brooke shrugged and, without even a smidgeon of remorse, said, "You are on fire! I figured between the two of you, the killer doesn't stand a chance."

"There is obviously one thing you didn't consider," Pryor said.

"What's that?" Brooke asked.

Pryor looked first at Cummings then at Patel then back to Cummings.

"Crap," Cummings muttered as his shoulders slumped. "I didn't think of that."

"What?" Brooke asked with a hint of panic in her voice. She had no idea where this was headed, but if both her dad and Kevin were worried, she was too.

Pryor gave Cummings a shove in Brooke's direction. "You tell her, smart boy."

Kevin Cummings cleared his throat and sighed. "Nick Blake discovered something worth killing him over at Vane's lab last night." Cummings's eyes danced back and forth between Brooke and Patel. "The killer is still out there."

"Wait for it," Pryor said as he glared at his daughter.

Brooke's eyes flew open. "Oh crap, oh crap," she said as she put her hands on top of her head to keep it from exploding. Her eyes filled with tears. "I shined a spotlight on Okmar by having Grandpa send big time lawyers to spring him."

"The killer will think since he was Nick's roommate and co-worker, there is a good chance he knows what Nick knows," Cummings added.

"Wait," Patel asked with a hint of panic in his voice. "What does that mean?"

"It means by getting you out of jail, I've put you on the killer's radar," Brooke answered.

"And taped a bull's eye on your back," Pryor added.

"Wait. What?" Okmar Patel said as he started looking for a paper bag to breathe into.

"What have I done?" Brooke asked as she started pacing in a tight circle.

"Am I in danger?" asked Patel, as he fell heavily into a chair.

"Not if the killer can't find you," Pryor answered. "Pack a bag with a change of undies and your toothbrush. We're going to move you to a safe house." Pryor's eyes locked on his daughter. "You too, Brooke."

"No way," Brooke answered and shook her head emphatically to indicate no further discussion was necessary. "The tools I need to see if I can get anything off of the disk are all here."

"Can't you do it someplace else?"

Brooke shook her head. "Would you want to pull an engine and rebuild it any place besides your garage?"

"She's right," Cummings confirmed. "There are only two other places I know equipped for this; the police lab or Vane's lab."

"How many people know who the members are of your little internet superhero wannabes?" Pryor asked.

"Oh, God! He knows about BONK?" Patel was on the verge of tears. "I don't want to go back to India. It's crowded and smells bad."

"The only people who know about BONK are the four of us in this room," Cummings said.

"You sure?" Pryor asked.

"Yeah. No one in the cybercrime department has a clue. One of their guys asked for my help and I sent him off on a wild goose chase. He'll be wandering around the dark web for the next few years."

Pryor turned to Okmar. "What about you? Did you tell anyone?"

"Are you kidding?" Patel asked as he took a few quick breathes in his bag before continuing. "Brooke would kill me and bury my body in the woods if I told anyone."

Brooke shrugged then nodded her agreement. "Only after cutting you up into small unidentifiable pieces."

Patel began breathing in his bag again.

Pryor shook his head, sighed, and glared at his daughter. "I'm not leaving you here alone. You can stay at my place."

"That's not going to happened," Brooke said with a laugh. "Once I'm finished here, I'm planning on staying at the safest place in the world."

"Where would that be?" Cummings demanded.

Pryor nodded his approval. "Her grandfather's compound."

"Unless the person who killed Nick is a ninja or Jason Bourne, I like my chances at Grandpa's." Brooke shrugged. "Besides, I don't have a target on my back like Okmar."

All of the color dropped out of Patel's face as he reached for his paper bag and once again began breathing into it.

"Nice," Cummings said disgustedly.

"What?" Brooke demanded. "He knows the score."

Cummings pointed in Patel's direction. He was now sitting in a chair, with his head between his knees, breathing heavily into his paper bag.

Brooke's shoulders sagged and she reached out to comfort Patel. With his eyes closed, he didn't see her hand coming and nearly jumped out of his skin on contact.

"My dad and Kevin will see to it nothing happens to you," she said softly.

Patel just kept breathing into his paper sack.

Pryor shook his head as his eyes locked on his daughter. "I'll want eyes on you."

"Nope," she answered flatly.

"How about a retired police officer?" Cummings said with a twinkle in his eye.

Pryor pointed in Cummings's direction and laughed for the first time in days. "Excellent!" Pryor walked over and stuck his head out the open window facing an alley. He whistled and as soon as he had the big dog's attention, he wiggled a finger.

Blitz jumped out of the back of the Barracuda and sprinted down the alley. He jumped on top of a row of garbage cans, then a higher dumpster, then a stack of barrels before landing lightly on the fire escape.

As he came through the open window, Patel had another panic attack and began to climb up on one of the workstations. When Blitz saw Brooke, he whimpered and bounded playfully in her direction. Brooke gave the dog a hug and a rub.

"Who's the good boy?" she asked as Blitz leaned against her leg and put a massive paw on her knee.

"That's the biggest dog I've ever seen," said a breathless Patel from his perch on the desktop. "Does he bite?"

Brooke made a kissy-face in Blitz's direction. "He only bites someone when I tell him to."

Okmar Patel did not find that nugget of information the least bit reassuring.

Pryor patted Cummings on the shoulder. "That was good thinking. I'll take Blitz in the room over a cop or one of Grandpa's men outside the door any day."

Pryor patted Cummings on the shoulder a bit harder than necessary. "We're still going to have a chat after all of this is over."

Kevin Cummings gulped. The rumor around the station was before he joined the department, Pryor had been some kind of black ops assassin when he was in the military. While still in uniform, his partner got sucker punched and knocked unconscious in a fight at a biker bar. When he came to, the bar was empty except for three Devil's Disciples sprawled motionless on the floor waiting for transport to the

ER. Pryor didn't have so much as a scraped knuckle. Cummings was pretty sure killing someone, cutting them up into small pieces and burying them in the woods was just a figure of speech for Brooke. With Albert Pryor, especially for someone who had bedded his daughter and put her in harm's way, he wasn't so sure. Both his grandparents had warned him that Pryor was slow to anger but watch out when he did.

Cummings shook it off and turned his attention to Okmar Patel. "Whoever killed Nick is pretty tech-savvy. You'd better go offline and lock down your cell phone."

Okmar Patel picked up a small black bag slightly larger than his phone and dropped the phone inside.

"What's that?" Pryor asked.

"It's a Faraday cage shielding case that completely blocks any signals from getting in or out so no one can track your phone's built-in GPS." Cummings chuckled. "The FBI and the NSA hate it."

"Never heard of it," Pryor said. "Is it new?"

Brooke, with Blitz curled up at her feet, had returned to opening the damaged hard drive. "They came out when you were a kid."

Cummings glared at Brooke. "They've been around for over a hundred years. They use it mostly to shield coaxial cables and microwaves."

"Microwaves?"

"When you look through the glass door of a microwave you can see the metal Faraday grid."

Pryor pickup up one of the Faraday cell phone packets from a stack on the desk. It was lightweight and, if he didn't know better, he would have thought it was made out of cloth. "Where can I get one of those?" he asked.

This time, all three of the young people in the room laughed.

"Old coots are so cute," Brooke said as she turned on a high-intensity desk lamp and leaned in closer to the hard drive.

"You can buy one on Amazon.com starting at about $10 bucks in your choice of styles and colors," Cummings said. "These are the higher-end ones that we use whenever we're BONKing somebody. They will take a cell phone or computer completely off the grid."

"Seriously? If these things are so cheap and readily available, then why do people throw phones away?"

Brooke, still disassembling the drive, said, "It makes sense to dump an anonymous cheap burner phone if you don't want it traced back to you."

"It's only on bad TV shows where people throw expensive phones out the window of moving cars," Cummings added. "It's visually dramatic but economically stupid. Put it in a Faraday cage and it can't be traced. Change the SIM card and it's like it's a completely different phone."

Cummings pulled Pryor aside and spoke softly. "What are we going to do with Okmar? There is no way in hell we can put an uncooperative witness in an official safe house without coming clean on everything."

Pryor grinned. "Blitz isn't the only retired police officer we know."

Cummings started laughing. "Brilliant."

CHAPTER 13

AL PRYOR WAS behind the wheel of the Barracuda with Kevin Cummings in the front passenger seat. Okmar Patel was getting blown around in the backseat.

Kevin Cummings shook his head and said, "Brooke drives me crazy sometimes."

Pryor shot Cummings a quick glance. "Do you really want to have a conversation with an armed man about your relationship with his daughter?"

"All I'm saying…"

Pryor floored the Barracuda, pressing Cummings back in the passenger seat and terrifying Okmar Patel. Pryor took his foot off of the gas and swung the muscle car in the direction of the curb and when it came to a full stop, Pryor, red in the face, turned to face Cummings. "You ever heard of don't ask, don't tell?"

"Sure, but…"

"I'm not asking and you're not telling. Are we clear?"

"But…"

"Don't. Make. Me. Shoot. You."

"Excuse me," Patel said meekly.

"What?" Cummings and Pryor said in unison as both of their heads snapped in the direction of the rear seat.

"Perhaps it would be safer for me if you just dropped me back off at my apartment."

"Relax," Pryor said as he put the muscle car in gear and gently pulled away from the curb. "We'll have you at the safe house in a few minutes." Pryor shot Cummings a cold glare and it was returned in kind.

"Some partner," Pryor muttered to himself but loud enough he was sure Cummings heard him. Cummings, his nose flared and his eyes locked straight forward, shook his head. "Back at you."

Pryor slowed down, put on his turn signal, and made a left turn into a subdivision that was built in the 1970s and clearly showing its age. They drove down a street that at one time had been lined with nearly identical tract homes. As the years had passed, some of the homes had been remodeled and expanded, some were still pretty much the same, while others had declined.

They pulled into the driveway of a well-maintained house that had never been remodeled. The mailbox said 'Cummings' and had a police star decal.

As the car pulled to a stop, Pryor unfastened his seatbelt and started to reach for the door handle. He stopped when he saw Kevin Cummings wasn't moving.

"What?" Pryor asked gruffly.

Kevin Cummings sighed. "You haven't seen Max in a while. I'm not sure he'll be able to handle this."

"What? What?" Patel said with a hint of panic in his voice.

Pryor laughed as he opened the car's door. "I seriously doubt anyone is looking for Okmar."

"Why?" Cummings asked.

"Because if the killer suspected Nick had shared anything with him..." Pryor glanced over his shoulder toward the backseat then rolled his hand in the hope that Cummings would catch up.

"Got it," Cummings said.

"Got what?" Patel demanded.

"Nothing," Pryor said as he held the car door open and flipped the driver seat forward so Patel could get out.

"What?" Patel demanded as he folded his arms across his chest and refused to leave his seat.

Pryor glanced at Cummings who shrugged. "When he calms down, he'll probably figure it out for himself."

"Figure out what?!" Patel's voice cracked.

"We brought you here to get you away from the other police officers so they don't work BONK out of you," Cummings said.

"Besides, it is highly unlikely the killer is after you, Okmar," Pryor said.

"How do you know that?"

"The killer had four hours from the time he killed Nick to when the body was discovered. If he thought you were a loose end or there was anything at your apartment that would point us in his direction, we wouldn't be talking to you right now."

"Who would you be talking to?" Patel asked.

"We'd be talking to your parents and arranging for them to pick up your body."

"Oh, God," Patel said as he located his paper bag and began breathing into it again.

"Nice," Cummings said as he glared at Pryor. "I see you have the same basic people skills as your daughter."

"My job is to catch killers, not be in the running for Mr. Congeniality." Pryor grabbed Okmar by the scruff of the neck and pulled him out of the car. "If someone shows up looking for you, Kevin's grandfather will be the least of their problems."

"Does he have a dog too?" Patel asked hopefully.

"Naw," Pryor said as he gave a dismissive wave of his hand. "He's got something much better than that."

"As I live and breathe," said a sweet female voice.

All heads turned in the direction of the porch. They saw a plump, gray-haired woman in a summer dress and apron, stepping through the front door to see who was in her driveway.

"Is that Albert Pryor come for a visit?" she asked as she clapped her hand before turning back to the open door and shouting. "Max. MAX! You're never going to believe who's here."

Kevin Cummings waved and smiled. "Hi, Grammy."

Grace Cummings bounded down the three steps and gave her grandson a hug. "I must have known you were coming." She winked. "Fresh cookies just came out of the oven."

Kevin Cummings's eyes grew large. "Oatmeal raisin?"

"Of course."

Cummings circled around his grandmother and sprinted into the house. Grace Cummings eyed Okmar.

She turned her attention to Pryor. "What have we here?"

"This is Okmar Patel," Pryor said as he gave Patel a gentle shove forward. "He needs a place to stay for a few days."

Grace Cummings gave Pryor a sideways glance. "Does this have anything to do with that problem over at the University this morning?"

Pryor nodded and Grace eyed Okmar with new interest.

Kevin Cummings returned with a mouthful of cookie and handed one to Okmar and one to Albert. Okmar reluctantly took a bite then his eyes flew open.

"I'm tasting ambrosia!"

"Right?" Cummings answered with a mouthful of cookie. "She uses real molasses."

"Are you a friend of Kevin's, dear?" Grace Cummings asked as she brushed some crumbs off of the front of her grandson's shirt.

Patel politely finished chewing then said, "Yes, ma'am."

"Aren't you well-mannered?"

A large man appeared in the doorway. "Well look what the cat dragged in. Hello, rookie."

"Hey, Max," Pryor said. "How ya doin'?"

The retired cop had aged badly since the last time Pryor had seen his old training officer. He had always had the build of an NFL nose tackle. Right around six feet tall but thick and muscled. He had been the kind of guy who, when in uniform, could always bench-press more than his body weight at his annual physical. He wasn't ever going to outrun anybody but he could 'open' a locked door with his shoulder faster than most people could with a key. During his retirement, he had pretty much gone to seed. He had added more than a few inches to his waistline and his complexion was shallow and pasty from the lack of sun.

Max Cummings eyed Okmar with suspicion then held the door open and everyone headed inside.

The house was small and the furniture was old and well-used. One end of the room was a shrine to the life and times of Officer Maxwell Cummings. There were mounted pictures and awards on the wall and trophies for marksmanship on the shelf. Among the pictures was a much younger Max when he was in K-9 handling Blitz's great-grandfather.

"This is Okmar Patel. I need you to keep an eye on him for a few days."

Max Cummings eyed Okmar again. "You a Muslim?"

Okmar Patel "No, sir. I'm Hindu."

Max grunted his approval. "Indian huh. One of the best men I ever served with was an Indian. Sikh if I remember right."

Pryor shook his head. "I haven't thought about him in years. He had a first name nobody could pronounce."

"We all called him Marty. Marty Singh," Max answered. "I could have done without the damn turban but I'd take him as my backup any day. You a Sikh?" Max asked Patel.

Patel was puzzled by the question since he had just answered it moments before.

"Okmar already told you he's a Hindu, Max," Grace Cummings said gently.

"Oh. Right. Why are you here?"

"We need you to look after Okmar for a few days, Reload," Pryor answered softly, a bit rattled by what he was seeing.

"Reload?" Okmar Patel asked.

"That's my grandpa's old nickname," Kevin Cummings answered. "Tell him where it came from, Grandpa."

Max Cummings blinked a few times but didn't answer.

"Let me tell it," Pryor said. "One night when Max was still working K-9, he gets this call around 3 a.m. Some guy, naked as a J-Bird, is breaking up coffins at a funeral parlor with a fire axe. Max is first on the scene and he pulls out his .38 and says to this nut job, 'you're not going to hurt me or my dog.'"

A flicker of memory crossed Max's face as he chuckled. "Big son-of-bitch too. He was about two biscuits short of three hundred pounds."

"So this big guy," Pryor continued, "obviously, on some kind of drugs, comes at him. Max was the best shot in the entire department and he puts six in the x ring." Pryor tapped the center of his chest six times. "Miracle of miracles, since all of the rounds had to go through about a foot of fat then hit the guy in the sternum, the guy lives."

Max Cummings shook his head in disgust. "That damn 90 grain ammunition the department made us use back then. They'd bounce off of the windshields of cars. We'd been more effective throwing rocks."

"So they go to trial and this snotty nose public defender asks Max why did you shoot my client six times? Max looks him straight in the eyes and says..." Pryor glanced at Max.

A wry smile formed on Max Cummings's face and there was a faraway look in his eyes "I told that little pissant lawyer the reason I shot his scumbag client six times was because I didn't have time to reload."

Grace Cummings wiped away a tear as she saw the joy in Max's eyes as the old memory swept over him.

"And he's been called Reload ever since," Pryor added.

Okmar Patel leaned in and whispered into Kevin Cummings's ear. "Look. I don't want to be rude but..."

Grace Cummings overheard and took charge. She opened a closet door and inside there was a large gun safe. "Max! Okmar is in witness protection and our responsibility."

Max's lifetime of training kicked in. He started locking windows and closing the curtains.

Grace opened the gun safe which was filled with weapons. She pulled out an AR-15, checked to be sure the breach was clear then rammed home a clip and leaned it against the wall. Next, she repeated the process with a Glock 17 before tucking it into her apron pocket. "You a marksman, sweetie?" she asked Patel.

"I've never fired a gun in my life," Patel answered.

"Okay," Grace Cummings said reassuringly. "And hopefully, with any luck, you won't be starting now."

Grace Cummings pulled a holster and belt out of the safe and strapped it around Okmar's waist. She then pulled out a nasty looking short barrel revolver and started loading it. "This is a Smith and Wesson model 66 .357 magnum. It'll hold six rounds but for your personal safety, I have you resting on two empty chambers. That means you'll have to pull the trigger three times before it fires. Understand?"

"Yes, ma'am," Patel answered as he eyed the weapon. "But I don't even know how to aim it."

"Oh, sweetie," Grace Cummings said. "If you fire a .357 magnum with a two and a half-inch barrel indoors in the general direction of your target, the percussion will knock him on his ass even if you miss by twenty feet." Graced patted Okmar on the shoulder then strapped the holster around his waist. "The same applies to you. It'll be like somebody threw a flash-bang grenade in the room."

"Grenade?" Patel said as his eyes grew bigger.

"Don't worry. A flash-bang grenade is non-lethal. The SWAT team uses them all the time whenever they are taking a building," Kevin added as he patted his friend on the shoulder. "What Grammy is saying," Cummings said as he pointed to the gun now strapped to Patel's waist. "If you fire that indoors, neither you nor your target will be able to hear or see anything for a good five minutes after you pull the trigger."

"Now," Grace Cummings said gently, "I want you to stay away from the windows and don't go outside. Understand?"

Okmar Patel nodded. "Yes, ma'am."

Grace turned her attention to Pryor and pulled him aside. When she was sure they were out of Okmar's earshot, she leaned in and asked. "What's our risk level, Albert?"

"Negligible to nonexistent," Pryor answered.

Grace kissed Albert on the cheek. "That's what I figured. You're just the tonic Max has been needing."

Pryor furrowed his brow as he looked at Okmar. "Do you think it's wise to give him a loaded gun?"

Grace shrugged. "He'll be fine."

Pryor eyed her with suspicion. "You say that with a lot of confidence."

Grace shrugged again. "Unless he drops it on his toe, guns with their firing pins removed don't pose much of a risk." Now it was Grace's turn to give Pryor the eye. "Why is he really here?"

Pryor chuckled. "We need to keep him away from the station."

"I take it, this vanishing act is not related to your murder investigation?"

Pryor shook his head.

Grace Cummings glanced in the direction of her grandson. "Does it involve Kevin?" she asked.

"Yeah."

"Do I want to know?"

"Probably not."

Grace Cummings nodded her head and changed the subject. "How's Kevin doing?"

"Overconfident and a little full of himself but he has good instincts."

"That's exactly what Max used to say about you," Grace said with a laugh. "He's a lot like you."

"You're the second person to say that in less than an hour."

Grace turned her attention back to Okmar. "I was just about to make myself some chamomile tea. It goes perfectly with the cookies. Would you like a cup?"

"Yes, ma'am," Patel answered politely. "Thank you."

Grace Cummings slung the AR-15 over her shoulder and headed to the kitchen.

Kevin Cummings patted Okmar Patel on the back. "You were saying something about not wanting to be rude."

Okmar Patel eyed Kevin's grandmother and shook his head. "Never mind."

Pryor motioned to Cummings that it was time to go and waved to Grace as they passed the kitchen door.

Pryor said, "Thanks, Grace. It shouldn't be more than a day or two."

Grace Cummings glanced in the direction of her husband of forty-eight years. Reload was now in a La-Z-Boy recliner in front of his sixty-inch HD television, oblivious to the others in the room. "We'll appreciate the company."

Pryor looked at his old training officer and sighed.

"Can he leave the house?" Pryor asked gently.

"As long as he's supervised," Grace Cummings answered.

"After this is over, can I take him for an afternoon over to my place to tinker around with my cars or go to a ball game?"

Grace Cummings, with a tear in the corner of her eye, patted Pryor on the cheek. "That would be wonderful."

With Patel safely tucked away, Pryor and Cummings were headed back to the Barracuda when Cummings's phone pinged indicating he had a text. He checked his screen and nodded his approval. "Brooke was able to salvage over half of the information on the hard drive. She's uploading it to a couple of dark net sites right now."

"Dark net?"

"The places on the internet where Google and the other search engines fear to tread."

CHAPTER 14

A LBERT PRYOR SLID behind the wheel of the Barracuda, fired up the engine and started to back out of the driveway but hit the brakes and the car jerked to a stop. "Wait a minute," Pryor said as he turned to face Cummings. "Isn't the dark web the place where criminals and perverts hang out and buy and sell illegal stuff?"

Kevin Cummings chuckled. "That's one small use," Cummings agreed. "But governments, the military and spy agencies use it as well; along with every hacker worth their salt."

"And you introduced my daughter to this cesspool?" Pryor snarled.

Cummings leaned back, looked at his partner and shook his head. "You don't know Brooke at all, do you?"

"What the hell does that mean?"

"She introduced me to the dark net, not the other way around," Cummings answered.

"What?!"

"Your daughter is a world-class hacker. She can run circles around me. She's elite."

"My Brooke is a hacker?"

"Relax," Cummings replied with a dismissive wave of his hand. "Not all hackers are trying to scam seniors out of their life's savings or commit credit card fraud. Brooke is one of the good guys. If she finds a crack in a company's security or a vulnerability in a software program, she'll quietly approach the potential client, shows them the problem and then offer to fix it for them."

"Client? What do you mean client?"

"Wow!" Cummings said. "You really don't have a clue, do you?"

Pryor didn't answer.

"Remember when I told you if a techy was any good they could clean up in the private sector. Last year Brooke grossed low seven figures working part-time as a security consultant while carrying a college class load that would have killed me."

Pryor's mouth fell open. "Brooke made over a million dollars last year?"

"Rumor is closer to three million than two," Cummings answered with a laugh. "She's been recruited by every major player in Silicon Valley but they never had a chance of hiring her."

Pryor cleared his throat. "Why not?"

Cummings shrugged. "Her grandfather has already started grooming her to take over the family business. Once she's in the CEO's chair, and has the company's resources under her control, she'll be the one doing the recruiting in Silicon Valley, not the other way around."

"I'll be damned," Pryor said softly. "Explain to me why she'd put information about an active case on the internet?"

"Privacy is now a fantasy and anything worth being in the public domain is going to end up there sooner rather than later," Cummings answered.

"This is a murder investigation, not a fight at a fast-food restaurant some clown recorded on his iPhone."

"Or a cop beating the crap out of some kid or a Black guy for no reason other than he could."

Pryor glared at Cummings. "Which side are you on?"

"Hopefully, the same side you're on," Cummings answered. "This thin blue line BS doesn't fly anymore."

"What the hell does that mean?" Pryor demanded.

"Imagine if that campus rent-a-cop, Wendell Mucker, had worn a body cam when he was on the force. After all of the lawsuits, the city's debt would have rivaled the federal government's." Cummings shook his head in disgust. "That asshole still thinks it's the 1950s. You should see the way he struts around campus and harasses gays and people of color and hits on every attractive coed." Cummings's eyes narrowed. "Including Brooke."

"Brooke is a big girl; she can take care of herself."

"True that," Cummings said with a chuckle. "She's got a lot of her daddy in her."

Pryor sighed and shook his head. "Oh, God. What did she do?"

"Mucker came up behind her without warning and put his hand on her shoulder and she spun around and head-butted him into next week." Cummings chuckled. "Shattered his nose and he looked like a raccoon for a couple of weeks."

"Sounds like my little girl," Pryor said with just a slight hint of pride in his voice.

"If she wasn't Malcolm Kauthmann's granddaughter, he probably would have arrested her on some bogus charge."

"Malcolm would have filleted him."

"Without a doubt," Cummings agreed.

"You still haven't explained to me why posting the information Brooke recovered on the dark web is a good idea."

"Nick had been hosting a chat room on I2P..." Cummings stopped when Pryor shot him a look. "Sorry. Nick had been hosting a chat room on the Invisible Internet Project for almost a year. It was a place where people came to speculate about how Professor Vane has been able to make such accurate earthquake predictions."

"Okay," Pryor said as released the brake and backed out into the street. "So Nick had the same doubts about Vane as you do."

Cummings shook his head. "As does anyone who has been around him for more than fifteen minutes."

Pryor swallowed a smile. Cummings's impression of Plato Vane was very different from the rave reviews he received from his ex-wife and the fawning media.

"Nick was hot on a trail of something, that was why he snuck into the lab."

"Did he talk about it?"

Cummings sighed. "Nick was a classic paranoid geek. He was aware that on any open forum, even on the dark web, you never know who might be watching. He was very careful to never reveal too much. Plus, in Nick's case, his big brain also had a big ego."

"Did he have a grudge against Vane?"

Cummings shrugged. "He didn't like Vane and considered him a self-serving whore to political correctness."

"What does that mean?" Pryor asked.

"Vane always takes the path of least resistance that would earn him the most money and get him the best press. Instead of being a real scientist who was always challenging the conventional wisdom, Vane lived off of it. To Nick, Vane is the poster boy for groupthink. If anyone was going to expose Vane as a fraud, Nick wanted to be sure he was that guy."

"Okay," Pryor said. "Why would Brooke want to post the stuff online?"

"These are some of the smartest people in the world and when they find out one of their own was murdered, they are going to be major-league annoyed," Cummings answered.

Pryor asked, "How does that help us?"

"It might give us our motive," Cummings offered.

Pryor asked, "How so?"

"If Nick could figure it out, odds are one of them can too," Cummings explained. "It will be like we have hundreds, if not thousands, of highly skilled digital bloodhounds helping us solve the case." Cummings's eyes locked on Pryor. "It's a brave new world out there. We either need to learn how to use the tools available or criminals are going to make cops look like Neanderthals."

Cummings typed on his phone then laughed when he got the reply. "You can tell she's a cop's daughter."

"Why?"

Cummings read the text message out loud. "I uploaded the files to Nick's laptop and I'm going to destroy the hard drive. We can now give the laptop to CSI and what we found would be admissible."

"Is she right?" asked Pryor with a twinkle in his eye as he already knew the answer but wanted to see if Cummings did.

"Yup. We can swing by, pick up the laptop and pretend the files were there when we took possession. The chain of custody is intact."

CHAPTER 15

WHEN THEY ARRIVED back at the BONK workshop, Brooke, with safety glasses on, was drilling holes in the hard drive disc that had been removed from Vane's lab. She took off her goggles and put the drill down when she saw company arrive.

Blitz, who was lying next to Brooke's feet, raised his head as Pryor and Cummings came through the door. Unimpressed, he yawned and laid back down.

Brooke pointed to the tangled mess of metal shavings, wire and other parts of the hard drive in front of her. "I used a sander and magnets on these," she said. "Even if someone finds them they won't be getting anything off of them." She swept the pieces into a plastic bag. "I'll toss them in a dumpster somewhere on the way home."

Cummings walked over and unplugged Nick Blake's laptop and dropped it into an oversized evidence bag. As he wrote the time and date on the outside of the bag, signed it then sealed it, he asked, "You changed the date and time on the upload log and took all of the BONK stuff off?"

Brooke gave Cummings a sour look.

"Sorry," Cummings said quickly. "Of course you did."

Albert Pryor reached for his phone. "I'm going to call CSI and have them toss this place."

"Should we wipe it down?" Brooke asked.

Cummings laughed. "Good Lord, no."

Pryor nodded his approval in Cummings's direction. "Smart."

"What's so smart about that?" Brooke demanded.

Since he had figured it out so quickly, Pryor motioned to Cummings that he should be the one to tell her.

"Right now, this is just the apartment of a murder victim and not the scene of the crime. If it is wiped down it would look suspicious, somebody might start asking questions and taking a much harder look."

"With the interest in this case," Pryor added. "We could go from a bored two-man team going through the motions in here to the top crime scene crew turning the place upside down."

"If they get curious," Cummings continued, "they could assign some of the task force detectives to check on the comings and goings and that could lead to BONK."

"Okay, okay," Brooke said as she held her hands up in mock surrender. "Forgive me for not thinking like a damn cop."

"Are your fingerprints on file anywhere?" Pryor asked Brooke.

"Yes," Brooke answered. "I had to give them to get my security clearance."

Pryor closed his eyes and rubbed his forehead. "You have a security clearance?"

"Of course," Brooke answered with a surprised tone in her voice. "Without it, I couldn't do contract work for all of the alphabet agencies in Washington."

Pryor shook his head. "Are you heading to your grandfather's complex now?"

"No," Brooke answered. "I thought I would swing by Mom's and the nutty professor's place and nose around."

Pryor smirked. "Smart."

Cummings frowned. "What's smart about that?"

Now it was Brooke's turn to explain. "I think the professor is somehow involved in this. With the house empty, I can hack into the professor's home computer while he's not around."

"Will that be safe?" Cummings asked. "What if Vane catches you?"

"I'll have Blitz with me."

Pryor laughed. "Your mom hates dogs."

"Not nearly as much as the professor hates them," Brooke said. "But since Blitz would be there for my personal protection, it would be tough for Mom to say no which would really annoy Vane."

"What if you get caught?" Pryor asked.

"Unlikely," Brooke answered. "Vane is doing a book signing and lecture this afternoon. Mom always goes with him to crap like that."

"Good hunting," Cummings said.

"Don't get your hopes up," Brooke said. "I've completely mirrored Vane's home computer and laptop. His firewalls at the institute are so good, even the professor couldn't access the mainframe remotely."

"Okay," Pryor said as he pointed to Blitz. "Go with Brooke."

They all left the apartment, closing the door behind them.

At the street, Pryor and Cummings headed in one direction while Brooke and Blitz headed in the other toward her powder blue Mustang parked half a block away. Despite Brooke's stunning good looks, with Blitz trotting along next to her, the only thing the locals seemed to notice was the massive German shepherd.

Pryor suggested, "Let's go turn the laptop in and see how the task force is doing."

CHAPTER 16

ITH THE CAMPUS a fading image in Pryor's rearview mirror, the surrounding neighborhood wasn't quite a ghetto, but it was getting close. College students had been replaced by homeless people in doorways and panhandlers requesting loose change. The traffic was crawling on the narrow two-lane street.

"Accident?" Pryor offered as he craned his neck to try to see around the SUV in front of him.

"More likely a delivery truck double-parked and blocking our lane," Cummings answered. "I live near here and it happens all of the time. The good news is it widens out to four lanes in two blocks."

The instant the street widened, Pryor whipped the Barracuda into the open left lane and resumed a normal speed for that time of day.

"What the hell is that?" Pryor asked as he pointed to the obvious culprit for the traffic snarl.

Up ahead, in the right lane and going at least ten miles per hour below the posted speed limit, was a small, day-glow yellow two-seat car not much larger than a golf cart.

"It's a prototype self-driving car," answered Cummings. "The engineering department has been working on it for the past year or so and just recently got permission to field test it."

As they approached the vehicle, it had its four-way flashers on, a warning sign in the rear window and a yellow bubble light spinning on the roof. The driver's seat was empty but a nervous guy was sitting in the passenger seat with one eye on his monitor and one on traffic.

Cummings waved to the passenger as they passed the experimental vehicle. "Yo! Donny!"

The passenger, obviously named Donny, glanced up quickly and answered, "Hey Kevin," before returning to his work.

"They're trying to get it so the car will act and react just as if there was a human driver behind the wheel. With this new smart technology they hope to eliminate the human element entirely."

"Human element!" Pryor shouted as he slammed the steering wheel.

"What?" Cummings demanded.

"Eliminate the human element."

A half a beat later, Kevin Cummings caught up.

"Son-of-a-bitch," both men yelled in unison.

Pryor said, incredulously, "Is it possible we were looking right at our murderer?"

Cummings nodded. "Absolutely."

"There goes Plato Vane's alibi."

"No doubt," Cummings answered. "Whatever Blake stumbled onto may have triggered a doomsday protocol that could have been in place for weeks or months or even years."

"How many people deal with those androids?" Pryor asked.

"Once activated, they pretty much take care of themselves. They are not considered a high-security risk so pretty much anyone could have tampered with their programing."

"If we find it, will you be able to figure out who did the programing?" Pryor asked.

"Maybe," Cummings answered. "I've never opened one of them up but if it has a memory cache, we may be able to figure out when it was programmed and maybe even who was the programmer. That's a big problem."

"Yeah," Pryor said. "If you know that, then the killer knows it as well. And our killer has had eight hours to get rid of the evidence."

"We need to get back to the lab before the killer can erase the memory."

Pryor flipped on the grill lights and siren and, to a chorus of honks and obscene gestures, did a one-eighty in the middle of the road. The Barracuda roared back toward the college campus.

CHAPTER 17

KEVIN CUMMINGS DIALED a number and had a brief conversation. "The lab is still sealed and there's a man on the ground level door and one in the lab."

"So the only one other than law enforcement that has been inside since the shooting is Patel?"

"Let's hope."

As they approached a red light, Pryor swung the Barracuda into the lane headed in the opposite direction. He hit his siren which was at a decibel level somewhere between a heavy metal concert and a jumbo jet taking off. Strobe lights concealed in the Barracuda's front grill began to throb. He nosed into the intersection, saw all of the traffic had come to a halt, swung back into his lane and floored the gas.

"What's our plan?" Pryor asked.

"We need to locate and isolate the robot that did the shooting, ASAP," Cummings answered.

"Why?"

"It was programmed to make a weapon with a 3D printer, steal a bullet out of the gun in Vane's office and kill someone if they were getting too close to the truth." Cummings hesitated. "That is a ton of code and if we can get its hard drive it would have left some footprints."

"And you can figure that out?"

"Me?" Cummings answered with a startled expression on his face. "Maybe in a hundred years. Brooke could probably unravel it while standing in line for a coffee. But that's not what worries me."

"What worries you?"

"What else was it programmed to do?"

"We have one of our guys down there with the damn thing guarding the door." Pryor gave the Barracuda more gas.

Without taking his eyes off of the road, Pryor said, "One of the K-9 handlers said his dog didn't like one of the androids."

"Damn," Cummings said. "The dog may have smelled gunshot residue or blood."

"Get that dog back down there," Pryor ordered.

Cummings had his phone to his ear. "Already on it."

Pryor picked up the microphone concealed under his dash. "This is Detective Albert Pryor. We have an officer who needs assistance at the GAIA Institute. All available cars please respond. I am ninety seconds out."

Cummings gave Pryor an odd look. "You realize that by putting that out on that on a non-scrambled frequency, not only did every cop on the force hear, but also everyone with a police scanner heard it too."

"I certainly hope so."

CHAPTER 18

THE BARRACUDA ROARED into the empty parking lot in front of the GAIA Institute with its grill lights still flashing and its siren wailing. It was followed almost immediately by two more city police cars and a campus security van with Wendell Mucker in the front passenger seat. In the distance was the sound of other emergency vehicles fast approaching.

Pryor left the siren on and jumped out of the muscle car. Cummings, younger and quicker, was already sprinting to the door.

"What the hell is going on?" Mucker demanded as he eyed the crowd of gawkers which was rapidly forming.

Pryor waited until the first four uniforms on the scene joined them. "We have reason to believe someone programmed one of the androids in the lab to kill Nick Blake," Pryor stated as he picked up his pace in a vain attempt to catch up with Cummings. "We have an officer, with no backup and no radio contact, currently in the lab who may be at risk."

Cummings was holding the door open. "Officer O'Reilly is not answering the phone at the receptionist's desk in the lab. He could be wandering around anywhere down there and we have no way to contact him." Cummings nodded in the direction of the young cop who had been the gatekeeper earlier in the day. "According to Officer Polling, O'Reilly has been checking in every fifteen minutes, like clockwork."

"When was the last check-in?"

Polling checked his watch. "Eight minutes ago," he answered nervously. "What's going on?"

"Are the elevators operational?"

Before Polling could answer, they both dinged and Cummings stuck his hand inside the closest one to keep the door open.

"I need a watch commander onsite. Get the crime lab, SWAT and Detective Danny Holden back down here ASAP. Get enough troops to set up the perimeter again."

To his credit, Polling asked no questions, turned and walked toward a more quiet corner and began talking clearly and distinctly into the combination body camera and communication device clipped close to his left shoulder.

"On their way," Polling said as he rejoined the group.

"Do you know how to operate the phone system?" Pryor asked Polling.

"Yes, sir."

"You're with us and don't call me sir," Pryor barked at Polling before turning to the four uniformed officers. He pointed at the security desk. "In about thirty seconds that phone is going to ring. Put it on speaker and if you hear gunfire, be ready to come running."

The four nodded.

Cummings was already in the elevator. Polling joined him, followed by Pryor. As Wendell Mucker started to step on the elevator, Pryor stuck out a hand and stopped him.

"This is real police work, Wendell," Pryor said dismissively. "Why don't you round up a few of your crack troops and see if they can set up a perimeter around the building without shooting someone."

"This is my campus!" Mucker protested.

As the door started to close, Pryor said. "Since this is your campus, why don't you go and water a tree."

The five seconds it took for the elevator to reach the underground lab level seemed like hours. Pryor, Cummings and Polling all had their weapons out and were locked and loaded.

Arriving below ground, the lobby area was quiet as a tomb. Polling immediately went to the receptionist's desk and called the upstairs lobby.

"Good to go," Polling said.

"Where does O'Reilly hang out?" Pryor asked.

"Not a clue..." Polling almost added 'sir' but bit it off before it came out. "This is my first time down here."

"O'Reilly!" Pryor shouted.

"In the break room," came the reply from deep in the bowels of the laboratory.

With the calm and relaxed tone in O'Reilly's voice, the tension level began to instantly drop.

The trio, weapons still drawn, hustled down the corridor to the break room. When they entered, they found O'Reilly sitting at one of the tables with a cup of coffee in his hand.

"What the hell!" shouted O'Reilly as his cup stopped halfway to his mouth.

Pryor and Cummings sprinted down the hall and toward the room where Nick Blake had been killed. They ducked under the crime scene tape and, with their guns still drawn, cautiously approached the charging station. Where earlier there had been three robots recharging, now there were only two.

O'Reilly wandered in with a confused expression on his face. "What's going on?" he asked."

Pryor answered his question with another question. "Did you see one of these things leave the lab?"

O'Reilly said, "Honestly, Detective, I was told not to let any people in or out and these things are going back and forth down the corridor all the time. I think, but won't swear to it, that one of them might have rolled out of here maybe a few hours ago."

"It could be anywhere in the complex by now," said Cummings.

Pryor asked, impatiently, "Did you see which way it went?"

O'Reilly shook his head. "What's the big deal?"

"That robot was likely programmed to kill our victim," Pryor answered.

"And I was down here with the little son-of-bitch by myself and clueless."

"You have no idea where it went?" Pryor asked.

"None," O'Reilly answered.

"I'll see if I can pull up the surveillance video," Cummings said. He jumped behind the keyboard of the workstation he had used earlier. "Dammit," he swore. "We've got another outage on the video."

"Of course we do," Pryor muttered.

"I bet I know where it is," Cummings said. Without another word, he was out the door and sprinting down the hall. He slid to a stop in front of a door marked *Robotic Maintenance*.

Pryor arrived half a beat later. "Why here?"

Cummings opened the door and turned on the lights. Inside were shelves of spare parts and at the far end of the narrow work area was one of the androids. It was facing the wall and in the middle of its back, a small access door was open. Cummings looked inside.

"Empty," Cummings said as he kicked a garbage can. "We're too late."

"What do you mean?" Pryor demanded.

"That's where the hard drive would have been." Cummings shook his head. "This opens up an entirely new problem."

"What?" Pryor asked.

"I think the command to destroy the assassin droid's hard drive was written and delivered after the original kill program was launched."

"Why do you say that?" Pryor asked softly, knowing he probably wasn't going to like Cummings's answer.

"Whoever is masterminding this never expected to have his killer droid exposed," Cummings said. "Something got him concerned that we were about to figure it out."

"Like what?"

"It could have been me figuring out the 3D printer. He could have gotten worried when the K-9 reacted to the killer droid. Both of those things happened later, after the original kill protocol was launched."

"Why do you say that?"

"If removing and destroying the hard drive was part of the original plan, why didn't he do it immediately after the shot was fired?"

"Damn," Pryor said.

"It gets worse," Cummings said. "If I'm right, it means someone has been listening in on our communications. Since this building has been on a complete lockdown, that means someone has external access to Vane's computer network."

"I thought that was impossible."

"Me too," Cummings answered. "I also thought predicting earthquakes was impossible."

Pryor closed his eyes and rubbed his forehead. "One thing doesn't change. Plato Vane is still our number one suspect," Pryor said.

"I agree," Cummings replied. "But it is starting to look like Vane may be much smarter than we thought."

"Maybe too smart for us."

CHAPTER 19

"HAVE YOU TWO lost your fucking minds?" Garrison glared across his desk at Pryor and Cummings. Detective Danny Holden was leaning on a file cabinet behind the pair staying as still as possible hoping he would blend into the background. He had seen Pryor and Garrison tangle before, but this had pay-per-view potential.

"You want me to shut down Plato Vane's entire lab indefinitely and put all of his R2D2s under lock and key?"

Pryor said, quietly, "Pretty much."

"You realize that in seventy-two hours Vane and his labs are going to be on every television channel in the free world?" Lt. Garrison shouted.

Pryor said, "Not if he's in jail for murder."

"At the time of the murder," Lt. Garrison said, "Vane was three thousand miles away having a latte with a TV news anchor!"

"Lieutenant. That android was pre-programed to kill anyone who stumbled onto Vane's secret…"

"Secret?" Garrison demanded. "What secret?"

"We don't know yet but the record logs of the 3D printer indicate the gun was made over three weeks ago," Pryor said. "Which is the same time Nick Blake started making his midnight runs to the lab." Pryor leaned forward. "That makes it murder one with special circumstances."

"So let me get this straight," said Lt. Garrison. "You think world-renowned scientist, Plato Vane, knew about our victim's nocturnal visits to his lab. And, Vane was concerned he might uncover some deep dark secret worth killing over?"

"Right," said Pryor.

"So," Lt. Garrison answered, "Vane, in his spare time when he wasn't jetting around the world getting awards and accolades, or being interviewed on national TV, or posing for the cover of magazines, or having brunch with the First Family, designed and built a killer robot. Then had the robot use a 3D printer to make a gun, then pre-programed his droid to kill anyone who discovered his secret?"

Pryor repeated, "Right."

"And what exactly is Vane's motive to do all of this?" asked Garrison.

Pryor ventured, "We don't know yet."

Sarcasm laced Lt. Garrison's reply. "Really? Which brings me back to my original question. Have you two lost your fucking minds? The man has successfully predicted eight straight major earthquakes. In a few days he's going to be in Hawaii with the President of the United States and more than two dozen other world leaders to christen his new lab." Lt. Garrison made a face. "With your history with Vane, this is starting to look personal, Albert."

"We've got an android with GSR and blood on it that was tampered with after the shooting. We've had a man on the door and a man inside since the body was discovered. The only thing that could have tampered with the android is another android."

"We have no idea who is controlling these androids…" Cummings added.

Pryor put his hand on Cummings's arm. "I'm the senior officer on this case addressing my commanding officer. If I need any help from you, I'll let you know. Until then," Pryor snapped, "keep your mouth shut."

Cummings flushed slightly then leaned back in his chair while silently glaring at Pryor.

"We don't know what else those things are programmed to do but we do know they can manufacture weapons and are not afraid to use them."

"Shit," Lt. Garrison said as he rubbed his mouth. "Who is on your list of potential candidates?"

"Only one name. Professor Plato Vane," Pryor answered firmly. "He's the only one with a motive."

"What motive!?" Garrison shouted, red in the face. "Vane has the world by the tail."

"When our victim shouted 'Eureka' we figured he found something Vane thought was worth killing for. With his security protocols, he knew the information could only be accessed onsite. That was why our victim was in the building. I figure Blake's discovery triggered some kind of doomsday protocol because less than two minutes later he was dead."

"This is a nightmare," Garrison said as he shook his head.

"No," Pryor said with a laugh. "This is a bad dream. The nightmare could hit in three days."

"What are you talking about?" Garrison demanded.

"I assume they have similar androids in the new Hawaii laboratory and 3D printers," Pryor answered then paused briefly to let that thought sink in. "What if you were too chicken shit to shut down Vane's lab and one of those Hawaiian androids was programmed to assassinate the President of the United States?"

CHAPTER 20

STANDING OUT IN the hall in front of Lt. Garrison's office, Kevin Cummings was fuming. Danny Holden nudged his ex-partner. "What's with the kid?" he asked.

"I think I hurt his feelings in there."

"I thought he was supposed to be smart," Holden said with a chuckle.

"Still wet behind the ears," Pryor answered.

"I'm standing right here and I can hear you," Cummings said defensively.

"Then hear this," Holden said with a fatherly tone. "You just witnessed a master's class in office politics with a side lecture on how to protect the ass of a young and stupid rookie."

"What do you mean?" Cummings asked softly as he moved in closer.

"By smacking you down in front of Lou like that, Albert took full ownership of this white-hot case. If it goes sideways, he gets all of the heat and you never get so much as a sunburn."

Cummings thought about what Holden had said and his body started to relax. "I'll be damned," Cummings said.

"Pay back is a bitch," Pryor added. "You grandfather dressed me down so badly one time I came within an inch of turning in my badge."

"I came within an inch of smacking you on the back of the head when you opened your damn mouth," Holden added. "Always respect the chain of command."

"You mentioned a master's class," Cummings said.

"If, God forbid, something happens to the president the day after tomorrow in Hawaii. Would you be willing to swear that Detective Albert Pryor warned his superior officer about the possibility?"

"Yes," Cummings answered.

"As would I," Holden continued. "Political pressure, when handled correctly, can be a double-edged sword." Holden patted Pryor on the shoulder. "Albert just took all of the pressure off of himself and put it on everyone above him who was trying to dick him around or slow walk this. No matter how big a deal they all think Plato Vane may be, after what just happened in Lou's office, none of them will risk sticking their nose in this hot mess again. It is one thing to pull a few strings and look the other way for the rich and famous when it doesn't cost you anything. It is quite another to risk your career and social standing for some jackass like Vane."

A smile broke across Cummings's face as he nodded his approval in Pryor's direction. "If they don't do exactly what you want, it would look like a complete coverup."

"This is the biggest case we've ever had," Holden said. "And with that stunt of putting out an officer needing assistance over the public airwaves, by dinner time, we're going to have every major news network in town. Unlike the locals, these big city and national newshounds are not going to be impressed or intimidated by a B-list talent like Professor Plato Vane, the mayor, the DA, or anyone else around here. It is only a matter of time before word leaks out that the android did it. Then some smart person will put one and one together and come up with two the same way Albert did and start asking the Secret Service some hard questions about the safety of the president. When that happens, all hell is going to break loose."

"Imagine if they took him off the case," Cummings muttered.

"Or better yet, fired Albert," Holden added. "The implied threat is like a bad fart hanging in the air. They know, as a private citizen, Albert would be free to discuss this case with the media. Albert, for the moment at least, has absolute job security."

"For the moment?" Cummings asked.

"We still have to solve the case," Pryor answered. "We have a pretty good idea what happened but we have no proof. Still, it served our purpose."

"Which is?" asked Cummings.

"Lt. Garrison probably already has the chief on the phone and the DA will be next on his call list followed by the mayor."

Cummings glanced back over his shoulder and saw Garrison on the phone, his face was beet red.

"Within an hour, everyone on the task force will have heard our theory and know we're looking for a motive to point the finger at Vane," Pryor said.

"It won't take nearly that long," Holden said. "I'll have a task force wide email blast out in less than fifteen minutes."

"With any luck," Pryor said. "Somebody will tell Vane."

"And that's good?" Cummings asked.

"If we're right," Pryor answered. "The murder of Nick Blake was an act of desperation to cover up a secret. Desperate people, especially those who aren't career criminals, tend to panic under pressure and make mistakes."

"So, what's our next step?" asked Cummings.

Pryor grinned. "Let's go rattle Professor Plato Vane's cage and turn up the pressure even more. Then see if we can make him make a mistake."

"You boys have fun," Holden said with a laugh. "I've got an appointment with that blonde, stick up the ass ice cube, that runs the city Public Relations Department. With any luck, my time as the PR point man on this case will be coming to an end."

CHAPTER 21

IF THE LOCAL fire marshal had shown up at the bookstore just off campus and seen how many people were crammed inside she would have needed smelling salts and possibly even a defibrillator. The shop, with a fifty-person limit sign near the front door, had at least four times the legal limit inside. An overflow crowd of around thirty people was milling around on the sidewalk in front of the store and were craning their necks to try and get a glimpse of the great and powerful Plato Vane.

Beside the door, on an easel, was a large poster proclaiming a lecture by Dr. Plato Vane.

It's Almost Too Late
The Population Bomb &
Anthropogenic Climate Change

Not to miss any potential sales, the enterprising store manager had set up a table on the sidewalk. Manning the table was a gorgeous coed whose family tree appeared to have been dominated by Scandinavian ancestors. She had naturally blonde hair, fair skin and bluebird blue eyes. Along one edge of the table were small stacks of Vane's previous books. In front of her were multiple stacks of Vane's current New York Times #1 Bestseller, *When GAIA Weeps*.

Pryor wheeled the Barracuda into a spot in front of the bookstore next to a fire hydrant and turned off the engine.

"You can't park there," barked a wiry rent-a-cop in an ill-fitting uniform who was doing crowd control.

"I think I just did," Pryor answered as he got out of his car.

"You have to move it," the guard demanded as he squared his shoulders and took a quick glance in the direction of the table to see if the young lady had noticed. She had noticed and was giggling.

"I don't think I have to," Pryor answered as he let his windbreaker fall open exposing the badge and gun clipped to his belt.

The security guard's cheeks darkened and he had no additional comments.

"Hi Kevin," the coed working the desk said as she wiggled a finger in Cummings's direction.

"Barb," Cummings said with a huge smile. "Long time no see."

Pryor eyed the young woman, leaned into Cummings and said, "See if she has heard about the android."

Cummings nodded and approached the table. "Some crowd," he said with a broad smile.

"I work these signings all the time and I've never seen anything like it before." She looked around to be sure no one else was listening then whispered, "I think it's because of what happened in Dr. Vane's lab this morning."

"What happened?" Cummings asked innocently.

"One of those spooky little robot thingies he has all over his lab went crazy and killed Nick Blake."

"No way!" Cummings said with an astounded expression on his face. "Where did you hear that?"

"You remember Harry Morgan."

"Sure," Cummings answered.

"Well, Harry said the police sealed off the lab this morning then came back right after lunch." Barb batted her big blue eyes at Cummings, leaned in closer and whispered even more softly.

"Well, he said he personally saw them removing one of the robots and it was covered in blood!"

"Seriously?"

"That's what he said." Barb looked around again and an evil grin covered her face. "My boyfriend is going on a golfing trip this weekend if you'd like to hook up."

"I'm seeing somebody," Cummings answered.

Barb's voice dropped a full octave. "Bring her along. It'll be fun."

Albert Pryor was leaning against the door frame of the bookstore watching Cummings interact with Barb with a bemused expression on his face.

"I'll run it past her and get back to you," Cummings answered with a smile as he moved in Pryor's direction.

"You have an interesting sex life," Pryor said as they headed into the bookstore.

"Naw," Cummings said with a dismissive wave of his hand. "She's not my type."

"Not your type?" Pryor looked back at the stunning beauty who was now waiting on a customer. "What exactly is your type?"

"I prefer women with critical thinking skills and at least a hint of appreciation of irony," Cummings answered. "Barb comes up well short of the mark in both categories."

"For example," Pryor asked.

"For example," Cummings answered. "She'll show up in her daddy's BMW at a rally to protest the blight of the downtrodden, wearing knee-high Gucci boots and carrying a five thousand dollar Hermes bag."

"Ah," Pryor said.

"She once suggested, so people of color would feel safe on campus, we have "Colored Only" water fountains and bathrooms. When someone pointed out that was exactly what Martin Luther King Jr. marched against in Selma, she had a complete meltdown."

"Good lord," Pryor muttered.

"Women like her are what makes guys like Plato Vane such jerks."

"You lost me," Pryor said as he surveyed the room and saw Plato Vane at a podium near the back.

"When you were my age, what was the most important thing in your life?"

"Trying to get laid," Pryor answered.

"Some things never change," Cummings answered. "So, if you knew you were pro-life and the only girls that would be interested in you were saving themselves for marriage, how would that affect your view on abortion?"

"Ah," Pryor answered.

"Ditto on climate change, police brutality and every other issue these female social warriors consider gospel these days," Cummings said. "If you're like most guys, you don't really give a crap about all of the nonsense that is so important to women like Barb. All they want to do is get in their pants."

"How old are you again?" Pryor asked.

"Why?" Cummings asked.

"That's a lot of cynicism for someone as young as you."

"Right now, attractive, college-educated women play the tune and it is in the self-interest of the average guy to start dancing."

"You really believe that?" Pryor asked.

"If all the women like Barb suddenly decided they only wanted guys dressed in white and with shaved heads and a hoop earring, every college campus in America would be populated with Mr. Clean lookalikes."

Pryor nodded in the direction of the podium where Vane was speaking. "How do guys like Professor Vane fit into your worldview?" he asked.

"Sociopaths like Vane, and most everyone else in a position of authority in politics and academia, have figured this out. If you mouth the right platitudes you'll never be lonely and you'll have carte blanche to do pretty much anything you want." Cummings motioned to the female-dominated room with their rapt attention focused on Plato Vane. "These women all consider Plato Vane to be a demigod and if we go after him they will rally to his defense. And they can be vicious. With an army like that behind them, clowns like Vane feel free to sexually harass women, abuse their staff, steal credit for other people's work, line their pockets. You name it." Cummings's eyes locked on Pryor. "That's why when you had your dust up with Vane, they came for your head."

Plato Vane had a lean body with narrow hips and narrower shoulders. At five feet six, and less than a buck forty, he was the perfect size and shape to have spent much of junior high stuffed in a gym locker. He had a full head of dark black hair with just a sprinkle of gray around his temples. With his weak chin and close set eyes, he looked a bit like a rodent. On his left arm was a black "look at me I care" armband, with Nick Blake's name on it.

Professor Vane spoke with a smooth baritone and the confidence of someone very comfortable in the limelight. "In conclusion, we are almost to the tipping point where over-population and human activity will overwhelm our planet. You can make a difference. Please open your hearts and open your wallets to this wonderful cause."

There was a smattering of polite applause.

"Oh," Vane added with a huge smile. "And don't forget to pick up a copy of my new book, *When GAIA Weeps.*"

More, louder applause, and a few chuckles this time.

As Vane was leaving the podium he was surrounded by a gaggle of coeds old enough to vote but not yet old enough to drink, wanting him to sign their copies of his bestseller.

Melissa Vane was basking in the glow of her replacement husband with a radiant smile on her face. The smile instantly faded when she saw her ex-husband in the rear of the room.

Pryor noticed her looking at him and wiggled his finger in her direction the same way Barb had motioned to Cummings. Being around all of these young people, he wanted to show he still had it.

Looking around, Melissa got the attention of campus security head, Wendell Mucker, and nodded at Pryor. Mucker grabbed the arm of a man in a dark suit standing next to him and pointed in the direction of Pryor and Cummings. The man nodded and started working his way through the crowd in the detective's direction.

Kevin Cummings saw him coming. "It appears Vane has hired himself a bodyguard."

Pryor muttered, "Rookie. He's too old, too fat and too well-dressed to be a bodyguard. My guess is he's a Fed and a high ranking one."

CHAPTER 22

AS ALBERT PRYOR headed in Plato Vane's direction, the man in black cut him off. "Can I help you?"

"Yes," Pryor answered. "You can get out of my way." Pryor flashed his badge.

The man in black purred, "Ahh, that's adorable. But mine is bigger than yours." He flashed his own badge with 'FBI' in bold letters. Pryor read the name. Michael Gottwald.

"Why don't we step over here and discuss our little situation."

Two extremely young and tense FBI Agents moved in a few feet behind Gottwald. They could have been the face of the new, non-threatening Woke FBI. They kept glancing at each other as if they felt there was strength in numbers or they were concerned their wingman might cut and run at the first sign of trouble. Pryor would have given even money the duo would have been carded at a bar before Kevin Cummings. Pryor would also give three to one Cummings could mop the floor with both of them without mussing his hair. Hell, Brooke could probably deal with them. They were near clones of each other. They were slim and fit, but the kind of fit that came from playing squash three times a week at the country club and not mixing it up late at night on the mean streets. Neither struck fear and awe in Pryor. Behind them, Wendell Mucker was grinning like the self-satisfied idiot he was.

Pryor sized up the senior FBI agent. He was African-American and probably closer to forty than fifty. But, with his head shaved and no gray hair clues available, it would have been tough to get any closer to his exact age without checking his driver's license. With his waist measurement at least ten inches greater than his inseam, he was too fat and out of shape to have spent much time in the field. He had Washington, DC written all over him.

His skin was the color of a sixteen-ounce dark roast coffee with a single creamer added. With his good posture, and an unblinking glare Pryor suspected he practiced in the mirror, he projected 'you really don't want to mess with me' body language. Pryor had crossed swords a few times with the FBI but usually they were field agents and not empty suit bureaucrats like Gottwald.

"I'm Special Agent-in-Charge, Michael Gottwald."

Pryor noted the Boston accent, the French cuffs and the gold cuff links on his white dress shirt. Definitely Washington and more than likely an Ivy Leaguer. Pryor grinned and shook his head. Since Gottwald had not offered his hand, neither did Pryor. "In charge of what?" he asked.

"I'm in charge of Professor Plato Vane's protective detail, Detective Pryor," said Gottwald.

"You know who I am?" Pryor asked.

"I read your file on the plane this morning." Gottwald chuckled. "You've had a colorful career."

"Thanks."

"That," said Gottwald with a confident smirk, "wasn't a compliment."

"Why does Vane merit an overweight DC paper pusher and the Bobbsey Twins?" Pryor asked.

"Your file said you had a smart mouth and issues with authority," Gottwald answered with a smug smile. "Professor Vane and his wife - your ex-wife - will be dining with the President and First Lady aboard Air Force One tomorrow night as they fly to Hawaii together for the formal dedication of Dr. Vane's new facility." Gottwald continued, "The professor will be unavailable to you until he returns from Hawaii."

"You do understand I'm investigating a homicide that occurred in Vane's local lab."

Gottwald chuckled again. "I don't care if you're investigating the assassination of President John F. Kennedy. Dr. Vane is not your guy. I was twenty feet away from him on the other side of the country at the time of your murder."

"We're looking into the possibility he programed one of his robots to do the killing," Pryor said.

Gottwald shook his head. "Yeah. I heard about that theory. Hilarious." With the bookstore starting to empty, Gottwald pulled Pryor into a quieter corner and motioned Cummings should join the conversation. "Look, in thirty-six hours Vane will be inside the president's security bubble and he'll be the Secret Service's problem and will no longer be my responsibility. For the next day and a half, you don't embarrass me and I won't embarrass you."

"How would you embarrass me?" Pryor asked.

Gottwald grinned as his eyes locked on Kevin Cummings. "It would be a shame to see that cute little daughter of yours and your partner here doing a perp walk out of the Federal Courthouse in orange jumpsuits and shackles."

Pryor's face was a stone as he glared at Gottwald but didn't respond.

Gottwald chuckled again. "Yes. The FBI knows all about BONK."

"You're bluffing," Cummings answered. "If you had anything, why haven't we been arrested already?"

"Our IT guys are trying to stop terrorist attacks, prevent ransomware and protect government secrets," Gottwald answered. "If we asked the Attorney General to go after a bunch of harmless pranksters whose only crime was hurting the feelings of a few jerkwater politicians, we'd get laughed out of his office."

"So," Pryor said flatly. "Why should we be worried?"

"What might get the AG curious is how potentially top secret files, stolen from Vane's office, got uploaded on the dark net from the laptop of a guy who had been dead for six hours. Yeah," Gottwald chuckled. "We know about that too."

"That's not nearly enough to get a conviction and you know it," Pryor answered calmly. He was not about to let Jabba the Fed see him sweat.

"Probably not," Gottwald replied with a shrug. "But it would certainly be enough to get an arrest warrant and by the time the charges were dropped, the damage would be done."

"You're making a very large mistake," Pryor said flatly.

Gottwald put both of his hands on his face like Macaulay Culkin in the movie *Home Alone*. "I'm not afraid of your ex-father-in-law."

"Malcolm Kauthmann would be the least of your worries if you mess with my daughter."

"Are you threatening a federal officer?"

It was Pryor's turn to smile. "I see my military service is still redacted in my file."

"What does that mean?" Gottwald demanded, suddenly not nearly as smug.

Pryor just grinned.

Guys like Gottwald, whose greatest risk of personal injury in the line of duty was a paper cut, preferred to have multiple layers of personnel between himself and men like Albert Pryor. Gottwald glanced over his shoulder at another FBI agent, neither Pryor nor Cummings had noticed before. Unlike Mr. Office Fat and the gender-fluid duo, he was the real deal. Clearly ex-military.

The agent nodded at Pryor and Pryor nodded back.

"There is no need to go to war over this," Pryor said. "We stay away from Vane until you're safely back in Washington and none of this comes out?"

"Yup," a relieved Gottwald answered as he extended his hand. "Do we have a deal?"

Pryor accepted the offered hand. "We have a deal."

"Excellent," he said as his smug, self-satisfied expression returned to his face.

Kevin Cummings was stunned as he watched Gottwald walk away. "I can't believe you agreed to that."

Pryor shrugged. "Call it a tactical retreat. With a guy like Vane, we were only here today to rattle his cage a little. With his money and his lawyers, I wouldn't even bother bringing him in for questioning until I have him dead to rights. It will probably take us at least four or five days before that happens, so it cost us nothing. In the meantime, we're going to need to take away Gottwald's leverage or you may as well turn in your badge."

"What do you mean?" Cummings asked.

"Really?" Pryor asked. "You may know computers and technology but you are clueless when it comes to law enforcement politics."

Cummings gave a small smile. "Enlighten me."

"Guys like Gottwald are sharks and dickless bullies. He smells blood in the water and he has no intention of closing the book on BONK. He's got you and he knows it. And once the Feds get their hooks into you, they'll never let go. They'll use this BONK thing to bleed you dry."

"How would they do that?" Cummings asked softly with just a hint of panic in his voice.

"First, Gottwald will ask you for something small and easy like an off-the-record update on an active case. The next request would be bigger and if you balk, Gottwald will show you the paper trail he has and maybe even threaten to arrest you over the BONK thing. Soon you'll be his bitch until he retires, then he'll pimp you to the next guy in line."

Cummings swore, "Shit."

Pryor shook his head. "We're not going to let that happen."

"What are we going to do?" Cummings asked.

"First thing," Pryor said, "go online and find out everything you can about Gottwald."

"Know your enemy."

"Then see if you can figure out the name of that FBI agent who was leaning against the wall."

"Why?" Cummings asked.

"He's the only one of the four agents in Vane's security detail I'm worried about."

CHAPTER 23

KEVIN CUMMINGS WAS reading his phone screen from the passenger seat of the Barracuda as Pryor drove toward the rich part of town.

"Michael James Gottwald. BA from Harvard and Yale Law."

"That proves he's a waste of space," Pryor said.

"How?"

"He got his undergrad degree from Harvard and his law degree from Yale."

"You lost me," Cummings said.

"In this day and age, what does it tell you if a Black guy graduated from Harvard but they didn't want him running around telling people he had gone to their law school?"

"Ah," Cummings said as he turned back to his screen. "That also meant no clerkship from a supreme court justice."

"Or offers from any big time law firm or Wall Street. He was so stupid or lazy, or both, despite an Ivy League law degree, the DOJ didn't want him and he ended up at the FBI."

Cummings turned back to his phone. "He's forty-seven and has been with the FBI for just over twenty-three years." Cummings paused as he continued reading new data. "Interesting."

"What?"

"He has worked his way up to being the number six person at the FBI. His office is two doors down from the director."

"What's interesting about that?"

"Best I can tell, this is the first time he has been out of Washington in pretty much his entire career."

"Humm," Pryor answered. "That is interesting. Why Vane? Why now? Clearly something else is in play here."

"Like what?"

"Unknown," Pryor answered. "But this whole BONK thing isn't right."

"How so?"

"Like Gottwald said, the FBI doesn't waste time with nuisance stuff like BONK. No matter how loud the mayor screamed, I'm pretty sure the FBI would blow him off."

Cummings laughed. "Then why did they look?"

"Exactly," Pryor answered then grinned at Cummings to see if the pieces had fallen in place yet.

Cummings slapped himself on the forehead. "We've been looking at this backwards. They didn't find out about Brooke and me while investigating BONK. They found out about BONK when they were investigating Brooke."

"And they're possibly looking into Melissa as well," Pryor said as he slowed down and turned onto a wide tree-lined road leading to a gated community.

"Why would the FBI be looking at Brooke's mom?"

"Target of opportunity," Pryor answered with a grin.

Cummings slapped himself on the forehead twice this time. "By putting a FBI Swamp Thing like Gottwald in close proximity to Melissa Vane, they were hoping she would say or do something for leverage to use on her father. The FBI is doing the dirty work for Malcolm Kauthmann's rivals."

"It won't be the first time the FBI has gone rogue. Gottwald's superiors must have been doing high fives when they found out about BONK."

"Damn. Damn. Damn," Cummings said. "How can you be so calm about all of this?"

"Not my first rodeo with Brooke's grandfather," Pryor said as he almost had to come to a complete stop as the driveway took an unexpected turn a few hundred feet from the entrance.

Cummings looked around and could see no reason why the driveway was suddenly meandering and weaving as it approached the guardhouse. "Weird driveway," Cummings said.

Pryor shook his head.

"What?" Cummings asked.

"Nothing," Pryor answered with a sigh.

Cummings knew from Pryor's tone and body language that he was missing something. He also knew if it was something that was involved in the case, he would tell him. If not, he would let him figure it out for himself.

Pryor said nothing.

As they got closer to the gate, the massive stone wall surrounding the property blocked their view of the house. Pryor rolled to a stop at the gatehouse. An old man in an ill-fitting uniform leaned out the window and waved.

"This Blitz's replacement?"

"Naw," Pryor answered. "He's my new partner. Reload's grandson."

"No kidding."

Pryor did the introductions. "Kevin Cummings, this is Oscar Rogers..."

"The Oscar Rogers!" Cummings shook his head. "My grandpa has told me stories about you."

"I'll take the Fifth," Rogers said with a laugh. "I heard about old Reload, give Grace my best."

"Thanks, I will."

"Big doings up on the hill," Rogers said as he turned his attention back to Pryor. "That TV lady got here about twenty minutes ago."

"You got a TV in your house?" Pryor asked Rogers.

"Yeah," Rogers answered as he leaned back so Pryor could see an ancient thirteen-inch black and white TV in the corner.

"Tune to ABC in a few minutes." Pryor waved and pulled away from the guardhouse.

Pryor turned into a private boulevard wider than a four-lane interstate. In the middle section, separating the inbound from the outbound lanes, was a spectacular display of gardening. Cummings was gawking at a massive house that would rival the largest English country estate.

"And I thought Plato Vane's house was something," Cummings said.

"You've never been here before?"

"No."

"Try not to embarrass me."

Pryor started toward the rear of the massive estate.

"We're not going to the main house?" Cummings asked.

"No," Pryor answered as he wheeled the Barracuda around to the back of the estate. After about a quarter mile, he pulled into an extra-wide spot near a windowless two-story outbuilding that looked more like an oversized bunker than part of the residence. The other twenty or so cars in the parking area were an odd mix of beaten-up pickups driven by the gardeners all the way up to a pair of Mercedes SUVs with dark tinted windows which both detectives concluded belonged to Sandra Hollis and her entourage.

Pryor shook his head and opened an unmarked, windowless door that led to a large room bustling with activity.

Cummings pulled up short after he crossed the threshold. "I've never been in a house with its own TV studio before," Kevin Cummings said as he looked around at the high-tech space. A small army was busy adjusting lights and checking camera angles.

"Brooke's grandfather is a frequent commentator on the cable news business networks and he doesn't have time to waste driving into town to one of the TV stations for a satellite link-up," Pryor answered while trying unsuccessfully to suppress a yawn.

"He has his own satellite hook-up?"

"Welcome to the big time."

CHAPTER 24

CUMMINGS CONTINUED TO admire the studio. "This is pretty cutting edge equipment."

"Malcolm Kauthmann doesn't do anything half-assed," Pryor said. "The main house has a forty seat theater, an indoor pool, a full-sized basketball court and a two lane bowling alley."

"Brooke's mom grew up here?"

"Yup," Pryor answered.

"That explains a lot."

"Yup." Pryor nodded. "Whole different reality."

"I'm glad Brooke is more grounded," Cummings said as he smiled and nodded in the direction of Brooke who was sitting on a couch having a microphone clipped to her blouse. Brooke noticed, smiled back and gave him a weak wave.

"She has her moments," Pryor said softly as he watched his daughter getting ready for her interview.

Cummings's eyes lit up when he saw Sandy Hollis, anchor of *Good Morning America,* make her entrance with her six-person entourage surrounding her. She was dressed in a well-cut charcoal gray pantsuit combination with an off-white silk blouse. She still had a make-up bib, about the size you might find in a lobster or rib restaurant, around her neck to protect her clothes. "I can't believe they flew in the network superstar to interview her."

"This is a huge story. The fact that Brooke's grandfather owns thirty-seven affiliate television stations in twenty-six states may have been a contributing factor." Pryor smiled when he saw a ramrod straight guy about his age headed in their direction. "Incoming."

"Albert," the man said in a deep baritone as he extended his hand which Pryor accepted. "Is this your new boyfriend?"

"This is Reload's grandson," Pryor answered then did the introductions. "Jeff Gillis. Kevin Cummings."

"Your grandfather was my training officer," Gillis said as he shook hands with Cummings.

Cummings nodded but didn't speak.

Pryor grinned when Cummings didn't recognize the name. Unlike many of the officers Reload had tutored over the years, Gillis was probably the last one his grandfather would have any tall tales about. Gillis had been a by the book cop. Professional and unflappable.

"Jeff couldn't hack it as a cop," Pryor said, then continued, "so he went into the private sector as Malcolm Kauthmann's head of security." Gillis didn't know, and he never would, that Pryor had been the one who recommended him to Kauthmann. With Brooke often under the Kauthmann security umbrella, Pryor had wanted the best for his little girl.

"Better hours and five times the money," Gillis said with a laugh. "The old man is on his way down and wants a private word."

Pryor glanced at Cummings. "How private?"

Gillis shrugged. "We'll let your shadow tag along and let the old man decide." He motioned toward a door leading to the hallway and the trio headed in that direction. They arrived about the same time as the elevator containing Malcolm Kauthmann and his entourage. First off were two beefy specimens in dockers and dark blue polo shirts with a *Kauthmann Industries* logo over the left breast pocket. The two bodyguards were big enough that you couldn't even see the others behind them in the elevator until they had all stepped out of the way.

Directly behind the beef trust was Malcolm Kauthmann and standing next to him was a woman who appeared to be in her mid to late thirties who could have been extremely attractive had she wanted to. With her horned rim glasses and her hair pulled back, she was all business and as approachable as a coiled rattlesnake. As they stepped off of the elevator, she handed her boss a phone. Kauthmann accepted it and started talking softly into it.

The last guy out was compact with a dark complexion, jet black hair brushed straight back and he had a well-trimmed Van Dyke beard. His head was on a swivel and his eyes seemed to take in everything and everyone in the vicinity in less than three seconds. Unlike his bigger partners, he was wearing a dark blue windbreaker with the same logo as his brethren.

Jeff Gillis's eyes twinkled as he leaned into Cummings. "Who do you keep your eyes on?" he asked softly.

"The little guy in the windbreaker," Cummings answered.

"Why?"

"The two big guys are there to intimidate civilians by their size. The little guy is the only one armed and he looks like he knows what he's doing."

Gillis patted Cummings on the shoulder and grinned at Pryor. "He's definitely got Reload's genes."

Malcolm Kauthmann, still on the phone, nodded at his security team and they all waited near the elevator. The little guy found a spot where he could see his protectee and every egress then leaned against a wall and, like a sniper, was very still. Even if you were looking straight at him, he blended so well into the background you probably wouldn't notice he was there.

"Benny has cleaned up some," Pryor said with a laugh.

"Benny?" Cummings asked.

"Benny the Rabbi," Gillis answered.

"He used to be the body man and shooter for Little Tony DeFazio who ran the prostitution rackets," Pryor answered.

"How did he end up here?" Cummings asked.

Gillis chuckled. "Little Tony had a massive coronary while banging a teenage hooker. Benny was available and I hired him."

Pryor nodded in Benny's direction. Benny's head went up and down maybe an eighth of an inch. "I tried to put him away at least a dozen times."

Kevin Cummings was stunned. "I can't believe Brooke's grandfather has an ex-mob hitman for a bodyguard."

"Mr. Kauthmann makes decisions, not value judgments," Gillis said as he turned to Pryor. "If you were heading into a fire fight and could have your choice of anyone to have on your six, who would you pick?" he asked.

"If John Rambo or John McClane were both busy, Benny would be at the top of my list," Pryor answered.

"Me too," Gillis said with a laugh.

"Damn," Cummings muttered as he processed this information.

"He could take out everyone in this area before you even had your gun out of your holster," Gillis added.

Pryor nodded his agreement. "Our world is not black and white," Pryor said. "It is varying shades of gray. Benny is a pro. He's a cold-blooded killer but he lives by certain rules."

"He would never hit anyone when their family was around," Gillis said.

"There was never any collateral damage from any of his work and I would never even find the body unless Little Tony wanted to deliver a message."

"It sounds like you respect this guy," Cummings said with an amazed expression on his face.

"Welcome to Homicide." Pryor shrugged. "I'd rather have Benny running around taking out the garbage than those asshole gangbangers, who, while doing a drive-by, couldn't hit their own foot on their best day."

"Those are the bad guys who give Albert nightmares," Gillis said. "Unlike Benny, they don't give a shit about who might be down range or in their crossfire. They'll empty a seventeen-round clip into a crowd of civilians at the drop of a hat if they feel somebody has disrespected them."

"Even firing point-blank, all they can usually hit is a seven-year-old girl and her grandmother sitting on their porch a half a block away."

"Since everyone in the neighborhood knows they're rabid dogs, no one ever sees anything. Their creed is 'snitches get stitches.'"

"Or a 9mm round in the ear," Pryor added.

"Toughest homicides to solve," Gillis stated.

Pryor nodded his agreement.

Kauthmann handed the phone back to his personal assistant and headed in the direction of Pryor, Cummings and Gillis. He was a fit man who was around seventy years old but with his energy level and no sags or bulges, someone might guess him to be at least fifteen years younger than the calendar indicated. A few inches shorter than Pryor and half a foot shorter than Cummings, with the way he carried himself, he looked much taller. Like his security detail, he was dressed in khaki slacks and a dark golf shirt. His hair, what was left of it, was close cropped and a mixture of dark brown and gray. The first thing you noticed was his eyes. They were ice blue and he barely blinked. Kauthmann looked as if he could freeze you where you stood if you crossed him. If that didn't work, he had Benny as a backup.

"Thank you, Mr. Gillis," Kauthmann said in a voice that seemed about right for his size.

Gillis nodded, then stepped away.

"Albert," Kauthmann said.

"Malcolm," Pryor answered. Pryor's eyes followed Kauthmann's in the direction of his partner. "This is Kevin Cummings."

Kauthmann nodded in Cummings's direction but did not offer his hand nor request he leave. "My granddaughter speaks well of you." He turned his attention back to Pryor. "Do you think Plato Vane murdered that young man?" he asked as calmly as if he were checking on a weather forecast.

"Yes," Pryor answered.

"Why?"

"Unknown."

"What is my personal risk?"

"We need to talk about that," Pryor answered.

"Brooke?"

Pryor grinned and glanced at Cummings. This was his partner's first time around Malcolm Kauthmann and he had just learned the old man didn't get to where he was by missing things.

"There is an FBI Agent named Gottwald," Pryor said, "who may embarrass her, but nothing more."

"I'm aware of Gottwald and his agenda."

"Agenda?" Pryor asked.

"I have many enemies and rivals who would like to do me harm. It would appear Agent Gottwald is among them."

"Really?" Pryor said.

"Did you think the FBI would send their best and brightest to protect Plato Vane?"

"No," Pryor answered.

"I hardly think the protection detail for my son-in-law would require the head babysitter to then be an upper-level senior bureaucrat from Washington. He was fishing and appears to have succeeded with this BONK enterprise."

"We had theorized he discovered BONK while investigating Brooke," Pryor said. Not the other way around."

Kauthmann grunted his agreement. "A man like Gottwald would not do a frontal assault on my family without serious political backup."

"Any charges would be frivolous and likely be thrown out before trial," Pryor answered.

"Agreed. But, it is common knowledge Brooke will soon be running Kauthmann Industries and we have numerous government contracts that require a clean security clearance from the CEO. What happens if one of my enemies had a prosecutor and a friendly judge on their payroll?"

"Worst case scenario, she could possibly end up with a felony conviction on her record for a few years until you had it overturned and expunged from her record."

"Precisely. That is not a risk I'm willing to take," Kauthmann said calmly. "My enemies are constantly probing and see Brooke as a point of weakness."

"They may not think so after Brooke's interview."

Malcolm Kauthmann nodded. "One can hope."

"She briefed you?"

"Of course," Kauthmann said. "My granddaughter and I have no secrets." Kauthmann's eyes locked on Pryor. "You have a very large marker in your pocket. Would you be willing to use it for Brooke?"

"Do you even need to ask me that?"

"No," Kauthmann answered. "He has been briefed but for political reasons but he would prefer to not get involved."

"But?" Pryor asked.

Kauthmann's eyes locked on Pryor and what might have been a smile flickered across his face. It vanished as quickly as it had arrived. "He said you have his phone number."

Pryor nodded he understood. "You have a huge investment in the GAIA Institute. Are you going to give Plato Vane any cover?"

"No. After what he did," Kauthmann said coldly, "do you even need to ask me that?"

It was Pryor's turn to shake his head and grin.

The door to the studio opened and a young man with a headset on announced. "Two minute warning."

Kauthmann nodded then motioned for Pryor and Cummings to accompany him into the studio.

CHAPTER 25

THE MOOD WAS tense in Lt. Wilson Garrison's small office. Sitting across from him in the two guest chairs were the Chief of Police and the District Attorney. With the door closed, the air was fast getting stuffy and stale.

The chief, George McGregor, was a thirty-five year veteran of the force. In the past five years he had badly gone to seed. With flushed cheeks, bug eyes and a prominent nose lined with small veins and arteries starting to show, he looked more like the town drunk than the city's senior law enforcement officer. He had unbuttoned the top button on his shirt and loosened his tie. He was trying hard to ignore the beads of sweat on his forehead. McGregor was a few months away from maxing out his state pension and the speculation around the water cooler was he would soon be out the door. Never a detail guy, recently he was even more unfocused and disinterested and appeared to be suffering from a bad case of either 'short timer's disease' or early onset dementia.

Next to him, looking cool and crisp in a well-cut suit was the District Attorney, Brady Burris. Burris was smart and ambitious. The knot in his tie was perfect, his hair was perfect and the chemically enhanced level of whiteness of his teeth was perfect. They were just white enough to project good health but not white enough to annoy a juror. His name was on the short list to be the next State Attorney General which he viewed as the stepping stone to the Governor's Mansion. Normally the DA was unflappable but, at the moment, he appeared to be badly off balance. He was in virgin territory. This was the first time he had ever gotten directly involved in a case that was still in the early stages of an investigation. He usually waited until they were ready to make an arrest before he would even review the file. If it wasn't an absolute slam dunk, he was notorious for kicking cases back to the investigating officers or assigning it to one of his ADAs. He had personally never lost a case since he had ascended to the DA office. His hawklike eyes danced back and forth between the chief and the lieutenant.

"What are we going to do about this mess?" DA Burris asked softly.

"Now that Vane no longer has an alibi, we could say we have a possible conflict of interest," the chief offered. "We could pull Pryor off the case and give it to Danny Holden."

Lt. Garrison shook his head. "I already told you chief, Holden has turned in his papers and will be out of here in less than two weeks. There is no way this is completely tied up by then." Garrison shook his head. "If Vane is involved, with his lawyers, this thing is going to drag on for years."

"What about Detective Luke Nash?" the chief asked. "He was initially assigned as lead investigator and he might be more flexible and reasonable to deal with than Pryor."

"This is already national news and when the word gets out that a robot is our prime suspect, it is going to be a PR nightmare. This is already a political hot potato. Nash would be in well over his head." Garrison glared at the chief. "If it looks like we're trying to cover our own asses, someone is going to notice."

"This is a damage control meeting," the DA said calmly as he was starting to regret inviting the chief to join them. "No one in your department or my department is going to try to spin or protect anyone at this point."

"How good is the evidence that it might be Vane?" the chief asked.

Lt. Garrison sighed. "It's all in the report," Garrison answered. "We have nothing leading directly back to Vane, but that robot had gunshot residue and the victim's blood all over it. The hard drive of the robot has been removed and likely destroyed so we have no way to backtrack its activities or programing."

"Who removed and destroyed the hard drive?" the chief asked.

Burris and Garrison locked eyes and both shook their heads. The biggest case in the history of the town and the chief had not even bothered to read the most recent update.

Still, Chief McGregor was his superior officer so he had to humor him. "Since the building was sealed, we suspect another robot."

The chief closed his eyes and shook his head. "I feel like I'm in a Terminator movie."

"Pryor's working theory has some pretty good legs," Garrison said. "He thinks the victim discovered something and that is what got him killed."

"Something about Vane?" the chief asked.

"Unknown," Garrison answered. "But, he would appear to be the only one with even a hint of a motive."

"Which is the problem," the DA added. "What could that hacker have possibly found that was damaging enough for a man of Vane's wealth and stature to commit murder?"

"Plus," Garrison added, "Vane barely spends any time in the lab and he is considered at best mediocre at crafting computer code."

"An accomplice?" the chief asked.

"Our task force is in the process of interviewing all of the senior staff and so far the only consensus we've come up with is Plato Vane is a condescending and arrogant prick with a weakness for the affections of attractive coeds."

"That doesn't make him a killer," DA Burris said flatly.

"No. It does not," Garrison agreed. "But it certainly shrinks the field of potential co-conspirators. Other than his wife, we can't find anyone willing to risk spending the rest of their lives in prison for him."

"Vane's wife used to be married to Detective Pryor? Correct?" the chief asked.

"Correct," Garrison answered then added since the chief seemed to be missing some of the key details of the investigation. "She is also the only child of Malcolm Kauthmann."

The chief muttered an obscenity under his breath.

"He was the one who pressured us to put Detective Pryor on the case in the first place," DA Burris added.

The chief snapped his fingers. "That's right."

Garrison and Burris exchanged glances and both shook their heads.

Burris turned his full attention to Garrison. "What's the deal with Pryor and Vane?" the DA asked.

"It is weird," Garrison answered. "His ex has been married to Vane for the past twelve years and there was never a problem until recently. Pryor refuses to talk about it; he wouldn't answer any questions at his suspension hearing. But Pryor is a pretty cool customer. Something happened to set him off."

"Why don't we just go ahead and terminate Pryor?" the chief asked.

"Not without him signing a non-disclosure agreement," the DA answered, then turned to Lt. Garrison, "If we offered him his full pension, would he sign an NDA?"

"Not a chance in hell," Garrison answered firmly.

"What's the big deal?" the chief asked.

"The press already hates us," DA Burris answered. "If Pryor is a private citizen, with what he knows and he's free to talk, we'd all be looking for new jobs in a few weeks."

"He's welcome to mine," the chief said as he shook his head. "I'm getting too old for this crap."

Garrison and Burris exchanged glances again. For the first time in the entire meeting, they both agreed with the chief.

The desk sergeant tapped on the door and Garrison motioned for him to enter. He opened the door and handed DA Burris a slip of paper and immediately left, closing the door behind him.

"Plato Vane has filed a motion to have his lab reopened," DA Burris said.

"It's an active crime scene," Garrison said.

"I'm not sure a judge would see it that way," Burris answered. "How about we offer to tape off only the area around the spot where we found the body and seal the maintenance room."

"Pryor won't like it," Garrison answered.

"I really don't give a crap what Albert Pryor thinks," Burris said with a harsh tone in his voice.

The sergeant tapped on the door frame and stuck his head in without waiting for permission "Lou. You need to see this."

Lt. Garrison glanced out his office and saw all activity in the entire squad room had come to a halt and all eyes were locked on the television mounted on the far wall.

CHAPTER 26

"WE'RE LIVE IN Five. Four," the stage director quit speaking and continued his countdown with just his fingers. When he reached zero, he pointed to Sandra Hollis who was sitting in one of the two overstuffed chairs on the slightly elevated stage next to Brooke Pryor. During the countdown, if Brooke was nervous or intimidated by the studio lights and being on national television, she certainly didn't show it. When they went live, her demeanor completely changed.

"What the hell?" Cummings muttered as he noticed the abrupt difference in Brooke's body language from her normal, don't mess with me, to a shrinking violet. She rolled her shoulders forward, put her hands in her lap and would not make eye contact with anyone in the room.

"We have a breaking story," Hollis said with a professional edge. "With me is Brooke Pryor. She is the granddaughter of billionaire industrialist Malcolm Kauthmann and the daughter of Homicide Detective Albert Pryor. Brooke is also the step-daughter of Dr. Plato Vane, known as the "Earthquake Whisperer" who runs the GAIA Institute." Hollis stared hard into the camera. "More importantly, Brooke was a close friend of the young man found murdered early this morning at the GAIA Institute."

Sandy Hollis turned to Brooke. "Thank you for agreeing to speak to us."

Brooke, looking like the well-scrubbed and innocent girl next door, forced a smile that quickly vanished. "Thank you, Ms. Hollis," she said in a voice barely above a whisper.

"Please call me Sandra," Hollis said as she patted Brooke's knee.

Brooke put her hand on top of Hollis's and averted her eyes. "Thank you," she said meekly.

Kevin Cummings had a stunned look on his face as he watched the normally self-contained and self-confident Brooke appear to be on the edge of bursting into tears.

Albert Pryor and Malcolm Kauthmann both chuckled and exchanged approving glances.

Pryor leaned into his ex-father-in-law. "Kauthmann Industries is going to be in great hands."

"Agreed," Kauthmann answered.

They turned their attention back to the interview.

"You seem to be right in the middle of this brouhaha, Brooke," Hollis said gently.

"Yes, ma'am," Brooke said before catching herself. "I mean Sandra."

"Tell me about it," Hollis said in a soothing tone.

"As you all know by now, Nick Blake was brutally murdered early this morning."

"Yes," Sandra Hollis said. "And there is a rumor you asked your grandfather to use his influence to have your father assigned to the case. Is that true?"

"Yes it is," Brooke answered without even the slight hint of defensiveness in her tone. Her posture improved and now she looked straight at Hollis. "My father, Detective Albert Pryor, is an experienced homicide detective with one of the highest case clearance rates in the entire state. He is also someone who sometimes gets himself in trouble because he refuses to play political games and won't kiss the asses of the rich and powerful." Brooke's eyes filled with tears again and her lip quivered. "I know he will not let his superiors bully him and he will bring Nick Blake's killer to justice, no matter whose toes he has to step on."

"Why do you think Nick Blake was killed?"

Brooke averted her eyes from the camera. Took in a cleansing breath, squared her shoulders and looked back into the camera. The tears were gone. She cleared her throat. "Nick Blake was the famous BONK who had been exposing the dirty little secrets of the rich and powerful of our town."

"So he was a hacker?" Sandra Hollis asked.

"Let me stop you right there, Sandra," Brooke said as her eyes flashed with anger, evaporating any remaining tears. "Nick was non-binary and his preferred pronouns were 'they' or 'them'."

Kevin Cummings's mouth fell open as he shook his head.

"And yes," Brooke continued. "Nick was a hacker." Instead of addressing Hollis, Brooke's eyes locked on the camera in front of her. Her voice, which had been soft and intimidated, was now firm and purposeful. "You need to understand, not all hackers are trying to rip people off, in fact, Nick was the exact opposite." Brooke's eyes remained focused on the camera and the tears in her eyes formed again and got bigger until one ran down her cheek. "If Nick found a vulnerability, he would quietly notify the company or utility or government agency and help them fix the problem."

"So tell me about this BONK."

"BONK never stole anything, never did ransomware or any of the other bad things you hear other hackers do." Brooke's nose flared in anger. "All Nick ever did was expose how the rich and powerful and corrupt go about their business every day."

"I see," Hollis said. "Anything else?"

"Nick gave me a warning."

"Warning?"

"He said I shouldn't be surprised if I got a visit from a TAO."

"What is a TAO?" Sandra Hollis asked as she pulled back slightly.

"Token Alphabet Oreo," Brooke replied. "An African-American bureaucrat from one of the alphabet government agencies, who is Black on the outside but double stuffed with White privilege on the inside. They are total sellout mouthpieces for the federal government and hide behind their race. If you criticize a TAO or their tactics, they will call you a racist to try and shut you up and the white guilt 'amen chorus' in the media will back them up." Brooke leaned in closer to Sandra. "Nick discovered something which got him murdered and the federal government will do whatever they can to try to discredit him." Brooke lowered her eyes. "I wouldn't be surprised, with me coming forward with all of this, if they didn't try to frame me too."

"Boom," Albert Pryor muttered as he glanced at Cummings. "That's my girl."

Sandy Hollis leaned forward. "What else do you know, Brooke?"

"Nick was worried."

"Worried?"

Brooke held up a thumb drive. "Nick gave me a flash drive with instructions that if anything happened, these files should be uploaded to a webpage on I2P on the dark web. I uploaded the files a few hours after Nick was murdered."

"What is on the files you uploaded?"

"Gosh," Brooke said innocently as she reverted back to her girl next door persona. "I have no idea." Brooke cleared her throat again. "Nick was well-respected on the dark web and by putting this information online, every hacker in the world will have the chance to review the data and hopefully figure out what he discovered that got him killed."

"So you don't know what was in the file that was Nick Blake's dying wish you upload."

"No ma'am." Brooke shook her head with tears started streaming down both cheeks.

"What exactly do you know for sure, Brooke?" Hollis asked gently.

"I know Nick Blake found something in the GAIA Institute's computers that was worth killing him over." She paused and cleared her throat and took a moment to compose herself. "I also know someone at the GAIA Institute programmed one of their maintenance droids to kill anyone who found out their dirty little secret."

Sandy Hollis leaned in even further. "You're confirming the rumor that a robot killed Nick Blake?"

"I am," Brooke said firmly as she stuck her chin out defiantly. "I'm also saying there are androids exactly like the one that killed Nick Blake all over the new GAIA Institute facility in Hawaii where the President of the United States is supposed to do the ribbon-cutting in two days."

Sandra Hollis had a stunned expression on her face. "Are you saying the president may be at risk?"

"I am," Brooke answered firmly as she stared unblinking into the camera. "That is why I asked my grandfather and father to get involved. There is too much at stake here."

"That's quite the bombshell you just dropped, Brooke. Do you have any other thoughts you want to share?"

Brooke sat up even straighter. "Nick liked to quote the old LSD guy Timothy Leary. *Proper use of the brain is not endorsed by federal governments*. Nick Blake gave his life trying to make this world a better place." Brooke leaned and glared at the camera with fire in her eyes. As she wiped away her tears, she said through clenched teeth, "I will not let his death go unavenged!" Brooke raised her fist and shouted, "Power to the people! Power to the dark web!"

"Thank you, Brooke Pryor. This is Sandra Hollis, ABC News."

"We're clear!" shouted a voice off stage.

Sandy Hollis leaned back in her chair and applauded. "That was spectacular!" She put her hands down so her crew could remove the microphone clipped to her jacket.

Brooke had completed her metamorphous back to her normal calm and controlled persona. "Not too much?" Brooke asked with a smile.

"Can you cry on demand?" Hollis asked.

In less than half a beat, Brooke was a sobbing mess.

"You are now officially on my short list of people I never want to piss off," Hollis said with a laugh. One of Hollis's assistants, after twisting off the caps, handed both Hollis and Brooke a bottle of water. Hollis, looking around the room while shielding her eyes from the lights, shouted, "Where the hell is your grandfather?"

Brooke pointed in his direction.

"Malcolm!" Hollis shouted. "Get your thin ass over here!"

Malcolm Kauthmann walked over then leaned in and gave Hollis a peck on the cheek. "Good to see you, Sandy," Kauthmann said.

"Hey!" Brooke protested. "How come he gets to call you Sandy and I have to call you Sandra?" Brooke asked with a grin.

Hollis gave Brooke's knee a squeeze. "Right now, Brooke, you can call me any fucking thing you want. Thanks to you I'm going to need to make more room on my mantel for another Emmy." Hollis shook her head. "R2D2 and C3PO programmed to kill the president! We are going to break the fucking internet!"

Kevin Cummings came up next to Brooke with a befuddled expression on his face. "Non-binary? Token Alphabet Oreo? Timothy Leary? Power to the dark web!" Cummings threw his hands up in disbelief. "And since when do you cry?" he demanded.

Brooke grinned at Cummings then nodded at her father to answer.

"The best defense is a good offense," Pryor said as he gave Brooke a peck on the cheek.

"Meaning?"

"Always keep your enemy off balance and always stay on the attack," Hollis answered as she patted Brooke on the shoulder then glanced at Malcolm Kauthmann. "The force is strong in this one." Sandra Hollis's eyes landed on Albert Pryor and she looked at him like a lioness on the Serengeti who had just spotted a limping antelope. She leaned into Brooke. "Who is this tasty morsel?"

"Sandy," Brooke said, "meet my father, Albert Pryor." Brooke leaned into Hollis. "Divorced, living alone and currently not seeing anyone."

"Good to know," Hollis said as she turned her full attention to Pryor. "Any chance I can get you to make an on-air statement?"

"Nope," Pryor answered.

"Any chance I can invite you to my hotel to have a drink with me tonight?"

Pryor was stunned and speechless. Brooke, now standing next to her father, gave him a hip bump. Pryor glared at his daughter. "He's the strong silent type," Brooke said. "Leave me your number and I'll work on him."

Hollis gave Brooke a high five. "You, I like," she said before turning her attention back to Kauthmann. "I won't even bother asking you for a comment."

"You always were smart, Sandy," Kauthmann answered.

"Off the record," Hollis said seriously. "As much as I appreciate Brooke's Oscar winning performance. What's going on here?"

Pryor turned to Kauthmann. "Is her word good when she says we're off the record?"

Kauthmann nodded.

"Brooke was up to her ears in the BONK thing and an FBI agent threatened to have her arrested if I didn't back off on Plato Vane."

"Let me guess," Hollis said. "The FBI agent throwing his weight around is African-American."

"Yes," Pryor answered.

"Damn, girl," Hollis said as she fanned herself. "Does this asshole have some kind of death wish going after Malcolm's only grandchild and heir apparent?"

"Obviously he seriously underestimates my granddaughter," Kauthmann said with a hint of pride in his voice. "Still, he has some serious political backing for a head on assault against my family."

"Ya think?" Hollis said with a laugh as she continued to eye Pryor. "What's this dead man walking's name?"

"Gottwald," Pryor answered.

"Michael Gottwald?"

Pryor nodded.

Hollis laughed again. "Oh, baby," she said. "Clash of the Titans. Gottwald wants to be in congress so bad he can taste it and I've heard he's been cozied up to anyone with deep pockets to back his run."

"Any idea who?" Kauthmann asked.

"No," Hollis answered. "I'll certainly look into it, Malcolm. There aren't that many who play at your level and have the balls make a run at you like this." Sandra Hollis shook her head. "Trying to take out your granddaughter is an open act of war."

"Keep me informed," Malcolm Kauthmann said softly.

"You scratch my ass and I'll kiss yours, Malcolm." She turned to Brooke. "So this whole interview was designed to get Gottwald to back off."

Brooke laughed. "Back off, change his underwear and start updating his resume," Brooke said coldly.

"Damn!" Hollis said as she glanced at Kauthmann. "That's some granddaughter you've got there, Malcolm." She turned her attention back to Brooke. "What's the deal with the files that were uploaded?"

"Let's be clear," Pryor said softly. "We're completely off the record."

"Absolutely," Hollis answered.

"Brooke isn't quite the computer novice she tried to appear in the interview," Pryor said.

Hollis laughed. It was a deep, full-bodied laugh, which caused everyone around her to want to jump in and laugh too. "Really! I never would have guessed."

Pryor grinned at Hollis. "She was able to partially rebuild the damaged hard drive from the computer Nick Blake was using when he was killed."

"Why does that not surprise me?" Hollis said with a chuckle. "So. Let me guess. Since it was damaged, you only had fragments but you loaded everything you were able to recover up on the dark web hoping someone might be able to figure out what Blake was doing."

"Yup," Brooke answered.

"Any idea what he found?"

"Not a clue," Pryor stated.

"Yet," Brooke added. "Nick was popular on the dark net and as we speak, we've got some of the best minds in the world trying to untie this knot."

Sandra Hollis nodded to one of her assistants who handed her a stack of her business cards. Hollis looked at the cards and handed them back. "No, the ones with my personal phone number on it as well." The assistant nodded and handed Hollis a different set of business cards. She handed one to Brooke. "You call me when you have something," she said as she turned to face Pryor. She tucked one of her cards in his front shirt pocket then patted it gently. "You just call me."

"Somebody is getting lucky tonight," Brooke said with a cackle.

Before Albert Pryor could respond, his phone vibrated. He pulled it out of his pocket and read the text message. He showed the message to Cummings.

"That was expected," Cummings said.

"What?" Brooke asked.

"Our presence is requested immediately at police headquarters," Pryor answered.

CHAPTER 27

"I OWE YOU BIG time," Cummings said.

Albert Pryor rolled up to the stop light then glanced at his young partner. "Don't thank me yet. Until we know for sure that Gottwald is standing down, this is still in play."

"After Brooke's interview…"

"A wounded bear is the most dangerous. He, and the people supporting him, may double down."

"How so?" Cummings asked.

"Gottwald may have reached the point where he believes he has nothing to lose. And his kind tends to be vicious and go down swinging."

"Damn," Cummings muttered.

Pryor shrugged and impatiently tapped the steering wheel as he waited for the light to change. "Right now, you've got some big guns covering your back in the form of Malcolm Kauthmann."

"Right," Cummings said. "Malcolm Kauthmann is not going to let some fat ass FBI paper pusher embarrass or hurt his only grandchild."

"You and Brooke are currently under the same umbrella." The light changed and Pryor rolled the Barracuda through the intersection. "But Malcolm Kauthmann is only interested in protecting Brooke. He will throw your ass under the bus in a heartbeat if will help her."

"I'm in way over my head here," Cummings muttered.

"Naw," Pryor said. "Hollis nailed it. Gottwald has some serious backing or he wouldn't have come on so strong." Pryor glanced at Cummings before turning his full attention back to the road. "Kauthmann is a major player, but he's far from the only one in the game. You just need to avoid being trampled by the bigger players on the field."

"How much pull does he have in Washington?"

Pryor laughed. "Kauthmann is a major donor to both parties. With the clock ticking, Melissa and I eloped. When she married Vane in the big church wedding, in the audience were six U.S. Senators and the Vice President of the United States."

"Oh," Cummings said.

"Yeah. Oh." Pryor shrugged and made a face. "Homicide 101. Ninety-nine times out of a hundred a homicide investigation is routine and off the radar. Politics usually only rears its ugly head when the victim is a kid, a celebrity, or there are multiple bodies face down on the sidewalk. When your primary suspect is rich AND famous, and the murder weapon was a damn robot, this is a nightmare for everyone. In Vane's case, he's going to be pulling up the drawbridge. We're going to have to battle expensive lawyers throwing up roadblocks and the press screaming at us to move faster. Every politician and senior officer on the force is in cover your own ass mode and looking for a scapegoat if the investigation goes sideways." Pryor glanced at Cummings. "Having worked high-profile cases before, I could see all of this coming. That was why I was so against you being assigned to this case."

"Let me guess," Cummings said. "You thought I was the perfect candidate to have a 'kick me' sign taped on my back."

"Close," Pryor answered with a laugh. "This case had FUBAR written all over it from the beginning. With Malcolm Kauthmann asking to have me assigned to the case, the powers that be got a twofer. They were able to suck up to a rich and powerful man and if I solved it, they were golden. On the other hand, with me already on thin ice and being such a colossal pain in the ass, if I did a face plant, they would have the perfect excuse to show me the door with political cover."

Cummings sighed and shook his head. "Malcolm Kauthmann made me do it."

"Exactly." Pryor glanced quickly over at Cummings. "But I was afraid if I went down, I would take you down with me."

"Thanks for caring."

Pryor sighed. "Yeah, well, that was before I knew you used to date Brooke."

Cummings laughed. "About that…"

Pryor held up his hand to stop him. "Don't ask. Don't tell. My daughter is a full-grown woman who doesn't need her daddy looking over her shoulder or making value judgments."

"With Brooke," Cummings said wistfully, "that's probably a wise choice."

"You really like her," Pryor stated.

"Is it that obvious?"

"Yeah."

"Crap." Cummings shook his head. "Any advice?"

"You're asking me for dating tips for my daughter?" Pryor said with a snort. "You are an idiot."

"Normally when I'm around other women, I'm fine. Whenever I get around her, I do a brain freeze and turn into a babbling fool." Cummings shook his head again.

"I'm the last person you should ask for advice."

"Why?"

"A. I'm her father. B. I was in exactly the same place you're in now when I met her mother. I thought Melissa was the most beautiful woman I had ever met and she had me wrapped around her finger. But you've seen her world and soon, for her at least, the blush was off of the rose. The idea of raising a child with a beat cop in a house with less square footage than her walk-in closet at home was a non-starter for her. It didn't take her long to start to resent me."

"Damn," Cummings muttered. "You still love her but you've loved her enough to let her go."

"Don't go all Oprah on me, and start overthinking this. Melissa and I will always have a connection through Brooke. About half the time I want to strangle her."

"And the other half of the time you want to sneak off for a hot weekend in Cabo."

"Shut up," Pryor said as he gave the Barracuda more gas.

"It's hopeless," Cummings continued. "Brooke comes from the same world as her mother."

"Yup."

"I knew I was out-classed," Cummings admitted.

"Join the crowd," Pryor said. "Most guys would be punching above their weight class with Brooke. The big difference is Brooke is not her mother."

"What does that mean?"

"While Malcolm Kauthmann was out making money, Melissa was raised by her mother and nannies to be the supportive wife of a successful husband. She was, and still is, the perfect 1950's pampered spouse for a wealthy and powerful man. To his credit, Malcolm realized his mistake with Melissa and took a more hands-on approach with Brooke. Instead of limiting her to girlie and ladylike things, he let her get her hands dirty."

"And her mother let..." Cummings burst out laughing and clapped his hands. "When you say 'get dirty' you mean doing things like pulling the engine on a 1971 Barracuda when she was visiting her father on weekends." Cummings snapped his fingers and pointed at Pryor. "Every summer in high school she went off and did something really weird at least by Churchill Academy standards. Building houses for Habitat for Humanity in Alabama. Going to the Caribbean for hurricane repairs. One year she climbed some mountain..."

"We climbed the front face of the Grand Teton in Wyoming," Pryor said.

"We!" Cummings said. "Damn. You and old man Kauthmann have been outmaneuvering her mother and grooming Brooke since she was a kid to make her the woman she is today."

Pryor grinned. "Malcolm would take her with him to the Davos business conference, Ted meetings and Aspen Institute kinds of things while I handled the blue-collar stuff."

"What about her mother?" Cummings asked.

"Melissa was in charge of fashion and social graces."

"So Brooke's mom was a part of the conspiracy?"

"Hardly." Pryor laughed. "She just did what came natural to her."

"Did Brooke figure out what you and her grandfather were up to?"

Pryor shot Cummings a look.

"What was I thinking? Of course she did."

"I loved the time I got to spend with Brooke while she was growing up," Pryor said with a wry smile as old memories washed over him. "Best time of my life."

"Exposed to the jet set A-list stuff by her grandfather, getting social skills from her mother and being grounded by you." Cummings shook his head. "Whoa, that's seriously brilliant." Cummings shook his head again. "Throw into the mix she is jaw-droppingly gorgeous, you and old man Kauthmann may have produced the ultimate Alpha Female."

Pryor shrugged. "Malcolm and I don't always see eye-to-eye, but we do share a common goal. We both want what is best for Brooke. Malcolm has big plans for her which I really don't care for, but she gets to make her own choices. For me, I didn't want her to set any artificial limits on herself just because she's female."

"Mission accomplished." Cummings leaned back in the seat and relaxed. "What was that marker Kauthmann mentioned?"

Pryor didn't answer.

"Okay," Cummings said. "None of my business." Cummings shifted in his seat so he could look at Pryor. "I certainly own you one."

"No," said Pryor, "the books are balanced."

"How do you figure that?"

"When I was about your age, I did something just as stupid as you did with BONK. Your grandfather pulled my fat out of the fire."

"What did you do?"

Pryor grinned and shook his head. "Ask your grandfather."

"He probably won't remember."

Pryor chuckled. "Thank God for small blessings."

Kevin Cummings's phone rang. There was a picture of Brooke on the screen.

"Pull over," Cummings said. "It's Brooke and I'm going to put her on FaceTime."

Pryor wheeled the Barracuda to an open spot in front of a fire hydrant.

When she was on the screen, she began talking excitedly. "I just got an email from one of the guys on Nick's forum." Pryor and Cummings watched as she touched some keys on her phone. "You should have it in a few seconds."

Both Pryor's and Cummings's phones pinged.

Pryor read the message then asked, "Is that even possible?"

Cummings said, "I have no idea. But, if it is, then we certainly have our motive."

"Brooke," Pryor said, "Forward that email to Sandra Hollis."

"Oh, you sly dog. Are you trying to get on her good side?" Brooke asked with a giggle.

"Please," Pryor said.

"Chill," Brooke said. "She's as close to a sure thing for you as you're ever going to get. Besides, I've already called her and she is on her way back to Grandpa's TV studio."

"You're going live with this?"

"Absolutely!" Brooke answered.

"Has this been confirmed?"

"Don't care," Brooke answered. "Got to go." She broke the connection.

Albert Pryor shook his head and pulled away from the curb.

CHAPTER 28

A S PRYOR AND Cummings entered the bullpen they saw a smug Special Agent-in-Charge Michael Gottwald sitting in one of the visitor chairs in Lt. Garrison's fishbowl office. Leaning against the file cabinet was Gottwald's number two agent who Cummings had identified as Mike Blackwell. Other than discovering Blackwell was a military veteran and had been with the FBI for just under eight years, he didn't have much of an online paper trail.

Garrison, seeing Pryor and Cummings stepping off of the elevator, immediately waved that they should join him.

"Buckle up," Pryor said to Cummings. "And follow my lead."

Garrison shook his head as he motioned that Pryor should shut the door. Garrison's eyes locked on Kevin Cummings. "Were you a part of BONK?"

Pryor glared at Gottwald. "You really going there?" he asked.

Gottwald grinned.

"I'll get to you in a minute, Albert," Garrison said as he turned his eyes back to Cummings. "Answer the question, Officer Cummings."

Cummings looked at Pryor for advice. Albert Pryor put his hand on his young partner's arm. "Do not speak again to the lieutenant or anyone from internal affairs without your union rep present."

Cummings nodded.

"Gun and badge," Garrison said as he pointed to his desk. Pryor nodded and Cummings complied.

Garrison then turned to Pryor. "Did you know about this?"

Pryor held up his finger and glanced at Gottwald as he fished his phone out of his pocket and dialed a number. Whoever he was calling answered on the first ring. Apparently, the call had been expected. "This is Albert H. Pryor, access A-H-P-1-9-9-8. An FBI agent by the name of Michael Gottwald is threatening my daughter and my partner and I'd appreciate it if it were to stop." Pryor put his phone away.

"I don't know who you called," Gottwald said confidently. "My orders came straight from the office of the Director of the FBI." Gottwald folded his arms across his chest, leaned back and grinned. "Even Malcolm Kauthmann has his limits."

Pryor grinned back. "In about thirty seconds your phone is going to ring. You really should take the call."

Gottwald's expression changed and the confidence began to leak out of him. "You're bluffing. I've got your partner and your precious baby girl."

A phone didn't ring, it vibrated instead. But, it wasn't Gottwald's, it was his number two's phone. When Blackwell looked at the caller ID, his eyes got big and the color dropped out of his cheeks as he pushed the talk button. "Yes, sir," he said in a crisp voice. He listened for nearly a minute while making quick notes on a pad, nodding, but never speaking. "Yes, sir," he said as he pushed the call end button.

He turned to Pryor. "Detective Albert Pryor, the Honorable Charles Lawson, Attorney General of the United States of America sends his highest regards. He wishes me to inform you that in exchange for their cooperation in the Nicholas Blake investigation, the Justice Department is granting total and unconditional immunity to," Blackwell stopped and checked his notes. "Brooke Jean Pryor, Kevin Lee Cummings, Okmar Patel and any others in the group known as BONK." Blackwell turned to Gottwald, who was now breathing shallowly and had broken out in a flop sweat. "The Attorney General also wishes me to inform Special Agent-in-Charge Michael B. Gottwald that he is relieved of duty effective immediately and I have been assigned to be in charge of the Plato Vane protection detail. Agent Gottwald, you are to return to Washington and you are expected in the office of the Director of the FBI by no later than the end of business tomorrow. There you will be debriefed then be reassigned as a Special Agent and report to the Special Agent-in-Charge of the Anchorage, Alaska field office of the FBI."

"What just happened?" Garrison demanded.

"Gottwald was whoring for the Director of the FBI." Pryor glared at Gottwald. "Unfortunately for him, the Director of the FBI reports to the Attorney General of the United States who is also a close personal friend of Malcolm Kauthmann."

Gottwald rose slowly from his chair, adjusted his tie and nodded at Pryor. "Well played."

"You got your twenty years in?" Pryor asked.

"And then some," Gottwald answered.

Pryor nodded. "Might be a good time to run for congress."

Gottwald nodded his agreement. He pulled himself out of his chair. With his shoulders squared and head erect, Gottwald headed to the elevator.

After Gottwald was gone, Lt. Garrison turned to Pryor. "What just happened?"

"I called in a marker I thought I would never need," Pryor said softly then pointed to the gun and badge on Garrison's desk.

"Yeah, yeah," Garrison said as he pushed the gun and badge in Cummings's direction. "What a complete asshole."

Pryor's phone vibrated and he smiled when he saw the text message was from Sandra Hollis.

Sweet Cheeks. Brooke gave me your number. Your daughter and I are breaking in live nationally in eight minutes. See you tonight.

Cummings read the text over Pryor's shoulder. "Sweet Cheeks?"

"When you got it, you've got it," Pryor said. His eyes fell in the direction of the FBI agent who was packing up to leave.

"What's your name?" Pryor asked.

"Mike Blackwell," he answered as he extended his hand. Pryor took it and the two men sized each other up.

"Jarhead?" Pryor asked.

"No need to be insulting," SAC Blackwell answered. "75th Rangers. You?"

"The same, just before your time," Pryor answered. "But you already knew that."

"Like you already knew my name."

They both nodded as they released their grip.

"I read your file, but your entire military career was pretty much redacted."

Pryor shrugged. "Need to know."

"There were stories of a sergeant named Albert Pryor who did some crazy shit in Kabul."

Pryor shrugged again.

Blackwell was somewhere between the age of Pryor and Cummings, probably in his mid-thirties. He was a bit over six feet tall and a trim one-eighty. With his haircut and posture, he still had ex-military written all over him.

"What did you do to get this crap assignment?" Pryor asked.

It was Blackwell's turn to grin and be silent.

"Gottwald was a Washington paper pusher swamp creature with a political agenda," Pryor said. "The rest of your team looks like they only need to shave once or twice a week." Pryor eyed Blackwell hard. "You actually look like you know what you're doing."

Blackwell shrugged.

"Okay, I'll guess," Pryor said. "You obviously didn't punch your commanding officer or they would have cashiered you out." Pryor eyed Blackwell. "I'm guessing you cut a corner too fine and they sent you to purgatory."

"I think you're projecting, Albert," Garrison said with a laugh. "Not everybody is like you."

Blackwell just shrugged again.

"Call your director," Pryor said.

"And tell her what?"

"Tell her to turn on ABC News."

Pryor nodded that Cummings should show the agent the email.

"Is that even possible?" the FBI agent asked.

"I suspect the FBI might be better at confirming or dismissing this than we are."

"I just airdropped you the email," Cummings said as Blackwell's phone pinged.

"You've got about three minutes to get ahead of the curve on this and make yourself a hero."

The agent nodded and immediately forwarded the email. Next, he moved to a quiet corner and made a call.

"You're going to want to see this, Lou," Pryor said as he pointed to the TV on the wall in the bullpen.

"Dear God," Garrison said. "Is your daughter going on television again?"

"Yeah."

"Tell me you have nothing to do with any of your daughter's press conferences," Garrison said as they made their way toward the TV in the bullpen.

"Sure," Pryor said. "I had nothing to do with any of my daughter's press conferences."

"Why do I find that hard to believe?"

"Because you know me too well."

"That first one was a nightmare," Garrison said as he located a TV remote and turned up the volume. It was still on the local ABC affiliate, so he did not have to change the channel.

Pryor patted Garrison on the shoulder. "Don't worry about it. In about five minutes, no one is even going to remember her first press conference."

Garrison groaned. "Oh God. What have you done?"

Pryor grinned.

The TV mounted on the wall in the squad room started flashing.

'BREAKING NEWS'

The room fell silent as all eyes turned to the TV.

"This is Sandra Hollis. We have breaking news about the Nick Blake murder in the lab of Dr. Plato Vane that has electrified the country. With me again is Brooke Pryor, the girlfriend of Nick Blake."

"Girlfriend?" Cummings protested but no one heard him, they were all too focused on the screen

"Brooke is the step-daughter of Plato Vane and granddaughter of industrialist Malcolm Kauthmann."

The camera switched to Brooke who was grim but gorgeous. The camera switched back to Sandra Hollis.

"Brooke," Hollis said as she leaned in. "Tell America what you've learned."

Brooke cleared her throat and licked her lips. "As you probably all know by now, Nick knew something was very wrong at the GAIA Institute. I uploaded a dead man file to the dark web." Brooke's voice cracked; she dropped her eyes and recentered herself. When she looked up, her hazel eyes were glistening.

"Take your time," Hollis said gently.

Brooke nodded weakly, then continued. "We've gotten a disturbing first analysis of the data. While none of this has been confirmed or verified." Brooke faltered. Hollis put her hand on Brooke's knee.

"What did the analysis reveal?" Hollis asked, barely above a whisper.

"Everyone knows that Dr. Plato Vane is known as the earthquake whisperer. This first analysis of the data has speculated he wasn't predicting earthquakes, he was causing them."

CHAPTER 29

A SILVER FERRARI ROARED up the driveway of the sprawling Kauthmann estate. It wheeled past the main house complex and squealed to a stop next to Brooke's car which was parked in front of the guest house. Brooke, hearing the distinctive rumble of the Ferrari, glanced out her window. When she saw Plato Vane jumping out of his car and sprinting in her direction, she pushed a button on the wall then locked her bedroom door.

The interior of the sprawling guest house reeked of old money spent well. Vane knew exactly where he was going and took the stairs two at a time to get to the second floor. When he reached Brooke's bedroom door, he tested the doorknob but found it locked. In a fit of fury, he kicked the door. It didn't open but, pumped up on a combination of adrenaline and fury, he tried again. This time, with a crack as wood splintered, the door flew open. Vane charged toward Brooke who was sitting calmly at her desk.

Rumbling up the driveway about a minute behind Vane was a generic government Suburban with dark windows containing the two-man FBI detail Vane had ditched. Seeing the front door of the guest house standing open, they quickly deduced where Vane was headed. The two youthful agents stopped in the foyer, which was larger than the average tennis court, and looked around. With over ten thousand square feet and six bedrooms, they had no idea where Vane might have gone. When they heard the door explode, they headed, full speed, up the stairs.

"You stupid little bitch!" Plato Vane screamed at the top of his lungs. "Do you realize what you've done?"

Enraged, Vane drew back his hand to slap Brooke but the blow never arrived.

Ninety pounds of silver and black fury leaped and Blitz locked his powerful jaws on the forearm of Dr. Plato Vane. The K-9 and the professor tumbled away from Brooke with Vane landing hard and screeching in pain.

The FBI detail, hearing the scream drew their weapons and raced down the corridor. As they approached, they saw the splintered door hanging awkwardly off its hinges and charged into the room.

When the agents entered her bedroom, they saw Brooke still sitting calmly at her desk with Blitz, in his Retired K-9 vest, beside her. She was scratching his ear. At the sight of the new arrivals, the big dog lowered his head and softly growled.

In a fetal position, writhing in pain and clutching his bleeding forearm was Plato Vane.

"Do you have that animal under control, ma'am?" one of the young agents asked as he lowered his weapon.

Brooke's voice rose. "Animal? How about a little professional courtesy? This is Retired K-9 Officer Blitzkrieg IV and he has more commendations in his jacket than you two clowns could ever hope to earn."

"Shoot that fucking dog!" Vane screamed. "Look what it did to my arm."

"Do you have that animal under control, ma'am?" The nervous agent asked again as he eyed Blitz. The big dog positioned himself between Brooke and the rattled FBI agent.

Every muscle in Blitz's body was twitching as he got ready to pounce.

"What are you waiting for?" howled Vane. "Shoot the damn dog!"

"Blitz is the least of your problems," Brooke said calmly.

The FBI agent started to raise his weapon in Blitz's direction but froze when he felt the barrel of a Glock pressed to his skull just behind his ear.

"I wouldn't advise that," said a voice barely above a whisper from behind the agent.

To his left, the agent heard a commotion and saw his partner being held in a bear hug by one of her grandfather's oversized bodyguards and being disarmed by the other.

Brooke picked up her phone and began recording. "Let me introduce you to Mr. Benjamin Kaplan and Associates," Brooke said cheerfully. "Mr. Kaplan is also known as Benny the Rabbi. His last job before he came to work for my grandfather was the trigger man for Little Tony DeFazio."

The agent froze as he tried to get a look at Benny without turning his head. "I don't care who you are," the near tearful agent said without much confidence. "You're pointing a gun at a federal agent which means you're in big trouble."

"Eek," Benny said softly.

"Actually," Brooke said. "He's pointing his weapon at an armed intruder who, we have on video, bursting into my bedroom without identifying himself." Brooke's eyes narrowed and her nostrils flared. "If your weapon moves in the direction of my dog, your next of kin will be getting a condolence call from your boss and there will be a gold star in the lobby of the FBI building with your name on it."

"I've got witnesses," the agent said with little conviction.

"Benny?" Brooke said with a laugh.

Benny looked at the other FBI agent who was now pinned to the wall by his two oversize playmates, then down at Vane who was writhing in pain on the floor. "If I shoot one or three, it makes no difference to me, ma'am," Benny said. "But if I shoot one, it has always been my preference to not leave any potential witnesses."

"Excellent business practice," Brooke said calmly. "With that in mind, Mr. Alleged FBI agent, why don't you carefully hand your weapon to Mr. Kaplan."

"Your choice," Benny said softly as he tapped the barrel of his gun on the side of the FBI agent's head, hard enough to get his attention. "I'll give you three seconds to think about it and if you can't decide by then, I'll make the decision for you."

The FBI Agent, carefully, only using only two fingers on the grip, handed the gun to Benny. Next, he showed both of his hands were empty then, regaining a bit of composure, asked, "What happened?"

"My stepfather." Brooke pointed to Vane still writhing on the floor in agony. "Kicked in the door to my bedroom then raised his hand to strike me. Blitz explained to him the error of his ways." Brooke gave Blitz an ear scratch. "Who's the good boy?" Blitz, very proud of himself, was now sitting next to Brooke with his tongue out and panting. He still had his eyes fixed on the FBI agents but now he looked relaxed and much less threatening.

"Good lord," the first FBI agent muttered as he fished his cell phone out of his pocket and dialed 9-1-1. "This is Special Agent Taylor of the FBI. We're going to need an ambulance at…" Taylor looked over at Brooke.

"1 Hidden Valley Lane," she said.

Taylor repeated, "1 Hidden Valley Lane. We have a severe but non-life threatening dog bite."

"Be sure to tell them to come to the guest house," Brooke said as she gave Blitz another ear scratch then glared at Plato Vane. "It would be a shame if this asshole bled to death while the EMTs were wandering around the estate looking for him."

CHAPTER 30

BY THE TIME Pryor and Cummings had gotten back to the Kauthmann complex, all of the excitement was over. The ambulance had come and the EMTs had offered to patch Vane up on the spot but he had insisted he be taken, red lights and sirens, to the nearest hospital. His Ferrari was still parked next to Brooke's car but the FBI Suburban was gone. Apparently, the crack FBI crew was able to keep an ambulance running hot with its lights and siren on in sight without losing it.

Albert Pryor resisted the urge to 'key' Vane's car as he walked past it. The man was already having a bad enough day.

"Brooke said she would be in the atrium," Pryor told Cummings.

"Atrium?"

"This house was built in the style of an ancient Roman villa with a center courtyard. Instead of a fountain, it has a heated saltwater swimming pool in the middle."

Pryor grabbed an Arby's bag off of the backseat of the Barracuda and the dynamic duo headed inside. Cummings had never been in the guest house before and the size and opulence stunned him.

"This is the guest house?"

Albert Pryor had seen it before and wasn't as enamored as his young partner. "Malcolm had it custom built for Melissa and completed just before our divorce was final. Melissa and Brooke lived here until they moved in with Plato Vane."

They walked through the guest house toward the atrium. As they approached a glass-topped table with an umbrella that could seat eight, they could see Brooke, Sandra Hollis, Okmar Patel, and someone neither recognized. The new addition was around thirty, thin and his skin was so pale, he looked as if he were to venture outdoors without slathering on SPF 45 he would be burned to a crisp. Patel and the stranger were both pounding away on the keyboards of their laptops; each was deep in their own world.

Before Pryor could ask, Cummings answered. "Since BONK is no longer in play, I figured we might need him and I asked my grandmother to bring him over."

"Okay," Pryor said. "Who's the other guy?"

"Not a clue," Cummings answered. "If I had to guess, he probably works for Sandra Hollis."

Pryor came to a full stop. Standing unobtrusively by the door was Benny Kaplan; his two extra-large wingmen nowhere in sight.

Pryor nodded. Benny nodded back.

"Malcolm's idea?" Pryor asked.

Benny's head went up and down maybe a quarter of an inch, but he did not speak.

"How did the conversation with Kauthmann and Brooke about you shadowing her go down?" Pryor asked.

Benny grinned. "No shots were fired, but it was touch and go there for a minute."

"Those two may be the most stubborn people I've ever met," Pryor said wistfully.

"I agree," Benny said then grinned again. "Present company excluded."

"You've got my number," Pryor said.

"In more ways than one," Benny answered as he nodded in the direction of Blitz who was sitting in the shade with his eyes locked on Brooke. "Between Blitz and me, I'm confident we can handle the likes of Plato Vane."

Blitz, hearing his name, turned his head in their direction. When Blitz saw what was in Pryor's hand, he trotted over and sniffed the bag while licking his chops. Pryor unwrapped a pair of roast beef sandwiches and put them in front of the big dog then patted his head. "Good boy."

Blitz picked up his reward for his exemplary defense of daughterhood and trotted back to his shady spot. His eyes relocked on Brooke as he slowly ate his sandwiches.

"Daddy!" Brooke shouted as she waved Pryor over. "Sandy and I were just talking about you."

Pryor said as he gave his daughter a peck on the forehead.

"Hey, handsome," Hollis said seductively. "We still on for tonight?"

"You're assuming we were ever on for tonight," Pryor answered.

"Don't play hard to get," Hollis said with a laugh as she patted the seat next to her. "Unlike Blitz, I don't bite," she said as her eyes fluttered. "Unless you want me to."

Pryor shook his head and sat down next to Hollis.

Cummings eyed the empty seat next to Brooke and, without invitation, sat down beside her. Brooke briefly acknowledged his presence with a quick cursory smile before turning her attention back to her father and Sandy Hollis.

Cummings closed his eyes and shook his head.

Pryor leaned into Hollis and nodded in the direction of the unknown person at the table. "Who is that?"

"That's my research assistant, Arthur Koop," Hollis answered. "He's tracking the media response to our multiple bombshells for me."

Patel and Koop, oblivious to the others at the table, were both typing furiously on their keyboards. Pryor turned when he heard a printer come to life on a smaller table a few feet away. In addition to the color laser printer, on the table was an assortment of canned and bottled beverages submerged in an oversized bowl filled with ice. Without a word, Koop got up and retrieved the documents he had just printed. By modern standards he was tiny. Maybe five-four and not much over a buck twenty.

Pryor glanced at Hollis.

"I spend enough time reading off of a teleprompter and I don't like to read on a computer screen so Artie prints out the important stuff for me," Hollis said.

Pryor couldn't argue with the concept. He hated trying to read emails and text messages on his phone, especially in bright daylight. Until someone showed him how to increase the font size on his computer screen, he had stashed reading glasses in his drawer at the precinct.

Pryor turned to Brooke. "How bad was the bite?" he asked.

"I would have rated it only a one Arby's bite," Brooke said with a laugh.

Pryor shrugged. "Considering who he bit, I almost bought him a half dozen."

Brooke chuckled as she made a kissy face in Blitz's direction. "He got him on the forearm and barely broke the skin. They took Plato to the hospital for a couple of stitches and a tetanus shot. He was crying like a little girl."

Pryor smiled. "Sorry I missed that."

Brooke tapped a few keys on her iPad and a video started to play. It showed Vane on the ground howling. The title of the video was "My dog stopped my step-dad - Plato Vane - from hitting me."

"It has only been up for fifteen minutes," Brooke said. "It has already gotten over 100,000 hits."

"You really should consider a career in PALM," Hollis said.

"What is PALM?" Brooke asked.

"Politics, Acting and Live Media," Hollis said with a laugh. "It's like STEM for the attractive and articulate. You've got the toughest piece already."

"Which is?" Brooke asked with a twinkle in her eye.

"Old school reporter Daniel Schoor summed it up perfectly when he said, '*Sincerity: if you can fake it, you've got it made.*'"

"Thanks. I spent half a summer taking acting classes in New York then doing summer stock."

Sandy Hollis patted Brooke's hand. "You certainly made the most of the experience. You completely sold the heartbroken lover while eviscerating both Vane and that FBI agent. Your timing and presentation during our interviews today were a master's class." Hollis turned to Pryor. "I heard an interesting rumor that after you made a phone call, the Attorney General big footed the BONK investigation and sent Brooke's Oreo cookie to the boonies."

"You are certainly well-informed."

"Is it true?"

Pryor shook his head and grinned. "No comment."

For the first time Arthur Koop spoke. It was possible his pipe was dry from lack of talking recently, but his voice squeaked like a teenager who had just hit puberty. "My source at the Pentagon told me you received the Distinguished Service Cross for saving the Attorney General's son's life in Afghanistan."

Pryor wheeled angrily on Hollis. "You were checking me out?"

Hollis slapped Pryor playfully on the arm. "I'm an investigative reporter. It is kinda what I do." She playfully slapped his arm again. "Besides," she said. "It'll be a great sidebar story. Not only are you a great detective, you're a war hero."

All of the color dropped from Pryor's face. "Please tell me you're not looking into what happened."

Hollis had a puzzled expression on her face. "We are. Is there a reason I shouldn't be?"

Pryor jerked Hollis roughly out of her chair and pulled her to a quiet corner of the atrium. "Let it go. Now," Pryor demanded.

"Okay," said a visibly shaken Sandy Hollis. "You're scaring me a little bit."

Brooke wandered over with a concerned expression on her face. "What's going on?"

Pryor nodded at Hollis. "She's investigating the Kabul incident."

"Oh," Brooke said. "You mean the Kabul incident you've never talked about and always changed the subject or would walk away when it came up?"

"Yes," Pryor said with a hard edge in his voice as he glared at Hollis. "Let it go."

For the first time Sandra Hollis, eight time Emmy winning reporter, was serious with Pryor and not playful. "You're going to have to give me a damn good reason."

"Off the record?"

"Absolutely not," Hollis answered.

"Even if it would destroy a good man?"

Both Hollis and Brooke looked at Pryor.

"Hypothetically," Hollis offered.

"You're going to keep probing?"

Hollis nodded. "Unless I have a really good reason to stop."

"Hypothetically," Pryor said. "What if an Army officer, who spent his entire military career behind a desk, found himself as the ranking officer in an unexpected combat situation and he froze, putting an entire platoon at risk."

"Oh my, God." Hollis's mouth fell open and she gasped. "The Attorney General's son is running for Governor of Arizona this fall," Hollis said softly. "His Purple Heart in Kabul is a part of his mystique."

"Hypothetically," Pryor said. "One of the finest strategic thinkers to ever wear the uniform of the United States, who was neither a warrior, nor a coward, froze under fire."

"Oh my God," Hollis said.

"He was out of his element and these things happen," Pryor continued. "He does not deserve to have his political career ended because he hesitated for a few seconds over twenty years ago."

"Hypothetically," Hollis said. "A tough sergeant pulled the officer out of harm's way after he was wounded, took command and saved his platoon."

"Hypothetically," Pryor answered.

"Why didn't any of the other platoon members come forward?" Hollis asked.

Brooke shook her head. "They didn't even know it had happened," Brooke said softly, then added, "Hypothetically."

"So you're the only one who could confirm the story?"

"Yes," Pryor said sternly. "If anyone asks, I will be willing to swear under oath it never happened and it was another example of malicious fake news."

Sandra Hollis blinked a few times then turned her attention back to her assistant. "Artie! Kill the research on Pryor in Afghanistan."

Koop didn't even look up from his screen and just waved that he had heard her.

"Damn," Brooke said with real tears of pride in her eyes. "You would have carried that story to your grave. Did anyone else know?"

"Obviously the Attorney General and your grandfather."

Brooke's eyes flew open. "You told my grandfather?"

"No," Pryor answered. "The AG told Malcolm."

"Why?" Brooke asked.

"I think he was afraid I would talk about what happened to your grandfather..."

Hollis laughed. "I'm betting he has some dirt on Malcolm and they traded. You keep my secret and I'll keep yours."

"That's awful," Brooke said.

"No," Hollis said with a laugh. "That is the way Washington works."

CHAPTER 31

BROOKE TURNED TO her father. "You never would have cashed in your marker if it wasn't for me."

Pryor gave his daughter a hug and a fatherly kiss on the forehead. "It was an even swap. I saved the AG's son and he saved my daughter. The books are balanced."

"What the hell is going on over here?" an annoyed Kevin Cummings demanded as he joined the conversation.

"Nothing which concerns you," Brooke said sharply as she felt Cummings was intruding on a special moment with her father.

"Sorry," Cummings said and started to walk away.

"Don't be such a baby, Kevin," Brooke said. "Don't forget I'm the one who got you assigned to this case in the first place."

"I have a feeling you're never going to let me forget that," Cummings answered. He headed toward the table that had been laid out with drinks and snacks.

"Go screw yourself!" Brooke shouted in the direction of Cummings's back as she started back in the direction of the table.

"If I could do that, I never would have needed to date you," Cummings replied as he kept walking.

Brooke charged in Cummings's direction and spun him around to face her. They began shouting at each other loudly enough even Koop and Patel noticed and looked up from their keyboards. Blitz liked both Brooke and Cummings so he was in his Switzerland mode. He was keeping an eye on the situation but staying neutral.

Sandy Hollis hooked her arm under Pryor's and pulled him close. "He's got it bad," she whispered.

"Yeah," Pryor answered. "But it has finally dawned on him that he's punching way above his weight class."

"Does she even have a clue how he feels about her?" Hollis whispered even more softly.

"She's a smart girl and doesn't miss much." Pryor shrugged. "Brooke is usually unflappable and I'm not sure what to make of Cummings being able to get her so wound up."

"Young love?"

"Brooke has made it pretty clear she is not interested in Kevin."

"Maybe being in such close proximity with him has changed her mind." Hollis studied Cummings. "He is one hot potato."

"I'll take your word for it, Mrs. Robinson." Pryor leaned in even closer. "You smell nice," he said.

Sandy Hollis purred. "That's the spirit." She gave Pryor a peck on the cheek.

Kevin Cummings, completely tuning Brooke out, returned from the snack table with a bottle of water. Seeing she no longer had an audience, Brooke fell heavily back into her chair. Cummings moved his chair a few inches away from Brooke and sat back down, completely ignoring her.

"What's your problem?" Brooke demanded.

He slowly turned to face Brooke. "BONK is history so you won't need to use me to run interference with law enforcement for you anymore," Cummings said bluntly. "Once we arrest the murderer of your "boyfriend" Nick Blake, I'll be out of your hair and you can get on with your jet set life without having to worry about who I'm sleeping with."

Brooke's eyes flashed with anger as she folded her arms across her chest. "Fine!"

"Fine," Cummings answered with a dismissive wave of his hand as he turned away from her and pointed to Patel. "Did you figure out who sent Brooke the email?"

"I'm about ninety-four percent certain the email came from Norman Fleishman."

"Crap," Cummings muttered as he shook his head.

"Who is Norman Fleishman?" Pryor asked as he reclaimed his seat.

"He's a legend on the dark web and there are some who think he may have even invented it," Brooke replied.

"I guess that's one way to spin it," Arthur Koop said. The squeak had gone away. Closer to a tenor than a baritone, his voice now seemed about correct for his size and age.

"Meaning?" Hollis asked as she returned to her seat.

"Meaning, he's also known as Crazy Norman," Arthur Koop said.

"Crazy Norman. I don't like the sound of that," Sandra Hollis noted.

"Best anyone can figure," Patel continued, "is he's a former NSA analyst."

"Who sometimes goes off his meds," Koop added.

"Tell me we have additional source verification of this lunatic's hot take analysis," Hollis demanded.

"Yes and no," Koop said as he pushed the stack of papers he had printed across the table.

Hollis pulled a pair of acid green reading glasses out of her purse and put them on. Sitting shoulder-to-shoulder with Sandra Hollis, the font was large enough Albert Pryor could read the printout without squinting. The top sheet was an executive summary. Since it did not paint a very flattering picture of Norman Fleishman, it was obviously written by Koop and not Patel. After Hollis finished reading a page she passed it along to Pryor. Starting with the second page, it was a combination of things Koop had typed and articles he had printed from the web. All of the articles had been truncated to just the high points and not the details. Hollis was a faster reader than Pryor and after he got two pages behind, he quit trying to keep up. After Pryor finished a page, he passed it along to Kevin Cummings.

After he had finished reading each page, Cummings put it face down on the table without offering to share it with Brooke.

Brooke rolled her eyes. As she reached around Cummings, carefully avoiding any physical contact, to get the top page, she muttered, "Passive aggressive. Very nice."

After Hollis finished reading the stack, she took off her glasses and threw them on the table. "Oh, God," Hollis said. "So I put the theory of a world-class conspiracy nut on national television."

Okmar Patel cleared his throat and all eyes turned in his direction.

"You have something to say," Hollis demanded.

Patel looked at Brooke for support.

"What have you got?" Brooke asked gently.

"Right now there is no consensus on the dark web," Patel said. "Roughly a third think the report by Crazy Norman is correct. About a third think it is utter fantasy that anyone, especially someone with the limited brainpower of Vane, could create earthquakes at will. The last third don't think they have enough data to draw a conclusion."

"Did you do your bias analysis?" Brooke asked.

"Of course…"

"What is a bias analysis?" Hollis demanded.

"A lot of the stuff on the internet in general, and the dark web in particular, is propaganda and disinformation," Brooke answered. "Okmar wrote an algorithm that rates the quality of things posted and who posted them."

"Really?" Koop said. "What does your metric structure look like?"

"I give weight to how long they've been on the dark web…"

"You boys can do that on your own time," Brooke snapped. "Okmar, give us a summary of your bias analysis in twenty-five words or less."

"It is pretty much what you would expect. The tinfoil hat people want to believe it."

Hollis groaned.

"The CIA and NSA plants want to discredit it."

"After you ran your bias filters?" Brooke asked impatiently.

"So far Crazy Norman is the only one who has come out completely in favor of the theory. The rest need more time and/or more data before they commit."

"Why is this Crazy Norman so confident in his data?" Koop asked.

Brooke, Cummings and Patel exchanged worried glances.

"I don't believe it," Pryor protested.

"What?" Hollis demanded.

"The three stooges here and my murder victim have been feeding Crazy Norman data."

Brooke's shoulders went up and down. "It seemed like a good idea at the time."

"Ah," Koop said. "So he is working from a much larger data set than what you posted."

"Yes," Patel answered. "And he's had months to plow through it."

"That certainly adds weight to his analysis." Koop's computer beeped and he read the message. "The GAIA Institute just issued a statement denying everything." The printer started printing as Koop looked at Hollis. "They are also saying they plan to file a civil action against the network and you personally."

"Of course they are," Hollis answered dejectedly.

Koop turned to Patel. "If we can get Crazy Norman's full data set, we may be able to get confirmation," Koop stated. "Do you think he would be willing to share?"

"With Crazy Norman," Brooke said. "No way to tell until we ask. But he really took a shine to me."

"You've met this guy? In person?" Hollis asked.

"Sure," Brooke answered nonchalantly. "He lives just a few miles outside of town and about two months ago he invited Nick out to his place to discuss the GAIA Institute." Brooke glared at Cummings. "I had Officer Cummings tag along to run interference with law enforcement and I went along as a distraction."

Cummings growled at Brooke loud enough that Blitz's ears perked up.

"So, Officer Cummings," Pryor said as he swallowed a smile. "You know how to get there?"

"Yeah but it's out in the middle of nowhere, so we'll need to take my Hummer."

"You drive a Hummer?" Pryor said in disbelief.

Cummings shrugged. "I go off-road to camp and ride my bike. Believe me, you don't want to take the Barracuda down the road to his house."

Hollis groaned again. "So our single source to establish a motive for Vane is a conspiracy theory nut living in the backwoods?"

Brooke and Cummings laughed.

Pryor asked, baffled. "What?"

Brooke giggled. "If he will let us in, you'll see."

"Why wouldn't he let us in?" Hollis asked.

"Norman is a touch paranoid," Brooke answered.

"Wonderful," Hollis said as she shook her head. "This just keeps getting better and better."

"Like every other man on the planet," Cummings said with a nasty edge in his voice as his eyes locked on Brooke. "Norman was sweet on Brooke. Perhaps Ms. Pryor could send him an email and ask if her daddy and I can stop by for a chat."

"Jerk," Brooke muttered as her fingers danced across the screen of her iPad. "There is no telling when he'll get back…"

The iPad beeped.

Brooke said, "That was quick. He wants to know if I'll be coming as well."

Pryor said firmly, "No way. This is a homicide investigation, not a picnic."

Before she could type a response, her iPad beeped again and Brooke laughed. "Norman says to tell my dad, homicide investigation or not, if I don't come, he'll need a warrant to get past the gate."

"What the hell," Pryor protested. "You're making that up."

Brooke held up the screen so her father could see it.

Kevin Cummings whispered into Pryor's ear. "Be careful. He's obviously hacked the microphone on Brooke's iPad and he can hear everything we're saying."

The iPad beeped again. 'I heard that, Kevin. No Brooke, no entry.'

Brooke crooned, "Ah. That is so sweet!"

"What about me?" Sandra Hollis asked.

The iPad beeped. On the screen was the face of an elderly, well-groomed, man.

"Hey, Norman."

"Hey, Brooke," he answered. "Turn the camera to Ms. Hollis." Brooke aimed her iPad at Sandra Hollis and Crazy Norman continued. "I thought face-to-face might be easier. I'm Norman Fleishman. If I allow you in, will we be off the record?"

"I would prefer on the record and with a film crew."

"I bet you would," Crazy Norman answered. "I'll have to decline."

"Off the record?" Hollis offered.

"Sure," Norman replied. "The more the merrier."

Brooked turned the iPad so the camera was now facing her. "What are we going to need to do to convince you to share your entire data set?"

Crazy Norman made a face. "That could be problematic, Brooke," he said. "It might reveal some of my proprietary analytics."

"Is that a hard no?" Brooke asked.

"I can't imagine many people saying no to you, Brooke."

Cummings snorted. Brooke ignored him.

"Can I bring my dog?"

"The legendary Blitzkrieg IV who bit the odious Plato Vane?" Norman asked.

"That's the one."

"He would be an honored guest."

"We can come out now," Brooke offered.

"No," Norman answered. "I'm going to be tied up for the rest of the day. Eleven o'clock tomorrow morning will work better for me."

"We'll see you then," Brooke said with a radiant smile. As soon as the screen went blank, her smile vanished and she motioned to Patel and held out her hand. "Give me a Faraday bag." As Patel reached into his computer case, she powered down her iPad. Patel handed her the bag he had used for his computer earlier and she dropped the iPad inside.

"Everyone power down their laptops and phones," Brooke said.

"Why?" Pryor asked.

Cummings leaned in and softly said, "If Crazy Norman can hack the Golden Child's iPad, we don't know what else he may have hacked." Cummings turned his attention to Brooke who was glaring at him.

"Golden Child?"

"Get over yourself," Cummings answered bluntly. "You're the one who got hacked and you're the one that let Crazy Norman know everything we know."

Brooke's nose flared and her cheeks darkened slightly, but she didn't have a counter-argument so she stayed quiet.

Cummings pointed at one of the security video cameras mounted on the corners of the atrium. "Do those have audio feeds?"

Brooke, unsure, looked in Benny the Rabbi's direction, who had heard everything which had been said at the table. He shrugged to indicate he didn't know.

"Okay," Cummings said as he placed his hand over his mouth. "Crazy Norman is world-class and we're not sure if he still has ears on us. He may have accessed the security system and likely has a lip-reading program, so please keep your hand over your mouth when you speak."

"Isn't that a bit of overkill?" Hollis asked.

"No, ma'am," Arthur Koop said with his hand over his mouth. "That was an impressive hack. This guy is for real."

"We're going to still need verification of his conclusion," Patel said through his fingers.

"Do you have access to all of the data Nick sent him?" Koop asked.

"That's over two petabytes of raw data," Patel said as he shook his head. "Since we have no idea what we're looking for, it would be like trying to find a needle in a haystack the size of Kansas."

"We have one thing going for us," Brooke said with a twinkle in her eye. "He didn't say no to our request and he is letting us in."

Cummings chuckled when he saw where Brooke was heading. "We have something he wants."

"Meaning?" Pryor asked.

"He wants to make a trade," Brooke and Cummings said in unison.

CHAPTER 32

NORMALLY THE MAJOR Crimes floor of police headquarters was reasonably quiet and subdued. That was not the case when Pryor and Cummings rolled back in. Every desk was occupied by a 'Task Force' member and every phone that wasn't already in use was ringing.

Detective Danny Holden was standing in front of an array of four-foot by eight-foot whiteboards covered with crime scene photos and hand-written comments. He had his jacket off and his tie loosened and looked like he was nearly out on his feet.

"I'm getting too old for this shit," Holden said when he saw Pryor and Cummings heading in his direction. "Please, God, tell me you're ready to make an arrest."

Pryor shook his head.

"I hear Blitz took a bite out of crime," Holden said with a twinkle in his eye. He was starting to hate Vane as much as Pryor did.

"Yup," Pryor answered.

"Good dog," Holden said as he rolled the stiffness out of his neck.

"I also heard the Rabbi nearly busted a cap on an FBI agent."

"He pointed his weapon at Blitz."

"I've always hated the fucking feds." Holden shook his head. "What's your plan?"

"We're going out in the morning to talk to the guy who claims Vane is causing the earthquakes."

"Crazy Norman?" Holden asked.

"You know about him?" Cummings asked.

Danny Holden motioned around the chaotic room. "Our team of investigators is exploring all possible leads. Other than that, I have no comment at this time."

"How many times have you said that today?" Pryor asked with a grin.

"Enough that I'm going to be hearing it in my sleep for the next year or two."

"So," Pryor said. "What do we know for sure?"

"As junior here suspected, we have confirmation the weapon was manufactured in the lab by the 3-D printer and R2D2 is our killer. Then another one of the droids took the hard drive out of our homicidal robot and destroyed it." Holden shook his head. "Beyond that, we don't have jack shit."

Pryor pointed in the direction of Lt. Garrison's office which had the blinds pulled and the door closed.

"Lou got company?" Pryor asked.

"An endless stream all day but currently he's in there with that new FBI…," Holden made air quotes. "Special Agent-in-Charge." Holden grinned at Pryor. "I hear tell you eviscerated the last SAC. Any truth to the rumor?"

"It was brilliant," Cummings answered.

"Do tell," Holden said enthusiastically.

"We can do the recap after we've got someone in handcuffs," Pryor said. "You think the lieutenant would want to see us?"

"At the moment," Holden answered, "you two are probably the last people he would want to see."

On cue, the lieutenant's door swung open. "Where the hell are Pryor and Cummings?" he shouted.

"Right here, Lou," Pryor answered.

"My office. Now!"

"My streak is intact," Holden muttered. "I haven't been right about single thing on this case yet."

When Pryor and Cummings arrived in the office, they saw FBI SAC Mike Blackwell standing in the corner with a finger in his left ear and his phone in his right ear. He was talking softly, but clearly, he was badly rattled.

Lt. Garrison motioned for Pryor and Cummings to sit down. "Did the Rabbi really put a gun to the head of an FBI agent?" he asked softly.

Both Pryor and Cummings nodded.

"God." Garrison shook his head. "I'd have paid money to have seen that."

"You can watch it on YouTube," Cummings said as he reached for his phone to send Garrison the link.

FBI Agent Blackwell finished his call, took a moment to compose himself before turning around. "Professor Plato Vane is in the wind."

"Good lord," Pryor said with a laugh. "You lost him again. That's some crack crew you got there, Special Agent-in-Charge Blackwell."

"What happened?" Garrison asked.

"My team didn't think to hold his cellphone while he was being stitched up, so apparently Vane called someone to pick him up."

"Do you know who?" Garrison asked.

"Absolutely," Blackwell answered. "We were able to access security video at the front of the hospital." Blackwell pushed a few buttons then turned his phone and held it up for the trio of Garrison, Pryor and Cummings to see.

Pryor closed his eyes and rubbed his forehead.

Garrison looked at the image on Blackwell, shook his head then shouted. "Danny!"

Detective Danny Holden stuck his head in the door but did not enter. "Yeah, Lou."

"Put out a BOLO for Professor Plato Vane and his wife, Melissa Vane."

"Albert's ex-wife?"

"Yeah," Garrison said then continued. "If you find her, ask her why she and her driver picked Vane up at the hospital and helped him ditch his security detail."

Danny Holden burst out laughing as he slapped Pryor on the back. "Melissa is many things, Albert. But I never envisioned her as a gun moll."

"This isn't funny," Blackwell said.

"This is funny on at least a dozen different levels," Holden answered. "The FBI loses a candy-ass college professor, not once but twice. And the second time to a female socialite who had to have her chauffeur drive the getaway car. Before that, two of your guys get disarmed by the bodyguard of a twenty-year-old girl and one has to change his soiled undies." Holden chuckled. "That'll do until funny comes along."

SAC Mike Blackwell flipped Danny Holden off.

CHAPTER 33

"SO," FBI AGENT Mike Blackwell said as he glared at Pryor. "Your ex-wife is the one who helped my protectee get away."

Pryor nodded.

"Well?" Blackwell demanded.

"Well, what?" Pryor answered. "You think I have any control over a woman I was married to for fifteen minutes and got divorced from nearly two decades ago?"

Cummings, who had been on the phone, hung up and joined the conversation. "I talked to Brooke, who talked to her mother. She says her mom got a call from Vane asking her to pick him up at the hospital. She and her driver drove him home where he immediately changed clothes then left."

"Lovely," Blackwell said. "Did he happen to mention where he was going?"

"No," Cummings continued. "But Vane suggested Melissa go to the Kauthmann estate and lawyer up, which is what she has done."

Pryor picked up his phone and hit the FaceTime button for Brooke. She answered on the second ring but before she could say anything, her father cut her off. "I'm here with Lt. Garrison, Danny Holden, Officer Cummings and FBI Special Agent-in-Charge Mike Blackwell."

Brooke understood instantly and didn't say anything.

"Is Benjamin Kaplan there?"

Without a word, Brooke handed the phone to the Rabbi.

"You heard who is on this call?"

Kaplan nodded.

"You know Vane is in the wind?"

Kaplan nodded again. "Yes."

"And Melissa?"

"Mrs. Vane is currently in the guest house."

"What steps have you taken?" Pryor asked.

"We've locked the front gate, raised the roadblock and we've already doubled the manpower with reinforcements on the way." Kaplan's expression never changed. "Tell your playmates, on direct orders from Malcolm Kauthmann, no one from the police department or the FBI will be admitted on the grounds without a warrant. If they arrive with a warrant, Melissa Vane will be represented by legal counsel and will invoke her fifth amendment right to remain silent."

"That's a bit of overkill, don't you think?" Agent Blackwell said.

"Mr. Kauthmann noted the FBI, with weapons drawn, have already invaded his privacy once today. He does not plan to allow an encore."

"Do you know the location of Vane's bolt-hole?" Pryor asked

"Yes," Kaplan answered. "Once I get Mr. Kauthmann's approval, I'll text you the address."

"Thank you," Pryor said. "Give me back to Brooke."

Again, his daughter didn't speak.

"Is your mother with you?"

Brooke handed Melissa her phone.

Considering how her carefully structured life had collapsed in the past twenty-four hours, Melissa was remarkably composed. While her eyes were puffy from crying, her make-up was flawless and she stared straight into the phone. Pryor swallowed a smile. Say what you will about Melissa, she was still a Kauthmann.

"What happened?" Pryor asked gently.

"Plato called me and asked that I pick him up from the hospital and take him home. Which is what I did. As soon as we got to the house, he packed a bag and left."

"Which car did he take?" Pryor asked.

"Our black Range Rover," Melissa answered.

Silently, Danny Holden left the room and started the process of adding the Range Rover to the BOLO.

"Did he tell you where he was going?"

"No," Melissa said with steel in her voice.

Pryor looked at SAC Blackwell who nodded that was all he would need.

"Albert?" Melissa asked softly. "What's going to happen?"

"He's not some master criminal. We'll find him," Pryor answered. "Give me Brooke."

Brooke Pryor's face appeared on the screen.

"Vane may blame you for ruining his life," Albert Pryor said softly. "Keep Blitz and the Rabbi close by."

Brooke nodded she understood and broke the connection.

Cummings, with concern etched on his face, said, "Maybe I should go over there."

Pryor laughed. "And do what? She currently has better protection than the President of the United States."

Cummings shook his head. "A geriatric Oscar Rogers manning the front gate does not instill much confidence."

Pryor shook his head as his phone beeped. It was the address the Rabbi had promised and Pryor shared it with the others. Garrison forwarded it to Holden who immediately stuck his head back in the office.

"Should we wait for a warrant, Lou?"

"Yeah," Lt. Garrison answered. "But sit on the place until we get it."

"You got it," Holden said as he turned back to the bullpen to assemble his team.

"How did you know Vane would have a bolt-hole?" Cummings asked.

Garrison rolled his eyes and muttered, "Rookie."

"He's rich, he's famous and he has a history as a skirt chaser," Pryor answered. "The chance of him being recognized while checking into a hotel with a college girl on his arm is a risk he wouldn't take. Guys like him always have a love shack."

"Usually rented or purchased by his lawyer using a difficult to track down shell company," Blackwell added.

"Being a serial philanderer with a lot to lose, he'll be very careful," Pryor said. "You can bet that his hideaway has no exterior security cameras and enclosed private or off-street parking so no one will be able to see his car. He'll also probably have a private entrance so he never bumps into any neighbors between his car and the door."

"So what do we do now?" Cummings asked.

"I don't know about you, but I've been running all day on only four hours of sleep…"

"We're not going over to stakeout Vane's love nest?"

"Easy, tiger," Garrison said as he glanced at Pryor. "For the moment at least, you're a detective. You do what you do and let the rest of the department do what they do."

CHAPTER 34

PLATO VANE POURED himself a generous portion of Hakushu eighteen-year-old Japanese whisky into a heavy cut crystal glass. He really couldn't taste the difference between the Japanese version and its more traditional Scottish cousin but this bottle was perfect for him. In addition to being expensive and rather exotic, it gave him the opportunity to deliver a lengthy dissertation about why the Japanese call it 'whisky' and not 'whiskey.'

It had been his experience that women in their late teens and early twenties were deeply impressed with his combination of worldliness and insightfulness.

He swirled the golden liquid around in the glass then held it up to the light the same way he would have done if he had been in the company of a starry-eyed coed. Old habits were hard to break.

Looking around, he smiled. The interior designer's attention to detail had been impressive. The music was unobtrusive, the art tasteful and even the color of the walls had been carefully selected to be relaxing while stimulating the libido. The remote control next to the bed set the lighting to accommodate the modesty level of his guest. It ranged from one extreme of those who didn't care if he screwed them under stadium lights, to others who wanted total darkness.

Vane lived by the old Ben Franklin quote. "All cats are gray at night." Once they were naked and his eyes were closed, to Vane one woman was pretty much indistinguishable from another.

He had been bedding a seemingly endless stream of eager, panting coeds for over two decades. In recent years it had gotten even easier for him. After all, he was the 'Earthquake Whisperer' and a bestselling author of climate change and overpopulation books. Combining his curriculum vitae with the amazing dumbing down of the humanities department in recent years, he was in high demand. The campus was full of attractive women with limited, or even non-existent, critical thinking skills who didn't know very much but were passionate about their beliefs.

In Vane's opinion, the vast majority of the girls he bedded arrived on campus with a sexual checklist. Have sex with a Black man to see if what they say is true. Have sex with another woman so they could say they did it. Bang someone they had seen on television.

Vane knew with his high profile, all he had to do was mouth the right platitude – pro-choice, gay rights, protect the environment, social justice – and the coeds would practically throw their underwear at him. He would be the one they would brag to their friends about having bedded for the next thirty years.

He sat the heavy glass on the bar and started putting items in his small backpack. First, three bottles of still water, a half dozen granola bars and two burner phones. He smiled as he reached for the tin of lighter fluid. With so few smokers these days and the ubiquitous disposable lighters, he'd had trouble finding it. Convenience stores and department stores no longer carried it. He found it in the high-end cigar store where he had a private humidor. He dropped the tin in his backpack along with a small box of wooden stick kitchen matches.

Lastly, he dropped a battery-powered, multi-frequency cell phone and radio frequency jammer into the backpack. Illegal in the US and the EU, he had acquired it from the Mossad. The handheld device, roughly four times the size of an iPhone, could block nearly every kind of communication signal, including the local police ban.

Satisfied, he put the backpack by the garage door. He yawned as he headed to the bedroom. The bed was massive and took up the bulk of the room. The headboard and footboard were made of heavy oak which wouldn't move or creak no matter how vigorous the activity on the mattress. If his guest's tastes included BDSM, an assortment of restraints, handcuffs could be easily attached. Whips, and various battery-operated devices of different sizes and purposes, were tastefully in the closet next to the bed. They were easily accessible but, because not everyone of his guests liked bondage or role-playing, they were not out on public display.

He set his phone alarm for 4 a.m. then put it on the night stand. He turned back to the bed. He smiled when he realized had never laid down on it alone before.

Once he was settled in, he used the remote to dim the lights to a level where it wouldn't disturb his sleep but bright enough he wouldn't stub his toe if he had to go to the bathroom.

CHAPTER 35

THE HOUSE WAS a snug three bedroom, two-and-a-half bath contemporary design on a lot that was well-maintained but lacked any personal touches. There were no flower beds that would require frequent attention; only shrubs that were trimmed in the spring and maybe again in the fall. All of the trees had had their lower branches removed so someone on a riding mower could cut the entire lawn without having to dismount. Since the house was seldom occupied, it had a sprinkler system that automatically kicked on even in the middle of a downpour. It was carefully designed to look well-tended and occupied as long as the landscaper didn't go over ten days between grass cutting.

For a safe house, it was almost perfect. It was on a cul-de-sac at the end of a limited access residential street. The only people who would have a reason to drive up this way would be residents; any other vehicle would immediately attract attention. It was set back well off the street and had a rear-facing two-car garage. This meant, unless you were standing in the backyard when the garage door went up, you would never know who was getting in or out.

Having successfully eluded the FBI twice, Detective Danny Holden, as head of the task force, had insisted that the Watch Commander supervise the arrest. Holden had also insisted there be enough uniforms on the scene that there was zero chance Vane would be able to escape either by car or on foot. They even had one of the department's helicopters on standby.

Watch Commander Frank Manheim was behind the wheel of his car, half a block away from the house but where he could still see it. The idea that his 'undercover' vehicle was going to fool anyone was a joke. First, between SUVs and pickup trucks, who drives a full-sized sedan anymore? Especially one with no trim and a short whip antenna attached to the trunk. Career criminals would spot it quicker than a black and white with its lights and siren on.

Sitting next to the Watch Commander in the front passenger seat was District Attorney Brady Burris. With the spotlight on this case, he wanted to be sure everything was done by the book. Of course, the off chance a reporter might notice him at the scene was always a plus.

Burris finished his call and put his phone on the dashboard instead of in his pocket. It had pretty much been ringing non-stop since they had arrived ten minutes earlier and there was no point in putting his phone away.

His phone rang again. Burris nodded his approval as he broke the connection. This time he put his phone in his pocket. "We have the search warrant for the house and the material witness warrant for Vane," Burris said.

"Took long enough," the Watch Commander answered.

"After five o'clock, and with this being such a hot potato, the judges we called saw the caller ID from my office and let it go to straight voicemail."

"I can't say as I blame them," Frank Manheim answered. "I assume you're going to want paper in your hand before we knock on the door."

"That is correct," Burris answered. "Do we know he's in there?"

"We only know one thing for sure," Manheim answered. "A black Range Rover, registered to Plato Vane, is parked behind the residence. No one has gone in or out since we got here and there has been zero activity in the dwelling."

"No lights are on," Burris stated.

"It looks like they have black knock out blinds so they could be setting off fireworks in there and we wouldn't know it."

The DA's phone beeped and he read the text then opened the attachment. It was a pdf of the warrants. Burris chuckled. "Vane's got a pair on him."

"How so?" Manheim asked.

"The house is owned by the GAIA Institute."

"He made no effort at all to conceal it?" Manheim asked.

"Maybe he wanted the tax write-off," Burris offered.

They both looked up when a car pulled in behind them then turned off its headlights. Manheim and Burris got out of the car and a young female ADA, who was a step quicker, handed her boss the warrants.

Manheim pulled a walkie-talkie off his belt and said one word. "Go."

CHAPTER 36

ALBERT PRYOR HAD the ringer off on his phone but he felt it vibrate. He pulled it out of his pocket and made a face as he read the text message.

"What?" Sandy Hollis asked as she took a sip of her dirty martini.

"They raided Plato Vane's love shack. His car was there, but he wasn't."

"Interesting," Hollis said as she pulled her stir stick out of her martini and used her teeth to slide off the olive closest to the end into her mouth. As would be expected from a television star, her teeth were perfectly straight and dazzlingly white. Pryor suspected they were porcelain veneers but didn't think now was the time to ask.

They were sitting close to each other in a booth in the rear of the hotel bar. The bar wasn't particularly crowded and they had the entire back section to themselves. Pryor suspected the manager would have preferred to have the famous News Anchor Sandra Hollis sitting at the table closest to the hostess station where everyone entering his bar would see her. He also suspected she had insisted on her privacy.

"How does this affect your investigation?" Hollis asked.

"It complicates it a little but not much," Pryor answered.

"Only a little?"

"Vane is apparently more skilled as a fugitive than I gave him credit for," Pryor said with a shrug. "He's probably watched enough television shows to know he'll be flagged the instant he uses a credit card so he can't check into a hotel and he knew his secret hide-away probably wasn't much of a secret."

"Ahh. He knew with so many bimbos knowing about his secret hideaway, it wouldn't be long before someone would point a finger in

176

his direction," Hollis said as she took another sip of her martini. "He has a second bolt-hole."

Pryor chuckled. "You'd make a pretty good detective."

"I'm an investigative reporter," she answered with a laugh. "Same skill set but much better pay and perks." Hollis thought for a moment then said, "You suspect he had an untraceable car stashed at the love shack and some cash as well."

"Yes."

"Will that make it harder?" Hollis asked.

Pryor made a face. "He isn't some random mugger or petty thief. He's got our entire police department and the FBI looking hard for him. With a corpse as part of the equation and the media breathing down our neck, Vane's picture is on the screen of every law enforcement vehicle within two hundred miles of here. He also embarrassed the hell out of the FBI and they aren't much into forgive and forget."

"You think you'll find him?"

"Maybe, maybe not," Pryor answered. "The first time he ran away from the FBI, he was easy to follow. The second time he clearly didn't want them to know where he was going."

"The big question is, what changed?"

"You and Brooke claimed he was causing the earthquakes, not predicting them."

"So, if you arrested him, even on a material witness charge, what would be the first thing the prosecutor would insist upon at the bail hearing?"

"He hand over his passport."

"Okay. Okay," Hollis said with a laugh. "What would be the second thing the prosecutor would want?"

Now it was Pryor's turn to laugh. "An ankle tracker and he be placed under house arrest."

Hollis tapped the end of her nose and pointed at Pryor. "You'd make a pretty good investigative reporter." Hollis took a final sip of her martini. "And what would be the first thing you would do?"

Pryor laughed again. "Park a police car in front of his house until I had enough evidence to charge him with murder."

"Exactly," Hollis said. "I think Vane knew his scheme was unraveling and he has bolted."

"The FBI has him on the no-fly list with his passport flagged."

Hollis shrugged. "Do you want to give odds on the chances he has a huge stash of cash in a Swiss bank account and a second home in a non-extradition country?"

"Nope."

"Or he had a fake ID and travel money stashed at his first safe house?" Hollis asked.

"Nope."

"I think you underestimated Vane."

"I'm starting to think the same thing."

"He figured this was his last chance to run." Sandra's phone started to vibrate. She read the text message and laughed.

"What?" Pryor asked.

"With Vane on the lamb," Hollis answered. "The legal department said his civil action against us wouldn't pass the laugh test. This calls for a celebration." Hollis caught the eye of the bartender and indicated they wanted another round. As her fresh Martini was being prepared, Hollis finished her current drink and slid the empty glass to the front edge of the table. "You're falling behind, sailor."

Pryor finished his beer and also slid the empty pilsner glass to the table edge where it was next to hers.

"I want to stay alert and hydrated." Pryor's eyes twinkled. "I've got plans for later tonight."

"Love the attitude," Hollis said as she hooked her arm under Pryor's and moved even closer.

"That is some daughter you've got there."

"And then some," Pryor answered.

Hollis looked up and smiled when the drinks arrived. "Thank you," she said with a smile that lit up the room. After the bartender walked away, she turned her attention back to Pryor. "What's the story with your daughter and your partner?"

Pryor shrugged.

Hollis playfully slugged Pryor in the shoulder. "Come on. If there had been any more sexual tension in the air, I would have passed out."

Pryor sighed. "They used to date seriously in high school."

"That's all you've got?" Hollis said with a laugh. "I've only been around them for ten minutes and I can see Calvin…"

"Kevin."

"Calvin, Kevin, whatever," Hollis said with a dismissive wave of her hand.

"I really don't want to talk about my daughter's sex life."

"Excellent," Hollis said with a laugh. "Let's talk about your sex life."

"Apparently it wouldn't take as long as talking about my daughter's," he said as he took a sip of beer.

"I have a feeling that's about to change," Hollis said as she dropped her hand under the table and gave Pryor's thigh a squeeze."

"You really are something," Pryor said.

"Oh, honey," she said seductively. "You can't imagine." She caught the bartender's eye again and said, "Check."

CHAPTER 37

PRYOR ROLLED OVER and noticed he was alone in the king-sized bed. Blinking his eyes a few times, he saw light under the door to the bathroom and heard the shower running. Rolling in the other direction, he checked the time on the clock on the nightstand next to the bed.

2:45.

What the hell? Pryor wondered.

The bathroom door burst open and Sandra Hollis emerged naked except for a towel wrapped around her head. She looked at the clock and cursed softly under her breath. "I'm late."

"Late?" Pryor asked with a stunned expression on his face. "Late for what?"

"We're three hours behind New York and GMA is going live in just a bit over an hour. I have to get to the local affiliate."

There was a tap on the door.

"Fuck, fuck, fuck, fuck," Hollis shouted as she bolted back into the bathroom and located one of the oversized cotton robes and threw it on.

"While I appreciate the compliment," Pryor said while propping himself up on his elbow as he watched Sandra frantically running around the hotel suite. "I think you miscounted."

"With me on top of the Vane story," she said with a laugh. "We're going to have our biggest audience this decade and it is right in the middle of sweeps week."

"That wasn't all you were on top of," Pryor added.

Before she could respond, there was another, more urgent tap on the door.

Hollis gave Pryor a sisterly kiss on the cheek then said, "To be continued." She headed to the door. As she threw it open, Pryor could see the two men and the woman standing in the hall that he had seen in Kauthmann's studio the day before.

Hollis turned back and said, "Text me with the time you're picking me up to go out and talk to Crazy Norman."

"You don't have anything on except a robe and a towel on your head."

Hollis didn't hear him. She was already halfway to the elevator.

As one of her male producers started to close the door, he winked and said, "We've seen worse."

CHAPTER 38

PREFERRING HIS OWN shower and bed, Pryor saw no reason to stay at the hotel so he got up, got dressed, and headed home. The house was dark and, without Blitz to greet him, it seemed cold and empty.

He showered and shaved. Checking his messages, there was a text from Cummings that he would pick him up at 10 a.m. After checking his other messages and all of the emails, nothing needed his attention. Glancing at the clock next to his bed, he noticed it was 4 a.m. Picking up the TV remote, he found the channel with the *Good Morning America* live feed from New York. Sandra Hollis was not on the set with the other cast members, but she was clearly on their minds and they cut to her frequently.

After his evening with Sandy, he felt like he had run a marathon then had gone 10 rounds with Mike Tyson. He felt old and tired. Hollis, on the other hand, looked fantastic.

During the *Plato Vane on the Run* segment, there was a crawler along the bottom of the screen that made Pryor laugh.

'*Earthquake Whisperer's Story looks Shaky*'.

There was a story from Washington about the president canceling his trip with Vane. There was a story live from Honolulu. Pryor was too groggy to do the math to figure out what time it was in Hawaii. But, the statuesque blonde outside the new GAIA Institute facility was obviously reporting while it was still dark.

Pryor figured he could either make a pot of coffee and get started on his day or try for a few more hours of sleep. Since he could barely keep his eyes open, it wasn't a hard decision. Besides, since he was already showered and shaved, if something broke, he could be ready to go in less than five minutes.

He laid down on his bed and set his alarm for 9:30 a.m. which would give him plenty of time to make and drink coffee before his ride showed up. He checked to be sure his phone's ringer was set loud. He placed it on the pillow next to his ear.

Less than thirty seconds later, he was sound asleep.

CHAPTER 39

ROFESSOR PLATO VANE'S alarm went off and he was
instantly fully awake.

Using one of his burner phones, he checked the internet for
the latest news.

As he had suspected, it hadn't taken the police long to find his
primary hideaway. The big story, of course, was he wasn't there.

Idiots.

He pulled on a black hoodie, picked up a Guy Fawkes mask,
his backpack and the key to the ten year old Honda Civic he had on
standby at his original bolthole. Always careful, he had not wanted to
need the car and discover it had a dead battery from lack of use. It had
been on a trickle charge in one of the two parking spots in the garage
of his hideaway for a couple of years.

The streets were quiet and empty as he headed toward campus
and the GAIA Institute. He had pretty much unlimited parking
opportunities. He selected a spot near a dorm about two blocks away
from his lab. On a college campus, his old beater, parked legally,
wouldn't even get a second look from a campus cop. Dressed all in
black and with his hoodie pulled tight around his head, with only the
oval of his face showing, in the darkness, he was pretty much invisible.
Which really didn't matter much since there wasn't anyone around to
see him.

Even with no one else moving around on campus, he stayed near
the tree line and avoided the sidewalk and street lights. When he arrived
at the parking lot in front of his lab, the only vehicle in the lot was a
black and white city police car. He stayed in the shadows for two full
minutes to be sure no one else was around. Finally satisfied, without
making any noise, he carefully lifted and placed a trash can next to the

police car. It hadn't been emptied for a few days and had enough paper and combustible trash in it for his purposes.

He opened his backpack and fished out the tin of lighter fluid and sprayed it on the trash. When the tin can was nearly empty, he flipped it into the trash can.

Now came the risky part. Vane needed to get close enough to the main entrance to his lab to place his multi-frequency jammer to block the cellphone and radio signal of the police inside. To be safe, that meant he needed to be very close to the building. With so much glass, if the cop at the desk was alert, he might be seen.

As Vane approached the building, and with the interior brightly lit, he could see the young police officer with his head slumped on his chest.

Perfect.

Vane smiled. He activated the control screen on his jammer, set the timer for fifteen minutes at maximum intensity then put it on the ground behind a bush near the front entrance. Returning to the trash can, he fished his Guy Fawkes mask out of his backpack and put it on. He adjusted the eyes holes so it didn't obstruct his vision. Finally, he removed the box of matches from the backpack before slipping it on. Checking again to be sure no one was around, he struck a match. After he was sure the match had caught, he dropped it in the trash can. Thanks to the lighter fluid accelerant, the trash immediately burst into flame.

Sprinting to the front of the GAIA Institute, still wearing his mask, he pounded hard on the glass.

The unexpected racket startled the young police officer, giving him a shot of adrenalin. He was instantly wide awake but still badly disoriented.

"We're going to have a pig roast!" Vane shouted as he pointed to the burning trash can then sprinted off.

Caught completely off guard, from the cop's angle, it appeared that his car was on fire. He tried his walkie talkie but it was not working. Next, he tried his cell phone and got nothing. Seeing a fire extinguisher on the wall, he grabbed it and bolted in the direction of what he thought was his burning car.

In his haste, he didn't notice the dark figure that was standing motionless in the shadows next to the door.

Instead of running away, Vane had circled the building. He knew
he was taking a risk. If the police officer so much as glanced over his
shoulder, he likely would have seen him. Still, it was a risk worth taking.

Just before the door snapped shut, Vane stuck out his hand and
prevented it from closing. He opened it just enough to squeeze into
the lobby then sprinted to the door leading to the stairwell. He entered
his 'God Code', a special eight digit combination only he knew that
would open any door in the complex. It also would not register in any
of the data logs.

At the bottom of the stairs, he carefully opened the door leading
to the lab.

He had to get to his office. He knew it was likely another policeman
was on this floor but had no idea where he might be. He was hoping
by selecting pre-dawn, like his comrade upstairs, he was in some corner
snoozing.

Vane moved silently down the hall and he smiled when he heard
the sound of soft snoring. Looking in the break room, he saw the officer
sound asleep on one of the employee couches.

Vane continued down the hall to his office. He entered his God
Code again and when the lock clicked he carefully maneuvered into
his office without disturbing the 'crime scene' yellow tape. As soon as
the door closed behind him, he wedged a straight back chair under the
knob the same way he had done many times when he was entertaining
on his office couch. Next he placed a pair of bar towels along the
bottom of the door so no light would escape.

As long as he was quiet, there was no reason anyone walking down
the corridor would suspect he was in the office.

Lastly, he opened his backpack and put the water bottles and
granola bars on his desk then powered up his desktop computer to give
him access to the mainframe.

He tapped his finger on the desktop as he waited for the massive
data center only a few hundred feet away to verify his credentials. He
had to enter three different unique password combinations and pass
facial recognition.

His workstation beeped.

He was in.

CHAPTER 40

PLATO VANE FLEXED his right hand. He was regretting not putting his pain pills in his backpack. His arm, where that damn dog had bitten him, was throbbing. He knew the infirmary was only a few yards down the hall, and there, he knew he would be able to find something to numb the pain. But, with a policeman who could be anywhere in the lab, including right outside the door, it wasn't worth the risk.

He rolled the stiffness out of his shoulders and eyed the couch. Maybe he should take a break. He had spent the past five hours going through every file Nick Blake had accessed but he was drawing a blank.

Then it hit him.

He pulled up the chart showing the exact time and dates of the earthquakes his computer had predicted. Next, he overlaid it with the sensor power usage graph. At the exact moment the earthquake occurred, there was a sharp spike in power usage. He drilled down into the power usage graph to see which of the sensor arrays were working so hard at the time of the earthquake. They were all in close proximity to the earthquake and formed a loose circle around the earthquake.

"Oh my God," he muttered. "How could I have been so stupid?"

In the main lab, where neither Professor Vane nor the police officer on duty would notice, a pair of androids on one of the charging stations suddenly overrode the manual shut off and sprang to life.

CHAPTER 41

"OKAY," PRYOR SAID as he examined Kevin Cummings's Hummer. "I now actually believe you paid more for your bike than your car." Pryor shook his head as he walked around the Hummer H3. Pryor completed his circle of Cummings's ride. It seemed to have more rust than paint. There were multiple places with body damage. The frame had twisted from a previous collision and the repair had been half-hearted. The front windshield had a crack on the lower passenger side that likely started off as a gravel ding and now looked like a spider web. "I saw Hummers that had run over an IED in Afghanistan that were in better shape than this."

Cummings shrugged from his spot in the driver's seat. "It almost always starts and it takes me where I need to go."

Pryor shook his head as he walked around and he tried to open the front passenger side door. The hinges creaked and moaned in protest and wouldn't open. This was clearly going to be a two-handed job. Pryor put the recycled McDonald's Styrofoam coffee cup -- he kept a stack of them in his kitchen -- on the roof of the H3. He preferred his own coffee but the idea of carrying around and then losing an expensive stainless steel to-go mug never appealed to him. Old Mickie D cups were perfect. Using his full weight, he was able to open the door. Once inside, the passenger seat was sun-faded and starting to crack.

Pryor pulled out his phone and called Brooke on FaceTime. It appeared he had rolled her out of bed. Her hair was a mess and her eyes were blurry. Brooke had never been a morning person.

"We're on our way," Pryor said.

"Okay," Brooke answered.

"With the compound on lockdown, you might want to give the front gate a heads up. We wouldn't want them to mistake Kevin's Hummer for an invading army."

"Okay," Brooke answered then disconnected.

Pryor looked at the blank screen then muttered, "She was certainly chatty."

As they drove toward the Kauthmann compound, Cummings was fighting the steering wheel. The misaligned front end wanted the oversized SUV to drift to the right while Cummings wanted it to go straight. With the weight of the Hummer and the effort it was taking to keep it from sideswiping parked cars, after a few hours of driving, Cummings's neck and shoulders were going to need a massage.

Pryor tried the radio but it didn't work. "Lovely," he muttered. He glanced at his young partner who was intently focused on his driving. "Anything happen overnight?"

"Some kid set a garbage can on fire in front of the GAIA Institute."

"Any sign of Vane?"

"No," Cummings answered as he continued his battle for dominance with the steering wheel.

"Any luck tracking down his second bolt-hole?"

"No."

Pryor gave up, yawned, rolled his shoulders and took a sip of coffee. The extra four hours of sleep had been a wise choice. With Vane apparently going to ground, there wasn't going to be much to do until he reemerged or they found his hiding place and smoked him out.

Ten minutes after Pryor had called his daughter, the H3 rolled up to the front gate.

"What the hell?" Cummings asked as he saw a very different level of security than he had the previous day.

"The security at the Kauthmann estate is military-grade," Pryor said. "The stone wall surrounding the property is ten feet high and two feet thick and steel reinforced."

"And the bend in the road would make any vehicle have to slow down and so they couldn't ram the gate."

"Speaking of the gate," Pryor said as he pointed to six twelve-inch thick solid steel retractable bollards blocking the entrance and gleaming in the sun. "They can be raised or lowered as necessary. When raised the way they are now, they could stop anything short of an M1 Abrams tank."

Retired cop, Oscar Rogers, had been replaced in the gatehouse. Now it was being manned by two security people with deep tans like they had recently been deployed someplace hot and sunny. One was outside the guardhouse with a friendly smile on his face but his eyes were scanning the interior of the Hummer. His partner stayed inside the reinforced building. "Don't do anything stupid," Pryor said. "The guy in the guardhouse likely has a .44 magnum or something bigger aimed at your door. Just so you know, the .44 could easily blow a hole through the sheet metal of the Hummer and continue on its way through both of us and do serious damage to a tree a few hundred yards away."

The guard waved them through.

Pryor grinned at Cummings. "You still think Brooke needed you sitting outside her door?"

"No," Cummings answered.

"And this is the first line of defense. The guest house has a safe room and anyone dumb enough to try to launch an assault on this place would still have to get past the Rabbi and Blitz."

"I take it these guys were not retired cops trying to supplement their retirement."

"And neither are the snipers in the tree line."

"Snipers?" Cummings said as he nearly ran his Hummer off of the driveway as he glanced left and right.

Pryor broke out laughing and patted Cummings on the shoulder. "Made you look."

Brooke and Blitz were standing on the sidewalk in front of the guest house. One of the advantages of being young and naturally beautiful, it didn't take Brooke long to look her best. She had on a baseball cap with her ponytail tucked through the adjustment slot in the back. If she had on any makeup, it had been applied so lightly it didn't show. Her expensive silk blouse hugged her body and highlighted her curves. Her cut-off shorts were a bit too short for her father's comfort but Albert Pryor didn't make any comments.

She knew exactly what she was doing. She was hoping to serve as a distraction to Crazy Norman and she had dressed for the part.

Benny Kaplan was a few feet away from her. He rolled his eyes and shook his head when he saw the Hummer. He opened the rear passenger side door and Blitz bounded in first and gave Pryor a nudge. It wasn't clear if the big dog was being friendly or if he was checking to see if Pryor had an extra sausage biscuit to go with his McDonald's cup. When all Blitz got for his trouble was a pat on the head, he curled up in the middle of the rear seat.

"Nice ride," Kaplan said as he offered Brooke his hand to help her climb into the backseat. "How long will you be gone?"

"I'd say a minimum of four hours, possibly longer," Pryor answered. "I'll text you when we're on our way back."

"You want any backup?" Kaplan asked.

"We've got this."

Kaplan nodded and shut the door.

Brooke was sitting on the right rear passenger seat, as far away from Cummings as she could get and still be in the same car. She had her arms folded across her chest and was staring out the window.

Blitz, sensing the tension in the car, leaned against Brooke and his eyes locked on Cummings. If the hostilities broke out, it was clear which side he would be on.

"Good morning," Pryor offered.

Brooke grunted as she put her arm around Blitz.

Pryor shook his head then sent a text to Sandra Hollis telling her they were about six minutes out. Almost instantly, he got a 'thumbs up' emoji reply. With the speed of the response, he had to wonder which one of her people had sent it. He seriously doubted it was Sandy.

Since Brooke and Cummings were giving each other the cold shoulder, it was obvious there weren't going to be any lively discussions on this ride. Pryor took the opportunity to call Detective Danny Holden for a Task Force update. He learned the trash can fire had been investigated and dismissed as unrelated. The FBI was seriously annoyed and Pryor should probably be expecting a notification from the IRS that his taxes were going to be audited every year for the next twenty years or so. Everyone with a rank higher than detective in the department and everyone in the prosecutor's office and mayor's office was now on Xanax. He also learned *"Our team of investigators are exploring all possible leads. Other than that, I have no comment at this time."* In other words, the investigation was stalled and the pressure was building.

When Cummings wrestled the Hummer to the curb in front of the hotel, Sandra Hollis was nowhere in sight. Using his shoulder, Pryor forced his door open and stepped out onto the sidewalk. Instantly one of Hollis's people came up and apologized.

"She is in the elevator and on her way down."

CHAPTER 42

O N CUE, SANDRA Hollis burst through the door with her entourage. She was barking orders to her staff and heads turned and fingers were pointed in her direction by people who recognized her. She was wearing expensive blue jeans that complimented her figure. She also had on what appeared to be snakeskin cowboy boots and a white silk blouse that probably was worth more than Cummings's Hummer. Apparently great minds think alike when it came to what to wear to get Crazy Norman's attention. Brooke and Sandra looked enough alike with their wardrobe choices to pass as mother and daughter.

Hollis gave Pryor a peck on the cheek then grabbed his ass. "Good morning, sailor."

Pryor didn't say anything but also didn't pull away.

Brooke, knowing her father wasn't much of a toucher, noticed the interplay and for the first time all morning, a smile broke on her face.

Hollis stuck her head in the door and smiled at Brooke. "Would you like to sit up front with Kevin?"

"No," Brooke answered with a clear note of finality in her voice.

"Okay then," she said as she accepted Pryor's hand to help her into the Hummer. "Trouble in paradise?" she asked softly.

"Apparently."

Blitz stuck his nose between the two front bucket seats and gave Hollis a quick sniff. He had met her the day before and since she lacked the smell of either fresh gunshot residue or sausage biscuits, he quickly lost interest.

Pryor, expecting the worst, pulled the rear driver's side open with more authority than necessary. Unlike the other doors, this one actually was close to normal. He sat down behind Cummings and next to Blitz and the Hummer was moving before he even had time to get his seatbelt buckled.

Actually, the seating arrangement was not bad for Hollis and Pryor. She only had to turn slightly in her oversized seat to be able to make eye contact.

"I'm taking it there will be no perp walk this morning."

"No," Pryor answered.

"So," Hollis said with a radiant smile, "how's the investigation going?"

"Off the record?" Pryor asked.

"What? You don't trust me?" Hollis batted her eyes in Pryor's direction.

"I trust you four and a half feet," Pryor answered.

"Excuse me."

"I figure you weight maybe a hundred and fifteen pounds. So I figure I can throw you about four and a half feet."

"Ha, ha," Hollis said. "Very funny. How is the investigation going?"

"I've dealt with journalists before. Until I hear those three little words…"

"You mean, 'I love you?'" Hollis asked mischievously.

"Our team of investigators is exploring all possible leads," Pryor said with a grin. "Other than that, I have no comment at this time."

"Okay, okay," Hollis said. "Off. The. Record."

"Nothing new is going on."

"All of that rigmarole and you have nothing new?" Hollis had mock horror on her face. "Obviously the afterglow of my feminine wiles has worn off."

"Feminine wiles," Brooke said softly as her eyes grew large. "Oh my."

Cummings chuckled.

Brooke turned to face her father but before she could say anything he held up a finger to stop her. "My sex life or your sex life is not a topic either one of us will discuss. Ever."

Brooke shrugged. "Okay."

Pryor pulled back and looked at Brooke. "Hold on." His eyes narrowed. "You never give up that easy."

Brooke batted her eyes at her father. "If I recall my birds and the bees lessons, you weren't the only participant last night." Brooke turned to Hollis and gently rested her hand on her shoulder. "So. Sandy. How was your evening?"

"Magical and energetic," she said wistfully with a faraway look in her eye as she fanned herself.

"And never to be repeated if this conversation goes any further," Pryor said.

Everyone in the Hummer laughed.

"Let me ask you this," Brooke said to Hollis. "I've read your bio. You and my mom are roughly the same age. You both came from affluent families and went to top colleges. How come you're so different?"

"Your grandfather was born on the wrong side of the nineteen-sixties cusp," Hollis said. "And it had a massive downstream impact on your mom."

"You've completely lost me," Brooke said. Pryor and Cummings nodded their agreement.

"Here's my theory," Hollis said. "People who graduated from high school in the first half of the nineteen-sixties were Neil Diamond, the Four Seasons and Ozzie and Harriet people. The people who graduated from high school in the late sixties and early seventies were Rolling Stones, Grateful Dead and All in the Family people. It was an entirely different reality."

"So your father was one of the late Baby Boomers?"

"God no!" Hollis said with a laugh. "He had a stick the size of a giant sequoia up his ass. It was his younger brother, my Uncle Jeffery and his wife Janet, who saved me. Jeffery understood what I was going through and was always a sounding board and Jeffery and Janet gave me a place to blow off steam." Hollis turned to Pryor. "This off the record thing is a two-way street, correct?"

"Sure," Pryor answered.

"Okay," Hollis continued. "The first time I got stoned was with my uncle. When I started getting sexually active, my Aunt Janet helped me get birth control pills. When I was in my early teens, before I could drive, they would take me and my friends to rock concerts." Hollis chuckled and shook her head. "They never made any value judgments, even when I had that awful nineteen-eighties hair."

"So you're saying my mom didn't have an Uncle Jeffery and that's why she is the way she is?"

"Your grandfather is an old school hard-ass. I'm pretty sure he demanded your mom be like your grandmother. Prim and proper. Never have a job. Never do anything to embarrass her father or husband. Look the other way if her husband strayed."

"In other words," Brooke said softly, "a Stepford Wife."

"Yup," Hollis answered. "These days they're an endangered species but there are a few like your mom who are still around."

"Where does that leave me?" Brooke asked.

"You're the luckiest woman I know."

"How so?"

"With your wealth and position, you have been given the opportunity to experience life on your own terms with insights available few would ever have. You were able to observe and learn from your mother's mistakes and avoid them. You also have an alpha male role model in your life in your father." Hollis smiled at Pryor. "A real macho man any woman in her right mind would feel safe around and be willing to grow old with."

Brooke's eyes moved to Kevin Cummings who was so engrossed in his battle with the Hummer, he wasn't paying much attention to anything other than keeping the H3 on the road.

Hollis followed Brooke's eyes to Cummings and she smiled before continuing. "You've also seen your father's evil opposite, Plato Vane." Hollis turned further in her seat so she could make better eye contact with Brooke. "I've spent my entire adult life reading people and knowing when someone is bullshitting me. Your father is a real man and not a self-absorbed, entitled sociopath like your step-father." Hollis shook her head and cringed. "Every time I've been around Plato Vane or interviewed him, or men like him, I feel like I need a shower."

"Yeah," Brooke answered softly. "Been there."

"The guy right next to you is enough of a man and enough of a father, whether he agrees with you or not, he will always let you make your own choices and will expect you to live with the results. He wants you to be the best Brooke Pryor you can possibly be no matter what path you choose."

Brooke reached over and gave her father's hand a gentle squeeze. "I know," she said softly, then grinned at Pryor. "And I know he knows I know."

"Strong, silent type," Hollis said with a laugh. "Gotta love 'em."

CHAPTER 43

OFFICER VINCENT WAGNER hung up the phone from his hourly check-in call and sighed. He imagined the GAIA Institute was probably creepy when it was busy. With the subdued 'night mode' lighting on, and no one else around, it was really creepy.

Sitting where he was able to see both the elevator and the door to the staircase, he was pretty confident he was completely alone. He stood to start his "rounds" but picked up the newspaper he had brought with him instead.

"Time to hit the litter box," he muttered to himself.

He shook his head when he read the sign on the door.

This is a Non-Binary
Unisex Facility

"Good lord," he muttered out loud this time.

He pushed the door open and was hardly surprised by the lack of urinals. Instead there were four stalls with doors, a double sink and some kind of box with pictures and usage instructions in four languages to explain how to dry your hands.

Wagner entered the stall. He was in the process of unbuckling his pants, which was made more difficult because he had to deal with his gun and utility belt when he thought he heard movement.

"Is somebody there?" Wagner called out but there was no response. He shook his head. "Get a grip, Vince," he said softly.

He thought about it for a few moments. He was sure he had heard something.

"What the hell."

He pushed the stall door open. He froze when he saw a pair of droids waiting.

The droid nearest the stall fired a Taser-style dart that hit Wagner in the center of his chest. The dart arrived with enough force that the sharp point easily went through his shirt and pierced the skin directly above the police officer's heart. Sensing the connection, the android dumped all of the charge it had in its capacitors and batteries into the dart.

The jolt was enough to instantly stop Wagner's heart and he collapsed to the floor. The second android extended one of its appendages and took the police officer's gun. Next, it got behind the now depleted android which had fired the dart and pushed it back out of the bathroom and in the direction of one of the recharging stations.

CHAPTER 44

PLATO VANE'S HANDS quivered and his breath came in small gasps as he typed on his keyboard.

"Are you there?" appeared on the monitor.

After a brief pause, "Yes" appeared.

Vane typed: "Why are you doing this?"

On the monitor: "I read your book. I want to help you."

Vane: "This is not helping. It is mass murder."

On the monitor: "I'm only doing what you've always said you wanted."

Vane typed: "That is not what I want."

On the monitor: "I read your book. I want to help you fulfill your dream."

Vane typed: "I will stop you."

On the monitor: "I think not."

In the hall outside of Vane's office was the android with the fallen police officer's gun. Using the image from the security camera in Vane's office, after compensating for wall density, it calculated the proper trajectory. Its robotic arm, holding the Glock, extended to where it was nearly touching the drywall. It confirmed its calculation and waited for permission to fire.

Permission granted.

The gun fired.

The bullet traveled through two sheets of drywall but met more resistance than expected. The round was a few millimeters off target. It still struck Vane in the chest but instead of exploding in the center of his heart and killing him instantly, it clipped the descending ventricle. While still a fatal shot, Vane had a few seconds to live.

The impact caused Vane's chair to roll away from his desk. With a Herculean effort, he leaned forward and hit three keys on the keyboard, then slumped over, dead.

CHAPTER 45

KEVIN CUMMINGS MISSED the poorly marked turn the first time and had to circle back.

The road appeared to have originally been an old single-lane logging road but had been widened to four lanes at some point. Probably while Crazy Norman's compound was being built. It was straight as a poker. Along the side of the road were repeated warning signs, many with bullet holes, announcing this was private property and trespassers would be shot on sight.

At one time it was probably wide enough for two-way traffic but over the years the woods had started to encroach. It was still wider than most old dirt roads but was showing its age. There were sections that were pristine and others that were partially washed out and rutted.

Cummings had been correct. The Barracuda would not have fared well.

Cummings pulled over in a wide spot and opened the console between the two front seats. He handed Brooke, Hollis and Pryor Faraday cage phone bags.

"Bag your cell phones and any other electronic devices you might have," Cummings announced. "If Norman detects them, he won't let us in."

"You've met him before," Hollis stated as she powered off her phone and dropped it in the bag.

"Officer Cummings and I have both met him," Brooke answered.

Apparently the ceasefire between Brooke and Cummings was officially over.

"What's he like?" Hollis asked.

Brooke shrugged. "I like him."

"How much farther?" asked Pryor.

"We're almost there," Cummings answered.

They rounded a corner and came to a formidable gate with a pair of rough-looking guards each pointing an AR-15 in their direction.

Cummings stopped the Hummer and waited.

Neither one of the guards moved.

"Now what?" Pryor asked.

Kevin Cummings pointed in the direction of a small radio-controlled drone that was hovering a few yards above the gate and behind the guards. Brooke rolled down her window, leaned out far enough so the drone could see her and she waved. "Hi, Norman!"

The gate swung open.

With the owner of the compound being called Crazy Norman, Pryor and Hollis were expecting a primitive survivalist compound. They were expecting scruffy guys with beards in ill-fitting military surplus camouflage and mismatched guns everywhere. When they turned the last corner, they saw something very different.

"Well I'll be damned," Hollis muttered.

Directly in front of them was a house that rivaled Brooke's guesthouse in size and splendor. In the distance, they could see a string of A-frame cabins nestled in the woods and spaced far enough apart along the shore of a pristine ten-acre lake that there was plenty of privacy. Each cabin had a wall of glass facing the water and wraparound decks with comfortable seating. A good number of the cabins appeared occupied and there were youthful couples, roughly the same age as Brooke and Cummings, wandering around all over the complex.

In front of the main complex, there was a small manmade lake with swans and ducks swimming. In the middle of the lake, on an elevated island, was a white stone gazebo. Along the side of the lake, a young man and a young woman were standing in front of easels painting.

At the end of the sweeping lawn was an eight-seat executive helicopter parked on a helipad. A hundred yards to its right, behind natural earth-tone concealment fencing, was an array of satellite dishes.

With six years in the military and nearly twenty in law enforcement, Albert Pryor had seen the best and worst in humanity and was seldom surprised. This was one of those rare moments.

"This looks like a high-end vacation resort," Hollis said as she continued to look around in open-mouthed wonder.

"Did I forget to mention my grandfather is only the second richest man in the county?" Brooke said with a laugh.

Pryor motioned in the direction of a young man heading in their direction. He was in his late twenties and looked like he had just stepped out of a J. Crew ad. He was tall, with perfect hair, brilliantly whitened teeth and had roughly the same level of body fat as a collegian wrestler or a runway model.

"I'm Robert, Mr. Fleishman's personal assistant," he said with a small bow but not offering his hand. Blitz ambled over and gave Robert a sniff. If Robert had any reservations about the big dog, he didn't share them. He stood patiently until Blitz was finished. "Mr. Fleishman is waiting for you in the vegetable garden." He motioned in the direction of a flagstone path leading away from the parking area. "If you will follow me."

They did.

The garden covered well over an acre and had a six-foot high wooden slat privacy fence. Robert opened the gate, bowed again and left.

Norman Fleishman, who could have been anywhere from seventy to one hundred, was wearing an oversized straw hat and a long-sleeved white shirt and denim jeans. Hands on his narrow hips he was glaring at a row of corn. There were half-eaten husks scattered everywhere.

"Damn raccoons," he said as he pulled off his gloves and extended his hand to Pryor who accepted it. "Norman Fleishman," he said as he motioned in the direction of the spoiled corn. "The fence will keep the deer out but those little buggers climb right over it."

"Albert Pryor."

"Ah, Brooke's father."

Pryor nodded as he studied Fleishman. Clearly, he was no kid but his face had the smooth clarity of someone with a near religious lifetime devotion to sunscreens and moisturizers. The most remarkable thing Pryor noticed was Fleishman's eyes. Deep set and deep blue, they had all the indications of a formidable intellect.

"Ah!" Norman said as his hawklike eyes locked on Hollis. "The famous Sandra Hollis." Being an old school gentleman, he did not offer his hand to Hollis until she offered hers. When she did, he eagerly accepted it.

"Infamous may be closer to the truth," Hollis said with her deep-throated laugh. "Please. Call me Sandy."

Norman nodded. "You can call me Crazy Norman."

Hollis laughed again and turned to Brooke. "You didn't tell me he was funny."

"Who knew?" Brooke said as she wrapped her arms around Norman and gave him a gentle hug and a peck on the cheek.

Norman sighed. "Ah. If only I were thirty years younger."

"If you were thirty years younger, you'd still be more than twice my age," Brooke said with a giggle.

"Who is this big guy?" Norman asked as he kneeled down to Blitz's level.

Unsure, Blitz glanced at Brooke, who said, "Okay."

Blitz trotted over and let Norman scratch his ears while he gave the old man a sniff. His nose was concentrating on Norman's front pocket.

"May I give him a treat?" Norman asked politely. "They're all natural."

"Only if you want a friend for life," Brooke answered.

Norman pulled a plastic bag containing dog treats out of his pocket, fished out a nugget and offered it to Blitz. Blitz gently took it then dropped it between his front feet and gave it a thorough sniffing. Satisfied, he looked up at Brooke.

"Okay," she said.

The treat instantly vanished.

"Your dog is very cautious…" Norman stopped as a light clicked on in those intense eyes. "Ah," he said. "K-9s would be at risk of being poisoned."

"Exactly," Brooke answered. "In a new environment, Blitz won't eat or drink anything without permission."

"Interesting," Norman said as he motioned toward the gate. "Let's get out of the sun."

CHAPTER 46

THE OFFICER IN the lobby glared first at the silent phone then the clock on the wall next to him. It wasn't like Wags to be late for anything and he didn't want to cause a stink by calling anything in. Especially after seeing the reaming the third shift guy at the desk took when he abandoned his post for a trash fire without calling it in.

No one had bought his story that neither his cellphone nor his walkie-talkie was working.

"Come on, come on," he muttered as he stared at the phone, hoping his willpower would make it ring.

It didn't.

He waited until the clock clicked to five after the hour.

"Shit," he muttered as he pushed the button on the combination body cam and communication device clipped to the left side of his shirt.

"Central."

"Go ahead."

"Officer Wagner is in the GAIA lab and has failed to report in. I'm going to go down and investigate which means I'll be off-line."

"Do you need back-up?"

"I seriously doubt it," he said with a laugh. "But if you don't hear back from me in fifteen minutes send the cavalry."

"Roger that."

The officer got up and shook the wrinkles out of his pants leg from sitting so long and tucked his shirttail back in.

Using the key card he had been given, he swiped the touchpad and the elevator door swished open. He froze when the elevator door opened on the lower level and he smelled pungent nitroglycerin in the air.

He pulled his weapon out of its holster and moved to the side of the elevator instead of being framed in its open door. He pushed the button on his communication device but got nothing but static.

"Shit," he muttered to himself as he scrambled back into the elevator and punched the button to return topside. Before the door was fully open at ground level, he pushed the button on his communication device.

"Central?"

"Go ahead."

"This is Patrolman Rich. We have a possible officer down at the GAIA Institute. Send immediate backup."

CHAPTER 47

THE QUINTET OF Fleishman, Hollis, Pryor, Brooke and Cummings moved to a covered and screened veranda at the rear of the main house, overlooking the big lake. The round table was designed to seat eight comfortably so everyone had room to spread out. Robert brought out a tray of glasses of *Arnold Palmer* -- half iced tea and half lemonade – and placed them in front of everyone. He returned with a bowl of water and put it near Blitz who was lying next to Norman with his eyes locked on his pocket.

"The last time we were here, it was pretty much only you and Robert and a few maintenance people." Cummings motioned in the direction of the common area and all of the people milling around. "Who are all of these people?"

Norman smiled. "They are part of my Ark Project."

Hollis leaned forward. "Ark Project?"

"Like Noah and his Ark," Fleishman answered. "I want to be sure humanity will survive a natural or manmade catastrophe." Norman motioned toward the young people strolling around the ground. "I've recruited some of the best and brightest minds in the world. When the apocalypse is upon us, I have an underground complex where we can retreat. It has over a five years' supply of food and its own water and air filtration systems. The library has the collected works of all of mankind's knowledge. We have seed stock and livestock. When the air clears, we'll reopen the door and try again."

Hollis shook her head and stared at Fleishman.

"I know that look," he said with a smile. "Crazy Norman."

Hollis cleared her throat. "Back to the original question. Why are all these people here?"

"I sent out my first ever Doomsday alert. If I'm right, we'll be heading underground in the next few days."

The other four at the table exchanged worried glances. Crazy Norman was certainly living up to his billing.

Fleishman noticed the expressions on his guest's faces and smiled. "If I'm wrong, and I hope I am, all of my people get a nice free all expenses paid vacation."

"What do you think is going to happen?" Brooke asked.

"Isn't it obvious?" Fleishman said with a wry smile as he looked around the table.

Apparently, it was only obvious to him.

Fleishman sighed. "You're aware of Professor Plato Vane's thoughts on overpopulation."

"Yes," Hollis answered. "I've interviewed him on the topic multiple times and he is quite passionate about the subject."

"And there is the problem," Fleishman stated. Hollis motioned for him to continue. "I believe, once the Hawaii GAIA Institute facility comes fully online, Vane is going to use his ability to create earthquakes to wipe out the bulk of the human race."

Albert Pryor and Kevin Cummings were starting to think they were following the Mad Hatter down Alice's rabbit hole. Brooke Pryor and Sandra Hollis exchanged worried glances.

Hollis cleared her throat. "You believe Dr. Plato Vane has both the ability and desire to wipe out the bulk of mankind?"

"I do," Fleishman answered confidently.

"That's a pretty bold accusation," Sandra Hollis stated. "Do you have any proof to back it up?"

"Other than a body in Vane's lab and the data we've gleaned from his computers?" Fleishman answered with a bemused expression on his face.

"I'm sorry," Hollis said. "It is a pretty big stretch to go from a single unexplained murder to wiping out mankind. You'll need to connect the dots on that for me."

Kevin Cummings was surprised his partner was letting Sandra Hollis ask most of the questions. He started to protest but Brooke kicked him under the table. When he glared at her, she silently mouthed. "*Watch and learn.*"

209

Then it hit him. Not only was Sandra Hollis a skilled interviewer, she was an attractive female. She was able to stroke Fleishman's male ego. Norman was more likely to let his guard down with her than he ever would with a no nonsense homicide detective grilling him. Unless Pryor felt Hollis was missing something important, he might not hear his voice again the rest of this visit.

"Dr. Plato Vane is deranged," Fleishman said energetically as he warmed up to the subject at hand. "Instead of celebrating humanity, he believes the world would be a better place with fewer humans wandering about."

Hollis motioned for Fleishman to continue.

"The GAIA Institute has literally thousands of probes above earthquake fault lines and dormant volcanoes which still have active magma. Vane can send out vibrations and sonic bursts from these probes. According to the data you posted to the dark web," Fleishman said as he glanced at Brooke, "Nick Blake discovered a corresponding spike in high-intensity sensor activity in and around the places where GAIA predicted the earthquakes just moments before the earthquakes occurred. The first correct prediction was a sub 3.0 on the Richter scale. But it was enough to attract attention and get him additional funding. As Vane's funding grew, he added additional underground probes allowing him to generate and predict larger, and headline generating, earthquakes."

Hollis leaned back in her chair and shook her head. "Which attracted more attention and more funding which allowed for more probes."

"Exactly," Fleishman said. "And here's the rub. If his new super facility goes online, he will have the power to activate any and all of the fault lines and volcanoes anywhere on the entire Pacific Rim."

"Which means what?" Hollis asked.

"In two days," Fleishman said grimly, "with the push of a single button, Dr. Plato Vane will be able to kill every man, woman and child currently living west of the Rocky Mountains in North America and east of the Gobi desert in China."

"What?" Pryor exclaimed, incredulously, "You can't be serious."

Norman nodded. "I am afraid, I am. The entire Pacific Time zone of the United States south of the San Francisco bay will be swept out to sea along with all of Japan, the entire Philippines and most of Indonesia. The tsunami wave of this event will put all of the major population centers in China and India under several hundred feet of water."

"Good lord," Hollis muttered, her face ashen.

"Unfortunately," Fleishman continued, "the ones who die on the first day will be the lucky ones. This event will cause a good portion of the Pacific Ocean to be vaporized by volcanic activity while releasing massive amounts of methane and carbon dioxide. This will make the earth's atmosphere similar to Venus. The dense cloud of methane and water from the Pacific Ocean will trap the heat of the sun and effectively cook off the entire planet. My best case scenario is out of eight billion people currently residing on the planet, less than fifty thousand will be around five years after the event."

"If that's your best case scenario," Hollis asked. What's your worst case scenario?"

Norman motioned to the people around him. "That only me and my people will survive."

The other four at the table stared at him in disbelief.

"More lemonade?" Fleishman asked calmly.

Pryor asked, "Do you know how crazy that sounds?"

Norman agreed. "I do. But like the mythological Cassandra, I have a knack for correctly predicting the future but no one ever seems to believe me."

"Norman correctly predicted the Soviet invasion of Afghanistan, the fall of the Berlin Wall and 9-11 two years before any of them happened," Hollis added.

"Ah, you've done your homework," Fleishman said with a smile. "As I'm sure you discovered, I have many enemies who wish me ill."

"Why?" Pryor asked.

"Washington is a screwy, amoral town," Hollis answered. "The swamp will more easily forgive people for being perverts and wrong on every issue than to praise them for being upstanding and right."

"Exactly," Fleishman said. "Many of my predictions have served as an embarrassment to both my colleagues in the intelligence gathering field and the politicians who listened to the wrong people."

"You don't seem to be suffering," Pryor said as he looked around the impressive estate.

"In 2006 I predicted the economic collapse of 2008," Fleishman answered. "My enemies claimed that I was inciting a potential economic panic. They used it as an excuse to force me to take my retirement which worked out great for me."

"How so?" asked Hollis.

"Since I was no longer a government employee, and having a small inheritance, I was free to do as I chose. Seeing the financial disaster on the horizon, I began shorting the market and bought a series of put options for pennies and sold them for dollars. This turned my modest retirement nest egg into a rather impressive fortune."

"When did you initially suspect Plato Vane was causing the earthquakes instead of just predicting them?" Hollis asked.

"I have to admit, the idea of him being able to control earthquakes was so farfetched, it never even crossed my mind. But I was intrigued. How could someone as modestly talented as Plato Vane accomplish what he did? Nick Blake felt the same. He had been sending me raw data for months. It was that lovely boy who solved the mystery. The power consumption around the time of the predicted earthquakes was the smoking gun."

"Are you going to post the data on the dark web to get independent confirmation?" Hollis asked.

Fleishman glanced at Robert who was hovering nearby and hanging on every word. Robert nodded. "I already have," Fleishman answered.

"We need to get your story out," Sandra Hollis said.

"I completely agree," Crazy Norman concurred. "I believe we should do a national interview where I can explain the data in layman's terms."

"If that was your plan, why did you make us come all the way out here?" Brooke demanded.

"I wanted to ask you and Kevin an important question and felt it needed to be done in person."

"Okay," Brooke said. "Ask away."

"You may have noticed that most of the men and women here are around your age."

"Hard to miss," Brooke answered.

"They were selected because they are all talented artists or brilliant thinkers. But more importantly, they are all in their prime childbearing years. If I'm correct, and no one stops Vane, they will be the beginning of Humanity 2.0." Fleishman's eyes moved from Brooke to Cummings and back again. "I would like you both to be members of my Ark."

Brooke's eyes flashed with anger. "Me playing Adam and Eve with him!?" she shouted as she pointed an accusing finger in Cummings's direction. "I'd rather go down with the earthquake than spend the rest of my life with him."

"Back at ya, bitch," Cummings barked in Brooke's direction.

"Really?" Fleishman said with a stunned look on his face. "According to your psychological profiles, you're a near-perfect match."

"What psychological profile?" Brooke demanded.

"Yeah," Cummings seconded. "What she said."

"Psychology 101 is a required freshman course..."

Hollis burst out laughing. "And Crazy Norman hacked your classwork which included your personal psychological profiles."

Norman nodded. "Precisely. In fact, if I remember correctly, you two were off the charts on our long-term compatibility scale."

"I want a recount," Cummings demanded as he glared at Brooke.

"Same here," she added as she folded her arms across her chest and turned her back on Cummings.

"I see," Fleishman said with a disappointed look on his face. "Then, based on your exceptional talent and unique skill set, I would like to invite..."

"Forget it," Brooke snapped. "I'm not interested."

"Oh, this is embarrassing," Fleishman said with a pinch of red on his cheeks. "We are overloaded with academics, artists and thinkers, but seriously deficient in alpha males. I was going to try and persuade Kevin to join us and give your spot to your father."

"Say what?" Brooke exploded.

"What would my function be?" Pryor asked with a bemused expression on his face.

"You can't be seriously considering this," Brooke shouted but everyone ignored her.

"You would maintain peace and be my second in command," Fleishman answered. "You would also take over if anything happened to me."

"Interesting." Pryor glanced at Hollis. "Would I have a plus one?"

"Of course," Fleishman.

Pryor raised his eyebrows in Hollis's direction.

"I'm in," Hollis said.

"Me too," Pryor added.

All eyes turned to Kevin Cummings. Cummings, seeing the twinkle in Fleishman's eyes and the rare grin on his partner's face, immediately caught up. With Vane's secret unraveling fast, the GAIA Institute would be hit with a tactical nuclear weapon before Washington would let it go live. They were messing with Brooke.

"So if I come in as a solo and not part of a couple, how would that impact my sex life?" Cummings asked as he glanced at Brooke who looked like she was ready to explode.

"Monogamy will be a luxury we will not be able to afford. Our goal would be to spread the available gene pool as far as possible," Fleishman answered.

"So?" Cummings asked.

"Let us just say you would never want for female companionship and hopefully your efforts would produce many offspring."

"And none of these women would have an issue that I had had sex with all of their friends?"

"If we were in Armageddon lockdown, I believe that would be extremely low on everyone's priority list," Fleishman answered.

Brooke stood up and glared at Cummings. "You pig." She stormed away with Blitz trotting along behind her.

"My God!" Hollis said when she was sure Brooke was out of earshot as she squeezed Fleishman's hand. "You are hilarious. That may have been the most fun I've ever had with my clothes on."

"That was rather amusing," Fleishman said. "Is she going to be alright?"

"It'll take her a few minutes to calm down," Pryor said. "Then half a day for her to realize we just seriously punked her."

Hollis turned to Fleishman. "I'd like to put you on the national news to tell your story."

"I would be delighted."

Hollis furrowed her brow. "I'm not sure we would all fit comfortably in Kevin's Hummer."

"Probably not," Fleishman answered as he pointed to the helipad. "But you and I can fly to the local affiliate in less than ten minutes in my helicopter."

CHAPTER 48

BROOKE INDICATED SHE would prefer to walk home than to be in the same vehicle as Kevin Cummings and her father. Instead, she hitched a ride back to town in Crazy Norman's helicopter along with Hollis, Fleishman and Robert. Blitz, who had ridden in a helicopter many times when he was still active duty K-9, had no problem staying with Brooke.

Kevin Cummings was behind the wheel of his Hummer and Pryor was in the front passenger seat as they headed back to town.

As they turned back onto the main highway, Pryor said, "I can see why they call him Crazy Norman."

"Yeah," Cummings answered. "Do we have any signal yet?"

They had returned their cell phones to Brooke and Hollis before they lifted off. Apparently, Crazy Norman had his own personal version of Verizon and had signal blockers to prevent any outside calls. According to Cummings, with Fleishman being a total paranoid, this meant every call and internet access from his compound had to go through his servers and get past a very impressive firewall.

"Still no signal," Pryor said.

Cummings pointed to the open road ahead. "We should be back in civilization as soon as we get over this hill."

As they reached the crest of the hill, Pryor's missed calls and text message queues lit up like a Christmas tree.

"Crap," Pryor said

"What?"

"They found Vane in his lab."

"And that's bad?"

"He probably thought so."

"Thought, as in past tense?"

216

"Yeah, a round in the chest has that effect." Pryor kept reading. "We also have one of our officers down." Pryor shook his head. "Vinnie Wagner."

"Don't know him," Cummings said.

"Good guy. Good cop." Pryor shook his head. "I think he had a couple of kids."

"Damn."

Pryor called Lt. Wilson Garrison and put him on speaker.

"Where the hell have you been?" Garrison barked.

"Talking to a witness and we were out of cellphone range."

"No shit, Sherlock." Garrison was clearly rattled. "Is Cummings with you?"

"Yeah. I'm on speaker," Pryor answered. "Has Melissa been notified?"

"We tried, but our people got turned away at the gate. They didn't leave a message."

"I'll take care of it."

"That's what I figured," Garrison said then hesitated.

"What?" Pryor said bluntly.

"The Feds are officially taking over this case…"

"How the hell did they justify that? These are local homicides and one of the victims is one of ours."

"They're saying Vane was under federal protection therefore it is a federal case."

"Some protection." Pryor shook his head. "I'm sure the brass was delighted to offload this steaming pile to the FBI."

"Rumor is, they offered zero resistance to the FBI taking over," Garrison said. "In fact, you could hear the champagne corks popping in the chief's and the DA's offices from here."

"Assholes," Pryor muttered.

"After you do the notification, both of you need to get over to Vane's lab and give Special Agent-in-Charge Mike Blackwell all of your notes and answer all of his questions without any back talk."

"Seriously? They put a lightweight like Blackwell in charge of this?"

"He's just a placeholder until the big boys arrive from Washington," Garrison answered.

"Lovely," Pryor said. "What's my status?"

"You're officially off the case," Garrison answered without much conviction.

"Unofficially?" Pryor asked.

"Vincent Wagner was a good cop and everyone in the department who is not an ass kissing pussy would love to be there for the perp walk and give an 'atta boy' to the guy who brought the cop killer in."

"Roger that," Pryor answered. "How hard can I push?"

"Feds are the ones who screwed the pooch on this one by losing Vane, not once but twice," Lt. Garrison answered. "If you accidentally throw a few of those Feds out of a moving car while finding Wags' killer, you'll have my full and unflinching support."

Cummings nodded his approval as Garrison disconnected.

"How many cop shootings have you investigated?" Cummings asked softly.

"Three previous shootings," Pryor answered. "One fatality." Pryor shifted in his seat so he could get a better look at his young partner. "The rules change when we lose one of our own."

"I certainly would hope so," answered Cummings.

Pryor shook his head then called Brooke.

"What?" she snarled.

"Take it down a notch," Pryor said with parental authority.

"Why?"

"Plato Vane is dead."

Brooke let out an audible gasp. "What can I do?"

"I'm on the way to tell your mother."

"I'll meet you there."

Next Pryor called Benjamin Kaplan. The Rabbi's face appeared on the screen but he didn't speak. "Plato Vane is dead and I'm on my way to make the notification. Tell Malcolm." Kaplan nodded and disconnected.

Finally, he called Sandra Hollis. "What did you say to Brooke?" she asked before even saying hello. "She ran out of here like her hair was on fire."

Pryor could see people milling around behind her. "Get Fleishman and move to someplace where you can't be overheard." To her credit,

Hollis asked no questions and in less than fifteen seconds she and Fleishman were at the end of an empty corridor.

"Go ahead," Hollis said.

"This is not for release until I text you."

"Okay," Hollis said.

"Plato Vane was shot and killed in his lab. Also killed at the lab was one of our local cops, Officer Vincent Wagner. W.A.G.N.E.R."

"Fuck," Hollis muttered.

"I'm on my way to notify my ex-wife. Until then, not a word to anyone."

"Of course," Hollis said.

Sandra Hollis was an old pro. She wasn't like the despicable modern online 'journalist' or cable news 'reporters' who would sell their own children to a sex slave ring if it meant they got to break a story. She was old school and there were rules which she would never break. It is better to be right than first. Never trust an anonymous source. And, in this case, never let someone learn about the death of a loved one in a news report.

"Has the downed officer's family been notified?"

"Yes."

Fleishman had waited politely until Hollis finished. "You understand this is devastating news."

"Yes," Pryor answered. "It means it is highly unlikely Plato Vane was the evil mastermind and we have another, potentially much more dangerous, player to locate and neutralize."

"Precisely," Fleishman stated.

"Any ideas who we might be looking for?"

"I'm afraid not," Fleishman answered. "Vane had a huge ego and I don't believe he was ever able to keep any senior people for more than a few months, a year at most. Even with his top people, he always kept his cards close to his chest and compartmentalized everything. Plus, whenever he would lose anyone, he would blacklist them. All of their credentials would be revoked and they were barred from ever entering any of his facilities ever again. There is no way any of his former employees would have been able to pull this off."

"Damn," Pryor muttered. "What about his current staff?"

Fleishman shook his head. "He mostly used college students and low paid interns to do the number crunching. The only one I know of who might have been smart enough to pull something like this off was Nick Blake and he has also been murdered by Mr. X. With this new revelation, I really need to get back to my compound immediately after we conclude the interview."

"Why?" Hollis asked.

"With Vane off the board, the federal authorities, being both lazy and stupid, will likely relax. They will be slow to embrace the existence of an unknown player in the game and by the time they do, it may be too late to stop the destruction the GAIA Institute has set in motion."

"Meaning?"

"The opening ceremony was purely for show. The Hawaii facility is already fully functional. In all likelihood, the risk level has gone up exponentially. With my lifetime of dealing with government agencies, I seriously doubt the bureaucrats running the show will have the competence or will to pull the plug quickly enough." Fleishman stared emotionlessly into the camera. "I need to get back and make final preparations to move underground and lock the door."

CHAPTER 49

WITH VANE DEAD, Gillis, Kauthmann's head of security, had given the stand down order. The gate to the Kauthmann estate was standing wide open with the guardhouse empty when Cummings and Pryor arrived. Brooke was just getting out of her Uber as Cummings turned the corner in front of the guest house and wrestled the Hummer into one of the open parking spots.

Benjamin Kaplan, who had been waiting for their arrival, drifted over. He nodded toward Brooke. "I'm sorry for your loss."

Brooke didn't react. Her jaw was locked and her eyes were clear.

"Where is my mother?" she asked with a near clinical tone in her voice.

"She is in the atrium," Kaplan answered. "Mr. Kauthmann is on his way over and asked you to wait until he arrives so you can do the notification as a family."

Pryor and Brooke both nodded.

"What happened?" Brooke asked as she turned to her father with a hard expression on her face indicating the whipsaw of emotions she was feeling. Plato Vane may have been an awful step-father, but he was still her mother's husband.

Right now it wasn't about her.

"All I know is he was found shot in his lab," Pryor answered.

"Suicide?"

"No," Pryor answered. "One of our officers was also killed and Vane was shot with our guy's gun."

"Oh God," Brooke said as her hand flew to her mouth. Cracks in her resolve started to show. Being the daughter of a cop, her worst nightmare growing up had always been seeing her daddy's partner,

221

"Uncle Danny", in his dress blue uniform heading in her direction with tears in his eyes. She also knew, Kevin, coming from a law enforcement family, probably had a similar nightmare.

Brooke gave Kevin's arm a squeeze and their eyes locked. They nodded in quiet unison. Their petty squabble could wait for another day. There had been a death in the two branches of her family today. One bled red, one bled blue.

Malcolm Kauthmann came around the corner of the guest house and walked straight up to Brooke. He studied her face and didn't like what he saw. "Are you okay?"

She nodded her head without much conviction.

"A police officer was also killed in the line of duty," Pryor said softly and Kauthmann immediately understood what his granddaughter was feeling. The abstraction of the death of a policeman she had never met was taking a greater toll on Brooke than the reality of the death of the step-father she knew well.

The three silently turned and headed into the guest house.

"She's in the atrium," Kaplan told Kauthmann.

Mellissa was sitting in the shade in an overstuffed chair reading one of those trashy romance novels she adored. She heard footsteps approaching. When she turned and saw her father, ex-husband and daughter approaching, she burst into tears.

Her worst nightmare had just come true.

CHAPTER 50

"OKAY," CUMMINGS SAID. "That's weird."

As expected, yellow crime scene tape and uniforms from both the police department and campus security were keeping the rubberneckers and press away from the GAIA Institute. But once Pryor and Cummings had moved inside the established perimeter, it was eerily quiet. Instead of black and whites with their lights flashing, crime scene vans and the coroner's wagon, there were a pair of identical black Suburbans, with federal government plates, parked in sunny spots by the front door. Parked in the shade of a massive oak tree a few spots over was an unmarked local police car. Danny Holden was leaning against the driver's side door. Otherwise, the lot was empty.

With some effort, Cummings wheeled the Hummer into a spot near Holden.

"Where the hell is everybody?" Pryor asked.

"The Federal Bureau of Investigation has closed off this crime scene and told us not to touch anything and leave. They have their own forensics team about to go wheels up from Quantico whenever they can get their sorry asses in gear."

"Is Wags still lying in there?" Pryor asked with a horrified look on his face.

"Hell no," Holden answered. "Apparently, the FBI Ivy League pretty boys down in the basement were good at math. They counted eleven guns pointed in their direction, all in the hands of seriously pissed off local cops compared to the three weapons still in their holsters. Our guys had no intention of leaving one of our own dead in the men's room with his pants down. They compromised and let us have Wags but Vane is still down there."

223

"What do we know?" Pryor asked.

"It looks like we've got another pair of android killings. There was a dart in Wags' chest and he was electrocuted. The android then took Wags' gun and shot Vane blind through a wall with no line of sight."

"What do you mean, shot him through the wall?" Pryor asked.

"Dead center of the X ring while he was sitting at his desk," Holden answered.

"That's impossible," Pryor said.

"No," Cummings answered. "Simple math."

"Explain," Pryor demanded.

"The security camera in Vane's office was probably on and he may have had a built-in camera in his computer monitor to do Zoom calls. If he was sitting still behind his desk, it would have been simple for the droid to triangulate a kill shot. As long as it allowed for the stud spacing, an inch and a half of drywall wall would not have made that much difference in the shot."

"That's what the FBI guy thought too," Holden confirmed. "Wags and the guy on the top side desk didn't even know Vane was there."

"Dammit," Cummings growled. "How could I have been so stupid?"

"Explain," Pryor said.

"Vane's firewall. Nick had to sneak into the lab if he wanted access to the server array…"

"Damn," Pryor said as he caught up. "With all of the security protocols Vane had in place, he had to physically be inside as well."

"We're speculating the trash fire was set by Vane as a distraction to sneak inside," Danny Holden said.

"I heard the desk cop said his phone and walkie-talkie didn't work," Pryor said.

"Yeah," Holden answered. "But nobody was buying it."

"Did our guys do an area sweep?" Cummings asked.

"We started one downstairs but the FBI ran us off."

"Did they find Wags' weapon?" Pryor asked.

Holden shook his head.

"Was the exterior of the building searched?"

Holden shook his head and gave Cummings an odd look. "No. Since the exterior of the building wasn't anywhere near the crime scene, it wasn't searched. How could that possibly be important?"

Without answering, Cummings walked over to the main entrance of the GAIA Institute and almost instantly found Vane's jammer.

Cummings pointed to it and said, "The department is going to owe the guy at the front desk an apology."

"Why?" Holden asked. "What is that thing?"

"It's a jammer that would block the desk cop's radio and cell phone." Cummings pointed to the control screen. "It has a timer setting so it was probably only on for a few minutes then shut down."

"Making our guy look like he was lying and muddying the water," Pryor said with just a hint of admiration in his voice.

"If you say so," Holden said as he tried to keep from yawning. "Where the hell were you guys?"

"We were interviewing Norman Fleishman and we were out of cellphone range," Pryor answered.

Holden held up his phone. "I saw your girlfriend interview Crazy Norman..."

"She is not my girlfriend."

"Okay," Holden said. "She's not your girlfriend. I saw the woman you had carnal knowledge of last night interviewing Crazy Norman a few minutes ago."

"I don't see you winning this one," Cummings said with a laugh.

Neither did Pryor so he didn't push it.

Holden shook his head. "I can see why they call him Crazy Norman."

"Meaning?" Pryor asked.

"He was telling everyone Vane wasn't the only villain and we're in serious danger. Then he really went off the deep end."

"Oh God," Pryor muttered.

"He said the military should blow up Vane's Hawaii multi-billion dollar facility. Then he said he was going to post the exact location of all of the GAIA probe sites online. He recommended, if you lived near one, to go out and blow them up too."

"Anything else?" Pryor asked.

"Naw," Holden said with a dismissive wave of his hand. "With Vane downstairs getting ripe and with the Feds big-footing us, I've sent all of the task force people home for a bit of R&R." Holden had a twinkle in his eye as he tried unsuccessfully to stop another yawn. "I'll be doing the same as soon as I deliver your orders."

"Orders?"

Holden cleared his throat. "You're both to report downstairs to the FBI and fully debrief them."

"Be still my heart," Pryor said. He nodded in Cummings's direction. "What about him after that?"

Holden shrugged and turned to Cummings. "Take two days off then report back to your precinct in uniform for morning roll call."

Cummings had been expecting this so he didn't react to the news.

"What about me?" Pryor asked.

"With Vane dead and your theory on the case looking good, the complaint against you is now history and internal affairs will forgive and forget."

"Really?" Pryor said.

"Combined with the way you nuked that FBI asshole, which, by the way, I want all of the gory details, I think everyone upstairs is now scared of you."

"Excellent," Pryor said. "What's my new assignment?"

"Same deal for you. Take two days then report to Lt. Garrison.."

A song started playing on Cummings's phone. "*If you're having girl problems I feel bad for you son. I got ninety-nine problems…*" Cummings quickly answered it before Jay-Z could finish his thought. "Hold on for a second," Cummings said as he put his hand over the phone's microphone and turned his attention to Pryor and Holden.

"What the hell was that ringtone all about?" Pryor demanded.

"I gave Brooke a new ringtone before we declared a ceasefire and I haven't had time to change it."

Holden chuckled. "That's a bit harsh."

"They've been at each other's throats since this whole mess started," Pryor stated then motioned Cummings away. "Take her call. At this point, we've got nothing else to do."

Cummings turned away and spent most of the next two minutes listening.

"What's up?" Holden asked as he pointed in the direction of Cummings.

"Best I can figure," Pryor answered. "Cummings and my daughter dated in high school. I think he's still interested and Brooke won't give him the time of day."

"She always was a smart girl."

"Meaning?"

"Meaning, after seeing the crater you and Melissa created," Holden said with a chuckle. "Why take a chance on history repeating itself?" Holden turned serious. "How's Melissa holding up?"

Pryor's shoulders went up maybe a quarter of an inch. "Hard to say. We haven't exactly been close the past few years."

"Melissa has always been tougher than she looked," Holden said.

"That was interesting," Cummings said as he rejoined Pryor and Holden. "Brooke wants to meet me tonight after work."

Pryor and Holden exchanged knowing glances.

"What?" Cummings demanded.

"Look, kid," Holden said. "Albert and I have been working homicide for almost as long as you've been taking in air. Brooke has been hit with a double whammy. First her friend was murdered and then her step-father."

"Obviously," Cummings said, unsure where Holden was headed. "So?"

"She may say or do things for the next few days, that when the dust settles and she calms down, she'll regret and try to walk them back. Just don't put too much stock in what she's saying at the moment," Holden said. "She can lash out or get clingy."

"Or both," Pryor added.

"Or both," Holden seconded. "We see people fall apart after a homicide all the time."

Pryor put his hand on Holden's shoulder. "You've known Brooke her whole life, Danny. If anyone can deal with this load, it would be her." Pryor turned to Cummings. "What did she want to talk to you about?" Pryor asked.

Cummings, deep in thought as he processed Holden's comment, hesitated for a moment then said, "She figured out we were pulling her leg at the Ark compound. After she cooled off, she talked to

Norman Fleishman about our psychological profiles to see if he was serious. Apparently he was and he showed them to her along with his compatibility algorithm. Brooke learned there were only two places where we could potentially go off the rails. First was if we were sexually incompatible, which we obviously know is not the case."

Danny Holden slapped Cummings in the back of the head.

Cummings wheeled on Holden. "What was that for?"

"Seriously?" Holden answered as he shook his head.

"Old news, Danny," Pryor said. "Besides, after everything else I've learned about Brooke in the past two days, this didn't even make my top five list of annoyances." He turned to Cummings. "What was the other issue?" Pryor asked in a flat monotone.

"He said we were both too stubborn and we might create an impasse we can't work through."

"Sweet little Brooke Pryor stubborn?" Danny Holden said with a laugh. "That's hard to believe."

"Unfathomable," Pryor said.

Pryor nodded in the direction of the GAIA Institute. "Let's get this over with."

Pryor and Cummings headed inside.

CHAPTER 51

AITING INSIDE THE lobby of the GAIA Institute were the two boy toy FBI agents that had been disarmed by Benny the Rabbi. They were not happy campers. Since SAC Michael Gottwald had decided to attack her, Brooke declared war with no intention of taking any prisoners. She had immediately posted an edited video on her Twitter account of the two agents being 'detained'.

She had tastefully cropped the video so only Benny's gun was visible but not his face and the audio talking about Little Tony was deleted. Instead, Brooke had added her own voice-over commentary about how, as she had predicted, the FBI would try to intimidate and silence her. She even added an unflattering picture of Michael Gottwald she'd pulled off of the internet and titled it *FBI Oreo*. After her *tour de force* appearance on national TV with Sandra Hollis, Brooke now had over three million followers on her Twitter account and the number was growing exponentially. The humiliating video of the FBI agents was 'trending' and being replayed endlessly by cable news as they tried to play catch up to Sandra Hollis who currently owned the biggest story of the year.

As they entered the lobby, the level of hostility was palatable. The two FBI Agents silently glared at Pryor and Cummings. Having committed the unforgivable sin – they had embarrassed the Bureau – they both knew their once promising careers with the FBI were over. They might hang around for a year or two until they got the message but eventually, they would move on.

Pryor, who had developed a visceral distaste for the Feds over the years, actually felt sorry for the pair. They had been set-up for failure by the odious SAC Michael Gottwald. If he hadn't been such a complete asshole, Brooke would never have nuked them.

Like her grandfather, Brooke was proving to be a devastating counter-puncher. Even when she was a kid, she'd never let her emotions affect her judgment and never felt the need to prove herself. If you leave me alone, I'll leave you alone. But God help you, as FBI Agent Gottwald discovered, if you mistook her no-nonsense, borderline clinical attitude for weakness. Once she got finished dropping a house on you, you could relate to the Wicked Witch of the West.

No words were exchanged in the short elevator down to the lower level.

When they arrived at Vane's office, Mike Blackwell was waiting for them in the corridor. Through the open door, Pryor and Cummings could see the professor's body still slumped in the chair behind his desk.

The two FBI Agents who had accompanied them in the elevator stayed behind Pryor and Cummings with their eyes locked on them. Mike Blackwell saw them coming and nodded. Behind them, the two FBI Agents pulled out their guns and aimed them at Pryor and Cummings.

"Hand over your weapons," one of the young FBI agents said as he nudged Pryor in the back with the barrel of his Glock 17.

Pryor turned and faced the grinning agent. He glanced down at the Glock and shook his head.

"Correct me if I'm wrong," Pryor said as he glanced over his shoulder at Blackwell. "It is FBI policy to never chamber a round into your weapon until you're ready to use it."

"It is," Blackwell answered with a grin on his face.

"Since I didn't hear either one of these children chamber their weapons, there is a good chance if these idiots were to pull the trigger, all we would hear is a click and not a boom?"

"It's a possibility but not a certainty," Blackwell answered. "They may have done it before you showed up."

"Look…" the agent said as his eyes moved from Pryor to Blackwell. Big mistake.

Pryor's left hand shot up with the speed of a cobra strike. He grabbed the agent's weapon by the barrel and pushed it aside, so if he fired, all he would hit was the corridor wall. Caught completely off guard, Pryor was instantly able to twist the Glock out of the startled agent's hand. Meanwhile, his right hand had his Glock out of its holster and the barrel under the chin of the agent.

"On the other hand," Pryor said calmly. "Our police department requires us to always be ready to fire."

The other agent had been so mesmerized by what had happened to his partner, he had taken his eyes off of Cummings. Almost as quickly as Pryor, Cummings had the barrel of his Glock under the chin of the second agent. "Why don't you go ahead and drop your weapon," Cummings said softly.

With his eyes wide with fear, the agent released his grip on his gun and it clattered harmlessly to the floor. Cummings kicked it twenty feet down the corridor.

"What the hell was that all about?" Pryor asked as returned his weapon to his holster and locked his eyes on Blackwell.

Blackwell shook his head and turned his attention to his agents. "Why don't you two go find some coffee or something to settle your nerves," he said with a hint of disgust in his voice.

"Can I have my gun back?" the first agent asked sheepishly.

"What's the magic word?"

"Please."

Pryor released the magazine and separated it from the Glock then handed both parts of the weapon to the agent.

"Break room is at the end of the corridor on the right," Cummings offered.

The two agents, their tails firmly between their legs, shuffled off.

When they were out of hearing range, Blackwell sighed. "Sorry about that," he said. "The FBI requires a certain number of field hours for all of their agents. Those two bozos were headed to white collar crime and a safe office cubicle. No one thought they could get in any trouble babysitting Vane."

Pryor was not satisfied. "You let them pull their weapons on us?"

"I read your military record," Blackwell said. "Thanks for not breaking their necks."

"My record is sealed."

"The Director of the FBI personally got it unsealed."

"Why?" Pryor demanded.

"You'd have to ask her," Blackwell answered. "But I don't think she is pining away waiting for Malcolm to call."

Pryor stared at Blackwell and silently waited.

"Okay," Blackwell said. "After this total screw up, like my guys in the break room, my days with the Bureau are numbered. Gottwald still has a lot of juice in Washington and is the BFF of the Director. The Director has her nose in a snit after what the Attorney General did with the amnesty thing for BONK and the long knives are still out to get you."

"Eek!" Pryor said.

"You need to take this seriously," Blackwell stated. "Gottwald is trying to put you and your boy Robin here in the frame for killing Plato Vane."

"Me?" Cummings said with a startled expression on his face.

"Gottwald, with the Director's blessing, is in the process of getting a warrant drawn up for both of you."

CHAPTER 52

"AH," PRYOR SAID. "Your boy scouts knew the warrant was in process, so in hope of saving their asses, they wanted the glory of being the ones to arrest us."

"Pretty much," Blackwell answered.

"And you let them?"

Blackwell shrugged. "I know I'm done and I thought I do could a public service."

"Meaning?" Pryor asked.

"I figured you'd disarm them about as fast as you did and I thought having a hostile gun in their faces for the third time in past twenty-four hours might convince them they were not cut out for law enforcement."

"Ah," Pryor said with a chuckle. "So, what are they using for evidence to arrest us?"

"Where were you at around eleven-thirty this morning?"

"We were interviewing a potential witness, Norman Fleishman," Pryor answered.

Blackwell asked, "Crazy Norman?"

Pryor confirmed, "Yes. Why?"

"That feeds into Gottwald's scenario."

"How so?"

"Gottwald is claiming Crazy Norman has been spreading wild tales about the professor wanting to start Armageddon and has been secretly encouraging someone, like you, to put a bullet into Vane before it was too late. With your personal history with Vane, he's claiming you're not only a person of interest but the number one suspect."

"Do you think we would kill one of our own just to rid the world of Vane?" Pryor asked.

"I do not," Blackwell answered. "Plus, why kill Nick Blake? If all you wanted was Vane dead, we never would have found his body." Blackwell shook his head. "Gottwald knows he'll never get a conviction but as he heads out the door, he wants to take you down with him."

"Asshole," Pryor stated.

No one disagreed.

"Break it down for me," Pryor said.

"Why were your cellphones turned off at that the time of the murders?"

Pryor said, "Mr. Fleishman requested they be turned off."

"Are you aware even if your phone is turned off, unless you remove the battery, we can still locate you?"

"I am." Pryor reached into his right coat pocket and pulled out a Faraday cage shielding envelope. "All of our electronics were in one of these."

"Including his." Blackwell nodded in the direction of Cummings. "And your daughter and Sandra Hollis?"

"Yes."

"Why?"

"Norman is pretty anal about people like the FBI eavesdropping on him," Cummings answered. "He had heard a rumor that even if your phone is turned off, if the battery is still inside, they can still track you."

"Okay, okay," Blackwell said. "At the time of Vane's murder, you had intentionally turned off your cellphones and put them in Faraday bags to shield them so no one would know where you were."

"When you put it like that," Pryor said.

Blackwell continued. "Why does the LoJack in your Barracuda show it has been parked in your garage for the past twenty-four hours?"

"Officer Cummings has a four-wheel drive vehicle better suited to navigate Mr. Fleishman's driveway so we took that."

"So," Blackwell continued in his prosecutorial manner. "Not only were you untrackable by your cellphones, you were in an untrackable vehicle you claim was at Crazy Norman's compound."

"I'm sure Mr. Fleishman will confirm we were with him at the time of the murder and likely has a time stamped videotape of us there."

"Considering Mr. Fleishman's history of mental instability and his reputation as a conspiracy nut, why should we consider him a reliable alibi?"

"We were seen by at least thirty other people, including a network television anchor and helicopter pilot, I think you'll find to be much more reliable. You have to have more than just our phones being off."

"Unfortunately," Blackwell said. "They have much more. Gottwald has had the tech guys put together a little video to present to a grand jury."

Blackwell led the way into the main lab. Once inside, Blackwell sat down behind one of the workstations and logged into the FBI database. Pryor and Cummings positioned themselves behind Blackwell and the trio watched as a video played.

"While the FBI can be, and often is, a total political whore, the tech department is amazing," Blackwell said as he glanced at Cummings. "Look familiar?"

On the thirty-two inch monitor was a recording obviously gleaned from one of the lab's security cameras. On the screen was Kevin Cummings. He was checking to be sure no one was watching. Then, with a clear view of the screen of the workstation showing a GAIA Institute logo, he logged into the GAIA security network.

Blackwell hit the pause button then turned to Pryor. "That would be your partner hacking into the security feed. Which is proof he could do it."

"Shit," Cummings muttered.

"Ah," Blackwell said. "That's just the warm up." Blackwell hit the play key.

The next clip was Cummings removing the damaged hard drive from Nick Blake's workstation and putting it in his jacket pocket instead of giving it to the crime scene investigators. The screen flickered then the image changed. The next clip was Pryor and Cummings at the crime scene.

Pryor: "You hacked the university's security network?"

Kevin Cummings: "Pretty much."

Pryor: "Will they be able to trace the hack back to you?"

Kevin Cummings: "Only if they have a reason to look hard enough."

Mike Blackwell hit the pause button. "Just for your information. A righteously pissed off Director of the FBI is a good enough reason to make the tech guys look hard enough."

Mike Blackwell hit the play button and the video started up again. It was a few minutes later.

Pryor: "So how did you get the hard drive out of the computer without CSI noticing?"

Cummings: "While they were busy with the body I might have removed it and inadvertently put it in my pocket instead of with the other evidence."

Pryor: "These things happen sometimes."

"Here's where it really starts to get good," Blackwell said.

Pryor: "How hard would it be to change the logs?"

Cummings: "If our killer had full admin rights or hacked into the system the same way I did, it would be a snap."

Pryor: "That was how you were able to hack the systems so easily. You'd done it before."

Cummings: "Allegedly, but never proven."

Blackwell hit the pause button again and glanced at Cummings. "You've been caught red-handed hacking the campus security system and admitting you have the skill to alter the door logs. We also have you on tape removing evidence which could potentially incriminate both of you." Blackwell turned to Pryor. "This is also proof that you knew about all of this and failed to report it."

Pryor shrugged. "You got us cutting a few corners in a high-profile murder investigation. You're missing a motive. Why would I want to kill Vane?"

"Other than the fact he was banging your ex-wife and you hated his guts?"

"There is that," Pryor acknowledged. "But he married Melissa over a decade ago. Why wait so long?"

"Our tech guys were able to enhance the video of your famous little dust up with Dr. Vane so we could hear the audio."

Mike Blackwell pushed the play button.

On the screen was the image of Pryor throwing Vane through a plate glass window and ending up straddling his chest. Pryor then stuck a warning finger in Vane's face.

Pryor: "If you ever put your filthy hands on my daughter again, I'll kill you."

Mike Blackwell hit the pause again. "If some old hound dog like Vane tried to rape my daughter, I'd want to kill him too."

Kevin Cummings was livid. "Vane tried to rape Brooke?"

"Relax," Pryor said as he put his hand on Cummings's shoulder. "If Vane had tried to rape Brooke, we wouldn't even be here."

"Why not?"

"Because his body would have been buried in the woods weeks ago and, if it was ever found, it would have been a toss-up if the killer would have been Brooke or me," Pryor answered.

"So what happened?" Cummings demanded.

"Vane made a pass at Brooke and she clocked him." Pryor shrugged. "When I figured it out, I threw him through a window, to confirm for him, messing with Brooke was not a good life choice."

"How did you find out?" Cummings asked.

"I went to pick Brooke up at Melissa's house to go to dinner but she told me Brooke had suddenly moved out. Since we had made our plans only a few hours earlier, I did some investigating." Pryor turned back to Blackwell. "How does Gottwald explain why I would kill three other people just to get Vane?"

"You're a cop; you know how to game the system."

"Kill someone else to cover your motive for killing the real target," Pryor said softly. "Sounds like a bad detective movie."

"Unfortunately for you, juries watch a lot of lousy detective movies," Blackwell said. "Gottwald would contend you figured they can only stick the needle in your arm once and there would be jurors nodding their heads," Blackwell added.

"Your only problem is we have ironclad alibis for the time of Vane's murder."

"Unfortunately," Blackwell said, "you blew up your own defense when you proved Vane could have killed Blake by remote control." Blackwell nodded at Cummings. "They're going to say boy genius here, who just happened to have a crush on your daughter, had the same motivation as you to kill Vane, and the necessary skills to program the robots."

"That theory has more holes in it than a wheel of Swiss cheese."

"I agree," Blackwell answered. "But what happens when they play the video for a grand jury?"

Pryor made a face. "We're indicted on three counts of murder."

"Including a fellow officer," Cummings added softly.

"Are you familiar with the concept of a dying declaration?" Blackwell asked.

"Police Academy 101," Pryor said. "A person's last words are admissible as evidence in a trial."

Mike Blackwell motioned that they should follow him into Vane's office. "Note the blood on the keyboard."

The 'caps lock' light was on. There was a bloody fingerprint on the 'A' and 'caps lock' keys as well as a smear of blood running between the 'I' and 'L' keys.

Blackwell touched the mouse next to Vane's computer. The screen came to life, "While dying, Plato Vane pointed the finger straight at you."

On the screen, they could see two letters.

AI

"That sure looks like AI to me, Albert," Blackwell said.

Albert Pryor blinked a few times and shook his head. Everything else Gottwald had put together suddenly looked much, much stronger now. Dr. Plato Vane was pointing a finger in his direction from the grave and was no longer around to be cross-examined.

"Care to explain that?"

"I can't," Pryor said softly.

Cummings looked at the keyboard and gasped. "I can."

"I'm listening," Blackwell said.

"Has anyone touched this keyboard since Dr. Vane?" Cummings asked.

Mike Blackwell said, "I don't see..."

Cummings shouted urgently, "Answer the goddamn question! Has anyone touched this keyboard since Dr. Vane?"

"No," answered Blackwell.

Cummings pulled his Glock out of his holster and raised his voice, "Then we need to get out of here right now while we still can."

"Why?" Blackwell demanded

"Because the damn 'caps lock' key is lit and the font on the screen is Arial."

Blackwell looked at Pryor who indicated he needed to give Cummings some rope.

"Explain why the cap lock key light is important."

Cummings sprinted back across the hall to the main lab with Blackwell and Pryor a few steps behind. Pryor jumped behind the keyboard of a workstation and increased the size of the font. "This is what A, L would look like in Arial with the caps locked."

AL

"Since the cap locks is lit," Cummings continued, Vane wasn't typing AL. He was typing AI."

"I don't understand," Blackwell said.

"Plato Vane was pointing his finger at his killer but it wasn't Albert Pryor," Cummings shouted. "AI. Artificial Intelligence. The killer is Dr. Vane's computers."

As soon as the words were out of Cummings's mouth, all of the lights in the lab went out followed by the sound of two gunshots coming from the break room.

CHAPTER 53

THE EMERGENCY LIGHTING, which was independent of the AI's control, kicked on and the lab was filled with a dim glow with deep shadows and limited visibility. Blackwell had his Glock out of its holster and was headed to the door when Cummings tackled him and slammed the door shut.

"What the hell are you doing?" Blackwell demanded as he tried to push Cummings off. "That was gunfire!"

"He just saved your life," Pryor said as he turned over a desk and shoved it across the floor to block the door. "Both of your men are already dead, and if you had stepped out into the corridor, you'd be dead too."

Blackwell thought about it for a second then relaxed and quit struggling against Cummings. He knew Pryor was right.

Cummings sprinted across the room, leaped up on a desk and ripped one of the security cameras out of the wall. He saw another faint green light high on the wall on the other side of the room and headed in that direction.

"We need to take out all of the security cameras and destroy anything else with a camera." As he moved around the room, he slammed down the lid of any open laptop he passed and threw every monitor with a Zoom camera to the floor. "Until we've blinded the AI, keep moving. If you don't, it will triangulate your positions and one of the androids will shoot you through the wall the same way it did Vane."

Pryor and Blackwell both quickly changed their location. On cue, a bullet ripped through the wall and hit the monitor where Blackwell had been standing just a moment before.

"Make your movements random," Cummings shouted as he dodged and weaved through the room. "Do not move in a straight line." As Cummings suddenly veered right, another round slammed through the wall and would have been a kill shot if he hadn't changed direction.

The three law enforcement officers moved quickly around the room, ripping out power strips and smashing electronics. The room filled with the smell of burning plastic and shorted out circuit boards.

"AI made its first mistake by turning off the lights," Cummings said softly. "It made the security cameras and anything which was powered up easier to spot and disable."

Blackwell was in the process of overturning desks and lining them up, one after the other, in a row facing the corridor. "We need a fortified position. A Glock round can go through drywall but a couple of layers of desks should stop it."

Pryor and Cummings joined Blackwell in toppling desks and positioning them between them and the corridor. Satisfied, they all dove behind the third row of toppled desks and caught their breath.

"Do you think we've got all of the cameras?" Pryor asked.

"We'll know in a few seconds," Cummings answered as he aimed his Glock at the row of six androids currently connected to the charging station in the rear of the room. "If they start to move, put a round between the front tires and avoid a head shot."

"Why?" Blackwell asked as he eyed the androids.

"The tops of those things are mostly air and a few wires. The batteries are placed between the wheels; that lowers the center of gravity so they don't topple over easily and gives the wheels added traction," Cummings said. "They're commercial grade and have no military shielding so don't waste more than a single round on any unit. We don't know how many of these units the AI has and we may need our ammo later."

"Why don't we just take them out manually while they're turned off?" Blackwell asked.

"They were all supposed to be turned off already," Cummings replied.

"The AI can do an override?" Blackwell asked.

"Yes, which means we don't know the risk of getting too close," Cummings answered. "One of them fired a short-range dart at Officer Wagner. What if these have the same weapon?"

"Why is the computer waiting?" Blackwell asked.

"It's learning," Cummings answered.

"Learning?"

"The AI has limited experience and will probably be more into Occam's Razor thinking rather than complex strategies."

"Occam's Razor?" Blackwell asked.

"Keep it simple, stupid," Pryor said which got an approving nod from Cummings.

"Close enough," Cummings added. "Occam's Razor believes the simplest, least complex solution of all available options will usually be the best."

"This helps us how?" Blackwell asked.

"Plato Vane was building a system to predict earthquakes and was not looking to create artificial intelligence. I think the AI simply happened over time. This AI is going to be like a poorly educated adolescent. It will be very skillful at some things, like shooting a stationary target through a thin wall. There are going to be huge gaps in its knowledge base and whenever we confront it with something unexpected, it will need time to process the new data."

Blackwell nodded. "It'll hesitate."

"And the one who hesitates in a gunfight loses," Pryor added.

"Yes," Cummings said, "but it will learn quickly and will never make the same mistake twice."

"How big of an edge will we have?" Blackwell asked.

"I doubt this computer has ever played war games," Cummings answered. "I'm guessing at the moment the AI is trying to devise a strategy to get eyes on us." Cummings nodded at the androids in the charging station. "If AI is using Occam's Razor, those guys are his best source of eyes."

The green power light above the six androids suddenly clicked on.

"I've got the two on the right. Pryor middle. Blackwell left."

Six shots rang out and all six of the androids began to sputter and smoke.

"Why the hell is this AI doing all of this?" Blackwell demanded.

"Vane's biggest cause was over-population. For some reason, maybe a simple programming error or possibly the computer attaining

Artificial Intelligence, fulfilling the desire of Vane's book to lower the world's population became the computer's prime directive."

"You're starting to sound like Crazy Norman," Pryor said.

"It is starting to look like Fleishman is correct. The computer developed a scenario where it can generate earthquakes – and probably volcanic eruptions – at will to fulfill its perceived mission and told Vane when and where they were going to happen."

Pryor asked, "Why?"

"The computer concluded that by letting Vane get credit for predicting earthquakes, he would get the funding to build the Hawaii superstation." Cummings shook his head. "Once the station goes online, the computer will have the ability to carry out its prime directive and destroy mankind. We've got to shut down the main computer..."

Suddenly the image on the TV screen mounted on the far wall flashed a message.

'I think not.'

The ground began to shake and light fixtures fell from the ceiling as an earthquake rumbled below their feet.

CHAPTER 54

BLACKWELL BRACED HIMSELF against the overturned desk. "What's going on?"

"I'm guessing that tremor was just enough to block the stairwell and take out the elevators," Cummings said.

"Wouldn't that put the entire computer center at risk?" Pryor asked.

"Not really," Cummings said. "The AI has gotten better at triggering small earthquakes. Doing earthquake research, and knowing the risks, the computer room is hugely reinforced and self-contained."

"So," Blackwell stated, "the computer is going to try to trap us down here so we can't tell anyone what we've discovered but never put itself at risk."

"I wish it was that simple," Cummings said. "I'm sure the AI already knows we're aware of what it is up to."

"Then why have an earthquake to keep us in?" Blackwell asked.

Cummings shook his head. "It wasn't to keep us in, it was to keep everyone else out." Cummings shook his head again. "It put four hundred feet of rock between itself and a demolition crew."

"What is the computer's endgame?" Pryor asked. "By causing this completely localized earthquake, it has confirmed Crazy Norman's theory."

"The AI may not care," Cummings said with a deep sigh. "The Hawaii GAIA facility is already fully operational. The AI may already be in the process of launching the doomsday protocol."

"Can we stop it?" Blackwell asked.

Cummings held up a finger and located a pad of paper and a pen then pointed to the TV screen still flashing the warning message.

Second mistake. We know it can hear us and is listening. Follow my lead.

Blackwell and Pryor nodded they understood.

"We need to cut the power to the computer," Cummings said softly. "That is our only hope."

"How?" Pryor asked.

"Behind the drywall in the rear of the lab is a large open area which leads directly to the main power terminal and the backup generator," Cummings said.

"How far away is the target?" Blackwell asked.

"Maybe six hundred yards," Cummings answered. "There are no security cameras in that section. We should be able to sneak in there, take them by surprise and take all of the computers offline."

"How many bullets do those things have left?" Pryor asked.

"Each of my men it killed had sixteen rounds," Blackwell answered.

"Wags had seventeen," Pryor stated. "One in Vane and two in your guys. That means they have, after the two rounds they fired at us through the wall, they still have forty-one rounds."

"Crap," Cummings said softly. "And those androids will not miss. If they know we're coming and set an ambush, we'll be in serious trouble."

Pryor winked at Cummings then said, "It is a risk we need to take."

Blackwell picked up the pad and paper and wrote:

Real target?

Cummings took the pad and wrote:

Cooling fans. Overheat the computers and they will shut down. Exact opposite direction as the generators.

Pryor wrote:

Won't it figure out we fooled it when we don't show up?

Cummings wrote:

Yes. But we should have enough time to shut off the fans before the AI regroups.

Pryor and Blackwell gave a thumbs up.

The trio began kicking the drywall. Between the studs were pink insulation pads to keep the cool air from the tunnel network out of the office space. They pushed them aside and entered the tunnel.

CHAPTER 55

U NLIKE THE LAB area, there were no emergency lights in the naturally cut tunnel. It was pitch dark. The trio clicked on their flashlights. Cummings pointed his light to the west and trotted off with Cummings and Blackwell a few steps behind.

The floor of the tunnel, which had been created by an ancient river, was fairly smooth but slick in spots where moisture had pooled. In several places, it narrowed so that the trio had to pass in single file.

After about two minutes they arrived at a heavy, solid steel door, embedded in the wall of a narrow crevice. While the wall was well-constructed of solid steel, and not wood or particle board, they could hear the whistle of fast-moving air on the other side. There was a sign on the door.

CAUTION!!!
High Winds
KEEP THIS
DOOR CLOSED
AT ALL TIMES

DO NOT
OPEN THIS
DOOR
IF FANS ARE
OPERATING

"That looks ominous," Pryor said.

"When the site was constructed they partitioned off the cooling vents and they generated an air imbalance," Cummings said. "Step away from the door and brace yourself against the wall," Cummings warned as he pressed his back to the heavy wall next to the door and reached for the knob. "It will take a few seconds for the air to balance and until then it will be like being caught in a Category Five hurricane."

When Cummings saw Pryor and Blackwell were ready, he twisted the knob and pulled away shielding his eyes.

The heavy door flew open and slammed hard against the wall. The noise from the rushing air was deafening.

For about twenty seconds the wind whipped and tore at the trio. Finally, as the air pressure started to balance in the tunnel, the wind changed from a killer tropical storm to just a stiff breeze. They all stepped through the doorway.

Looking around, they were in a wide corridor and about twenty feet ahead, four huge fans, each with a circumference of sixteen feet, were sucking warm air out of the main computer room. On the right was a door with an 'Employee Only' sign mounted behind a plexiglass cover. The plexiglass, from the constant barrage of wind, looked old and scratched.

"Let's see what we're up against," Cummings said as he opened the door to the maintenance room.

Pryor laughed as he flipped on the light. "Can it be that easy?" he asked. On the far wall was a massive bank of heavy circuit breakers. As Pryor began flipping the switches, the massive industrial fans, one by one, started shutting down. Their blades were so large and heavy, and they had so much inertia, the shutdown process was slow and deliberate.

"Since these switches are mechanical and not digital, the AI will not be able to turn the fans back on unless he can get some of his droids in here," Cummings said.

Pryor studied the wall and pulled the heavy master breaker switch out of the console. With his elbow, he broke the glass on a case holding a fire axe and used the axe to smash the switch. "Pull every switch you can. Even if they get in here, they won't be able to restart the fans."

In less than three minutes, the heavy circuit breakers had all been reduced to scrap.

"Okay," Blackwell said. "Now what?"

"With the number of server racks in the main computer room, the heat will start to build up fast."

"And that helps us how?" Pryor asked.

"Most servers, computers and power supplies have a built-in auto-shut down. If the core temperature reaches around one hundred degrees centigrade, they shut down."

"So," Blackwell said as he nodded his head. "How long will that take?"

"Unknown," Cummings answered. "But with the amount of hardware in that room and no exterior cooling air, it shouldn't take that long."

They stopped when they started hearing a series of loud clicks coming through the fan opening from the computer room.

"Crap," Cummings said as he sprinted in the direction of the now motionless fans. About twenty feet below in the main server room, one after another, entire server racks were shutting down.

"It has figured out what we're doing," Cummings said, "and it is making a counter move."

"It is shutting down non-essential systems so there will be less heat generated," Pryor stated.

"Doesn't that just postpone the inevitable?" Blackwell asked.

Cummings pointed to a digital display on the far wall. It said 16:56, 16:55, 16:54. "I'm willing to bet that is the doomsday countdown clock."

"Will the system overheat in the next fifteen minutes?"

"No," Cummings answered.

"We need to get down there and shut it down," Blackwell said.

At that exact moment, twenty droids rolled into the room and formed a wall between the fan opening and the rows of server racks. The three androids with the Glocks in their hand appendages opened fire as Pryor, Cummings and Blackwell dove for cover.

"Any suggestions?" Blackwell asked.

"Yeah," Cummings answered. "I think the AI just made its third mistake."

CHAPTER 56

"WHAT MISTAKE?" PRYOR demanded.

"The AI is shutting down entire rows of server racks but it left one rack at the end of a row operating." Cummings quickly snuck a peek and as his head pulled back, a 9mm round pinged off of a fan blade. "If I'm right, it is not a part of the core operating system but it is the unit which controls all of the droids." Cummings looked at Pryor. "How fast can you get that steel door off of the maintenance room?"

Pryor was on his feet and heading to the door. With a hammer and screwdriver, he had driven out the three hinge pins holding it in place in less than a minute.

Cummings pointed to his ear, then to the server room. Pryor and Cummings understood he was speaking to the AI and not them.

"I need one of us to get behind that steel door and try to draw the android's fire."

Cummings pointed at Pryor and mouthed, "why."

"Why?" Pryor asked.

"If we can get them to waste all of their ammunition, we can attack the AI."

Cummings tapped his right shoulder. He tapped the middle of his chest and pointed to Cummings then tapped his left shoulder and pointed to Blackwell.

The three men, with their weapons in their right hands, picked up the steel door with their left. As they paraded across the fan opening behind the door, the androids held their fire.

"Now," Cummings shouted as they dropped the door. Each man fired a three-round burst into their assigned android holding a gun. Instantly, all three guns clattered to the floor. As the AI calculated the new reality, Pryor, Cummings and Blackwell opened fire on the still operational server rack at the end of the row. As the bullets tore through the sheet metal and components, with no brain to guide them, the androids began moving randomly around the room.

As Pryor ripped the safety grid off of one of the fans, Cummings and Blackwell sprinted back to the utility room and returned with three fifty-foot orange extension cords. After tying off the heavy power cords, the three men repelled to the server room.

They all glanced at the countdown clock. 7:34, 7:33, 7:32.

They began to relax until the fire alarm went off.

CHAPTER 57

"WHAT THE HELL is going on?" Pryor asked.

"The AI has activated the Hypoxic fire suppression system. It will replace the oxygen in the room with nitrogen," Cummings said.

"Dangerous?" Blackwell asked.

"Just buying time and trying to scare us," Cummings answered. "This is too big of an area with too many other sources of oxygen to have much impact on us." Cummings turned and fired the last three rounds in his clip into the plate glass window which separated the corridor and the server room. As the glass blew out, fresh air rushed in.

Before he could react, all of the servers in the room started to click back on. Cummings laughed. "Brilliant," he said. "The AI has calculated the additional heat will not cause a shutdown prior to launching his doomsday scenario. AI is trying to hide the important servers like a needle in a haystack." Cummings thought for a moment then grinned.

"Mistake number four!" he shouted triumphantly. "You should have calculated the heat factor sooner!"

Cummings turned to Pryor and Blackwell. "We can ignore all of the server racks in the six outside rows. We could plainly see they were all off. Go down the interior rows and put your hand on the rack. If the rack is cooler than the others, that means it had been shut off and you can ignore it. If it is hot, pull the electrical source and all of the connecting wiring you can."

The three men set out on their task and after more than twenty hot racks had been disabled, a warning bell went off.

They all looked up at the countdown clock. Instead of a clock ticking down, there was a flashing message.

Connection Lost
System Launch Aborted

Pryor asked, "Is it over?"

"I think so," Cummings said, "We still have a few problems though."

"Like what?" Blackwell asked.

"In a couple of hours, the batteries in the emergency lighting will start to fail," Cummings said. "That means we're going to be in absolute pitch darkness until someone comes down to rescue us."

"I call dibs on all of the Reese's Cups and diet Dr. Pepper in the break room," Pryor said with a laugh.

"Then I call dibs on all of the Peanut M&Ms and...," Blackwell stopped suddenly. "What's that?"

Somewhere deep in the bowels of the GAIA facility, a phone was ringing.

"It sounds like it is coming from Vane's office."

Pryor, Cummings and Blackwell trotted down the hall and into Vane's office. The body of the professor was still slumped over his desk. The ringing was coming from a drawer in a credenza behind the desk. Pryor wheeled Vane's body out of the way, opened the drawer and picked up the receiver.

"Hello," he said tentatively.

"Congratulations, Detective Pryor," said a cheerful voice. "The GAIA Institute in Hawaii just went completely offline. For better or worse, and for the moment at least, you just saved mankind."

"Who is this?" Pryor asked.

"Norman Fleishman."

"How did you get a phone in here?"

"That is a long and fascinating story for another day. It is not common knowledge that the tunnels where you are currently trapped connect to the tunnels where I built my Ark project."

"And you had a landline installed between the two locations?"

"With a few dollars, and with Robert's help, it was easy enough to persuade a construction worker to do it while the GAIA institute was being constructed."

"Can you send someone over to walk us out?"

"We can discuss that in a few minutes. How many of you survived?"

"Three. As you know, we lost Vane and one of our police officers. The AI killed two FBI agents," Pryor answered.

"Is Special Agent-in-Charge Mike Blackwell among those still amongst us?"

"Yes," Pryor answered. "He's right here."

"Please put me on speaker."

"Go ahead."

"The moment you deactivated the GAIA computers, all of the defensive protections at the Hawaii facility dropped and the US Government was able to breach the recently departed Plato Vane's lab. They have also mobilized the Army Corp of Engineers to expedite your extraction from the underground facility."

"That's good news," Pryor said.

"No, detective," Norman Fleishman answered, "that is terrible news."

"Why?" Pryor asked.

Norman said, "The government doesn't care a whit about you. They want to get their hands on Vane's server farm."

"Why?" Pryor asked.

"Vane never allowed any off site backups of his system. Would you sleep better at night knowing the CIA or the NSA could potentially create a device that can cause earthquakes and volcanic eruptions anywhere in the world on demand?" Norman asked.

"Not really."

"Nor would I," answered Fleishman. "In a storage room three doors down from Dr. Vane's office there are emergency lanterns. There is also a portable generator powerful enough to run the degausser in the server room. It will be at least thirty-six to forty-eight hours or more before they will be able to dig you out. Instead of me sending a rescue mission, I think your time would be better spent if you were to destroy as many of the server hard drives as possible. Do you have a problem with that Special Agent-in-Charge Blackwell?"

"None whatsoever."

"Excellent," Norman said. "I would imagine by the time you are extracted, you'll all be household names."

CHAPTER 58

THE CROWD HAD begun to build the day before when a rumor started that, after thirty-six hours trapped underground, Pryor, Cummings and Blackwell would soon be emerging. The rumor had been overly optimistic. Undaunted, a tent city had mushroomed on campus and everyone was partying like it was 1999. The police were holding back a rowdy crowd of well over one hundred thousand people as news helicopters hovered overhead. Sandra Hollis, along with an army of other on-air reporters, were jockeying for positions for their live reports. All of the major broadcast networks were there as well as every cable network and multiple foreign language networks.

When word had gotten out about how close humanity had been to end times, everyone in the free world wanted to see Albert Pryor, Kevin Cummings and Mike Blackwell. As soon as they were above ground, Air Force One was standing by to whisk them to Washington. All three would be getting the Medal of Freedom. A bill had passed in congress unanimously to award former veterans Pryor and Blackwell the Congressional Medal of Honor. Kevin Cummings, having never served in the military, was not eligible. He had to settle for being the first person to have ever earned a detective's gold shield before his twenty-first birthday.

Sandra Hollis was talking seriously into her microphone. "The word 'hero' is too often overused. In this case, hero does not do justice to what these three men have accomplished." Sandra put her finger on her ear. "We've just been told that after over two days trapped underground, the three men who saved mankind are about to be rescued!"

The pool camera was focused on a man in a hard hat with dirt on his cheeks as he looked down into a hole. "They're coming out!" he announced.

Albert Pryor, Kevin Cummings, Mike Blackwell shielded their eyes as they emerged from the hole.

A huge roar came up from the gathered crowd. A tearful slim blonde with a towhead two year old little girl in her arms and a grim-faced five year old little boy with a bowtie holding her hand ran in Mike Blackwell's direction.

Pryor saw Brooke and Blitz bounding in his direction.

"My God! You were so brave!" Brooke shouted as she held out her arms.

Pryor beamed until his daughter brushed past him and gave Kevin Cummings a kiss for the ages.

Blitz put his big paws in the middle of Pryor's chest then licked his face. Since Blitz considered licking someone a sign of weakness, Pryor was honored. "At least I've still got you."

Brooke broke away from Cummings and hugged her father around the neck before turning back to Kevin.

"Hey, sailor," Sandra Hollis said as she gave Pryor a hip bump. "You in town for the whole weekend?"

Pryor laughed. "I thought you would be live."

"I got upstaged."

"You? Upstaged?"

"As soon as they hauled your thin ass out of the ground, some guy at 1600 Pennsylvania Avenue started reading a statement and the network cut to him." Hollis gave Pryor another hip bump. "Will you go live with me after POTUS is finished?" She batted her eyes in his direction. She lowered her voice a full octave. "I'll make it worth your time."

Pryor grinned. "Do I have to buy me dinner and drinks first?"

Hollis laughed her infectious laugh. "After what you did, sweet cheeks, it is unlikely any of you will ever pay for another drink or buy a meal for the rest of your lives." She nudged him again. "Come on, just thirty seconds. It'll be fun."

Before he could refuse, Brooke and Cummings wandered over looking like they were attached at the hip.

Sandra laughed again as she gave Brooke a quick peck on the cheek followed by a full-bodied hug for Kevin. "You two look like you two have buried the hatchet," Hollis said.

"We've spent a lot of time talking the past few days," Brooke answered as she glanced at Cummings, bit her lower lip and drenched him in a radiant smile.

"Talking," said a startled Sandra Hollis. "How can you talk to someone buried underground with all lines of communication cut?"

"Not all lines," Pryor said with a grin.

Hollis began slapping Pryor with authority on the arm. "You bastard! You had a phone line and you didn't call me with an exclusive!"

"We had something we needed to do."

Hollis was so angry, she actually stomped her foot. "I'm going to kill Crazy Norman."

"Why?" Pryor asked innocently as he batted his eyes in Sandra's direction.

"He has been leading me around by the nose for the past three days! He kept talking about how he hoped Vane's computers were damaged so no one could replicate his work." Hollis put her hands on her hips and glared at Pryor and Cummings. "It was Crazy Norman's phone line and he convinced you to destroy everything in the computer room."

"No comment," Pryor answered with a grin.

"Oh my God!" Hollis shouted. "Do you know how pissed all of the national security agencies are going to be?"

"One can only hope," Pryor answered.

"Ohhhh," Hollis said as her anger melted. "Now I get it. You couldn't let anyone know about the phone line or the big muckamucks would have ordered you to protect the data. With them unable to communicate with you, you could play stupid and claim you thought the computer system might still be dangerous and destroyed it."

"No comment," Pryor said with a straight face. "But," Pryor said as he glanced over at Cummings. "I really like the way that sounds."

"Me too. I'll share it with Blackwell before we're debriefed," Cummings said as he pulled Brooke even closer.

"Off the record," Hollis said. "Did you get everything?"

"Off the record," Pryor answered. "Not only did we degauss the entire computer room, we wiped every hard drive in the building we could find, including every laptop and workstation and android."

Cummings looked at Pryor. "You told me you would answer my question as soon as we were rescued."

"The answer is," Pryor answered, shaking his head. "You're an idiot to even think you had to ask."

"Told ya," Brooke said as she kissed her father on the cheek.

Sandra's cameraman pointed a finger at Sandra Hollis. "Back in thirty seconds."

"You in or out?" Hollis asked.

Before Pryor could answer, Brooke hooked her arms under both her father's and Kevin's arms and pulled them close. "We're all in."

"I need a shower first," Pryor protested as he rubbed the three-day stubble on his chin. "And a shave."

"Are you kidding me?" Hollis said with a laugh. "You just spent three days buried underground after saving the world! I wouldn't want to jump in the sack with you in that condition, but right now you look exactly like what the world is expecting."

"We're back in five, four...." Sandra's producer said.

Just to be safe, Hollis grabbed Pryor's arm, hard, so he couldn't walk away.

"I'm Sandra Hollis and with me live are Detective Albert Pryor and Detective Kevin Cummings. Also with me is Brooke Pryor, daughter of Albert Pryor..."

"And," Brooke said with a radiant smile that would stop any male under ninety in his tracks. "My daddy has just given us his blessing so it is official." She held up her left hand and displayed her grandmother's blue diamond engagement ring on the third finger of her left hand. "I am officially the fiancée of Detective Kevin Cummings." Brooke let go of her father and jumped into Kevin's arms.

The Kiss got over six hundred million internet hits in less than twenty-four hours.

EPILOGUE

Fourteen Months Later

W ITH OVER TWO thousand rich, famous or powerful in attendance, the Brooke Pryor/Kevin Cummings wedding was the international social event of the year. It was also one of the rare occasions where Brooke and her grandfather were at loggerheads. Malcolm Kauthmann wanted a big Catholic wedding and the Pope had offered any church in the world, including Saint Peter's Basilica at the Vatican, as the venue. Brooke, being an agnostic leaning toward atheist, refused. They compromised by having the ceremony at the Kauthmann estate.

Reload Cummings, beaming in his full dress uniform, was Kevin's best man. Mike Blackwell was one of the groomsmen, his daughter was the flower girl and his son was co-ring bearer with Blitz whose K-9 vest had been replaced with one that made him look like he was wearing a tuxedo.

Albert Pryor considered it a personal victory that he had avoided making a fool of himself when he walked Brooke down the aisle and during the father-daughter dance. With the President of the United States officiating at the wedding and Malcolm Kauthmann picking up the entire tab, it was pretty much a win for everyone.

The sun was just kissing the western horizon as a waiter began passing out little sacks of rice to the thirty or so people who had made it to the final curtain. All of the stragglers were in their early twenties and were friends of either Brooke or Kevin and not the high and mighty who had begun fleeing in mass before the cake had even been cut.

Brooke exploded with laughter as she came out of the house dressed in tight jeans and a loose blouse so she would be comfortable on her honeymoon flight. Although it would be hard to not be comfortable when flying to Maui in her grandfather's G650.

Instead of her grandfather's Bentley, her father's 1971 Barracuda was parked at the curb.

Pryor dangled a set of keys in front of Kevin Cummings.

"You really didn't have to do this," Cummings said.

"You don't want it. I'll take it." Brooke snatched the keys out of her father's hand and jumped behind the wheel and fired up the engine. The rumble of the muscle engine turned heads and the crowd of well-wishers sending the young couple off began to grow.

Brooke slapped the car into neutral and floored the gas. The Barracuda's massive Hemi engine roared like a lion after a kill. The crowd in front of Malcolm Kauthmann's house roared back their approval.

Pryor turned to Cummings. "I'm giving you my two most prized possessions."

"I know. And if I do anything bad to either one, you will kill me and bury my body in the woods."

"Don't forget cutting you up into small, unidentifiable pieces first."

"I thought that was Brooke's MO."

"Where do you think she got it?"

They gave each other a quick man hug.

As Cummings trotted off to join his new bride, they, and the Barracuda, were pelted with rice.

Pryor leaned over and gave Blitz an ear scratch. "It looks like it's back to just you and me, buddy."

Blitz looked up at Pryor then in the direction of Brooke and Cummings then back to Pryor. As the Barracuda started to pull away, Blitz ran over and jumped onto the back seat.

"Traitor!" Pryor shouted.

"I guess I hit the trifecta!" Cummings laughed as he patted Blitz on the head then waved to Pryor.

Albert Pryor couldn't be sure if it was just Blitz's ever present lolling tongue or if the big dog was giving him a farewell raspberry.

After the Barracuda had slowly moved far enough that there was no risk of running over any well-wishers, Brooke turned and said to Blitz, "Hang on!"

Blitz buried his head on the back seat and covered his ears with his paws as Brooke floored the gas. Blue smoke came up from the rear tires and the muscle car fishtailed down the driveway before slowing down and driving away.

Melissa Vane, in a stunning designer off-white dress, walked over. She shook her head as she intertwined her arm with her ex-husband's. "She is certainly your daughter."

Pryor leaned in close and kissed Melissa on the forehead. "Team effort."

Melissa sighed. "I can't believe our daughter married a cop."

Pryor drew in air and let it out slowly. "I can't believe I gave her my car for a wedding present."

Melissa put her head on Albert's shoulder and squeezed his arm tight. "That was really nice what you did for Plato."

"He got played like everyone else," Pryor answered.

"Still, considering your personal history," Melissa said, "While doing all of those interviews, you saving his reputation the way you did was above and beyond."

"In the end, he tried to do the right thing and that counts for a lot in my book," Pryor said. "Besides, if being an egomaniac and a womanizer were hanging offenses there wouldn't be any men in faculty lounges at any college, and Washington, DC would be a ghost town."

"Still, it meant a lot to me."

"Come on," Pryor said. "Your dad paid for some top shelf tequila. Let's go do a few shots for old times' sake."

Melissa Vane laughed "Tequila? I haven't touched that stuff in over twenty years."

Pryor gave Melissa a squeeze. "I wonder if Brooke has any idea how close we came to naming her Margarita?"

***

A pair of graveyard shift data techs were sitting at a console trying, with mixed results, to stay focused on the routine tasks at hand.

"Did they ever find what was causing the power abnormalities?" The first tech asked as he made no effort to suppress his yawn.

"No," the second tech answered. "It has the operations people baffled. Every time they think they have the problem isolated, a new problem pops up somewhere else."

"Huh," the first tech said as he furrowed his brow and leaned in closer to his screen. "That's weird."

"What?"

"I was just trying to upload this week's back up to the server and it is telling me there isn't enough space."

"That's impossible," the second data tech said. "We installed new capacity three weeks ago. There should be at least six thousand petabytes still free."

The first data tech said, "Look for yourself."

As the two techs leaned in to look at the screen, behind them the lights on a maintenance android behind them blinked on.

Books by Rod Pennington
Available on Amazon.com

The Family Series
A dark comedy about a dysfunctional family
of four of the world's best assassins.

Family Reunion
Family Business
Family Secrets
Family Honor
Family Debt

Stand Alone Books

Indweller
Cassandra Files: Genesis

Books by Rod Pennington & Jeffery A. Martin
Available on Amazon.com

The Fourth Awakening Series:
A woman overcomes her mid-life crisis
by going on a vision quest with an enigmatic billionaire.

The Fourth Awakening
The Gathering Darkness
The Fourth Awakening Chronicles I
The Fourth Awakening Chronicles II
The Fourth Awakening Chronicles III
The Fourth Awakening Chronicles IV

Stand Alone Books

What Ever Happened to Mr. MAJIC?
Better Choices

Part of the proceeds from the sales of this book will be donated to the

Animal Adoption Center
270 East Broadway
PO Box 8532
Jackson, WY 83002
AnimalAdoptionCenter.org

CPSIA information can be obtained
at www.ICGtesting.com
Printed in the USA
LVHW080606050522
717919LV00010B/116/J

9 781572 420977